Texas Bombshell

WHISPERING SPRINGS, TEXAS
BOOK ELEVEN

CYNTHIA D'ALBA

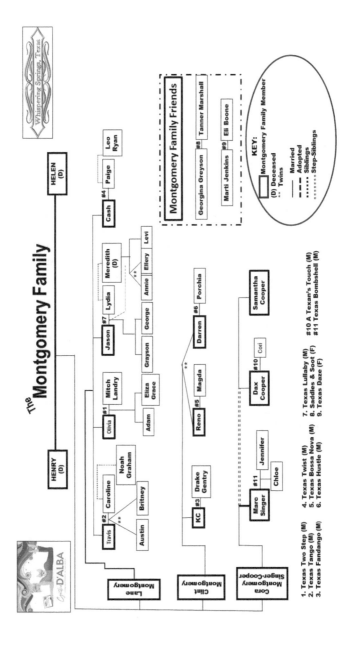

The Montgomery Family

Whispering Springs, Texas

Montgomery Family Friends

Georgina Greyson — #8 — Tanner Marshall

Marti Jenkins — #9 — Eli Boone

KEY:
☐ Montgomery Family Member
(D) Deceased
** Twins

— Married
— — Adopted
— Siblings
········ Step-Siblings

1. Texas Two Step (M)
2. Texas Tango (M)
3. Texas Fandango (M)
4. Texas Twist (M)
5. Texas Bossa Nova (M)
6. Texas Hustle (M)
7. Texas Lullaby (M)
8. Saddles & Scot (F)
9. Texas Daze (F)
#10 A Texan's Touch (M)
#11 Texas Bombshell (M)

Copyright

Cover Artist: Elle James
Editor: Delilah Devlin
Cover Models: Shane Rice
Cover Photo by Tom Tyson

One

Sheriff Marc Singer's jaw tightened as he reread the last sentence of the report. "The cattle rustlers remain at large with few leads."

He sighed and scrubbed his hand down his face. He'd bet his last dollar that most non-cattle people would never believe that cattle rustling continued to be a problem in the twenty-first century. Sure, the theft operations today were more sophisticated than the rustling of the eighteen-hundreds, but the end result was the same— a valuable asset stolen and sold for profit, leaving the rancher out the money.

The recent spree of cattle rustling had hit Whispering Springs County much harder than any of surrounding counties. That was bad enough, but this time, it was Montgomery cattle from his cousin's ranch. County judge Darryl Yeats had promised Marc all the men and resources he might need to track the crooks and the stolen cattle, but so far, there hadn't been enough evidence left at the scenes to investigate. Whoever was behind these thefts was professional and knowledgeable, not only about cattle but also about how cattle ranches operated.

"I'm getting ready to leave," a soft female voice said from his office doorway.

Marc looked up at his newest hire, a front desk clerk named Tiffany Yeats. All of twenty-two, Tiffany was a tall, blond beauty and the granddaughter of the county judge. Fifty years ago, she would have been called a bombshell. "Good night, Tiffany. Have a nice weekend."

She stepped into his office, closed the door, and leaned against it. "Today's been so hectic that I didn't get a chance to tell you happy birthday."

"Thank you," he replied, a little uncomfortable with the closed door, her sexy against it, and her sultry expression. As he was closing in on forty, he should have been flattered by the attention of a much younger woman. Instead, it made him wish he hadn't done the judge a favor and hired his favorite granddaughter.

"Are you doing anything special tonight...you know, to celebrate?" She licked her full lips.

Damn. She could be his daughter...if he'd gotten his first wife pregnant in high school when they'd been dating. Her flirting did nothing but remind him of their age disparity.

"I celebrated with my family last night, so no big plans for tonight. I expect a quiet evening at home."

He told this lie with conviction and a straight face, a valuable skill for a law professional. His home was in Whispering Springs, Texas, which boasted the strongest and most accurate gossip vine he'd ever experienced. For example, he knew last night's dinner with his family had been a subterfuge staged to convince him that the fancy dinner was the total of his family's celebration of his birthday, which happened to be today. He also knew there was a surprise party for him tonight with all his family and friends. He wondered if this blatant flirting by the attractive younger woman was part of the smoke screen.

"Well," Tiffany said, stepping forward until she could put both hands flat on his desk. She leaned forward, her ample assets on full display since she'd unbuttoned the top button of her shirt.

He was a red-blooded guy who loved women. Of course, he'd noticed her full breasts. It was almost impossible not to do so. He didn't smile or react, but he wanted to. This was a damned good ruse to throw him off, and that had to be what was happening here. His money was on his brother Dax setting up this act. This entire scene had his fingerprints all over it.

"My night's completely free," she continued in an enticing whisper, which forced him to lean toward her. "You want to have a few drinks? See what comes up? Celebrate your birthday in style?"

He jerked back in his chair with a choked laugh. "Thanks, Tiffany. That's kind of you to offer, but I never date my employees." He gave her a smile he hoped was professional while simultaneously discouraging further invitations.

"No one has to know," she said with a shrug as she

3

leaned a little closer over his desk. "It can be our little secret."

"Thank you, but no." He pressed his back firmly into his chair, and this time, gave her a stern look. "Have a nice weekend, and give your grandfather my regards."

She stood, stared for a minute, then smiled with a casual shoulder shrug and left.

He wondered if this was the first time in her life that any male had told her no. Hiring her had been a favor to Judge Yeats. Tiffany had been fresh out of college with an interior design degree, something there wasn't much of demand for in a place like Whispering Springs. Plus, she had a history of youthful indiscretions, like underage drinking, a couple of DUIs, and a drunk and disorderly. Her grandfather had successfully negotiated her out of those situations with only fines and community service. Marc hadn't approved of the sentences imposed, but that all predated his arrival and was in the past, or so the judge assured him. So far, until tonight, Tiffany had been a model employee. She was always on time and ready to work, so he wrote off tonight as out of character and assigned the blame to Dax. His brother would find out soon that payback was a bitch.

His cell phone rang at six. The caller ID read LEO'S BAR AND GRILL. Finally! The call to come to his surprise party. He was tired of hanging around the station, waiting to be summoned.

"Sheriff Singer," he said.

"Marc? This is Leo Ryan."

"What can I do for you?" Marc asked, a smile twitching at the corners of his lips.

"I've got a couple of underage drinkers—fake IDs, the whole shebang. I don't want you to arrest them, as I've given them non-alcoholic beer. But can you run by and put a good scare into them? My staff tells me this isn't the first time these boys have been here, and I don't mind them coming in to eat, but I'm not willing to put my liquor license at risk for a few snot-nosed college kids."

Marc chuckled. What a great story to get him to Leo's for his party. "I'm happy to do that. I'll shut down my computer and head your way. Won't be long...maybe ten minutes or less." He provided his arrival time to give the guests time to get into place to surprise him.

Taking his time, he shut down his computer and tidied up his desk before grabbing his hat and heading to his white, sheriff-branded SUV. The drive to Leo's Bar and Grill took a whopping four minutes, so he arrived about ten after six. As usual for a Friday night, there were few parking spots available. As he circled to the back, he glanced around for recognizable cars and trucks, but finding one in this sea of mostly trucks was difficult. However, he thought he saw his brother's new truck wedged into a dark corner near the trash dumpster.

Parking at the rear, he entered through the side and made his way to where the owner, Leo Ryan, stood behind the long, shiny mahogany bar pulling a draft beer. Leo gave him a head nod and then glanced toward a couple of young guys sitting on stools near the end.

Taking the seat next to the guys, Marc set his hat on the bar top. "Good evening, fellas."

The shoulders of the nearest kid stiffened. Marc heard him clear his throat before turning.

"Good evening, Sheriff." The kid's voice was unnaturally low, as though trying to make himself sound older.

It didn't work, and Marc rubbed the scruff on his chin to keep from laughing. "Don't think I know you, and I know most of the folks that frequent Leo's. New in town or traveling through?"

"New," one kid said while the other answered, "Traveling through."

Marc nodded seriously. "Got some ID on you?"

Both boys scrambled to pull plastic IDs from their front jeans pocket—a rookie mistake. IDs are kept in wallets, not loose in pockets...unless you think you'll have to produce them. The boys handed over their IDs.

"Hmm, let's see. Juan Valdez and Ricardo Montalbán." He gestured to the kid the furthest away. "You're Ricardo?"

"That's right," the boy replied in a much-too-loud voice.

"And Juan."

"Correct," the boy closest to him said.

Marc tucked the IDs into his shirt pocket. "I've always wanted to meet a coffee grower and a famous Mexican movie star."

The two boys exchanged glances, and the one beside him said, "Hey, give those back. Those are ours."

Marc chuckled. "Fake IDs are against the law, fellas. How about you pull out your real IDs before I run you to the station and do fingerprints to see who you are?" Of course, he had no intention of taking them to the station. Technically, they weren't drinking alcohol, and in Texas, they could drink what Leo had served. He doubted they were aware of that. And second, fingerprints to determine their identities? He'd bet these two watched enough wrong police TV shows that they'd buy it.

The two boys gulped nervously and pulled out their wallets. Each one passed over a Texas Driver's License.

"James Porter and Brian Nelson." A rough birthday calculation put them at seventeen. Marc handed back their driver's licenses. "Here's the thing, guys. You're lucky you stumbled into Leo's place. If you were drinking real beer, you'd be in big trouble. As it is, Leo served you non-alcoholic drinks. So, other than these terrible fake IDs, no laws have been broken." He sighed. "Get on back to Diamond Lakes, and don't let me find you in Whispering Springs again for another four or five years, then Leo will be happy to give you a beer. Leo," Marc called.

Leo walked down and stopped. "What's up, Sheriff?"

"These two gentlemen are not quite twenty-one. I'm sending them on their way. However, I assured them you would happily serve them in four or five years."

Leo nodded. "First beer on your twenty-first birthday is on the house."

The boys hopped off their stools. "Thanks," Juan, aka Brian, said.

After they'd gone, Marc pulled the IDs from his pocket. "Juan Valdez and Ricardo Montalbán?"

The two men started laughing.

"Which one tipped you off?" Leo asked. "The movie star or the coffee grower?"

Marc chuckled. "Thanks for the laugh. I needed

that." He stood. "Guess I'll head home unless there's anything else you need me to investigate?" He waited for Leo to direct him to the party room in the back. For all the cars in the lot, there were quite a few empty tables in the dining area.

"Nope. You solved my problem." Leo shook his head with an amused snort. "Juan and Ricardo. Jesus." He was muttering to himself as he walked away.

Surprised by not being directed toward the back party room, Marc started toward his car when his phone rang. The caller ID said, "Dax."

"Dax?" he said as he answered.

"Hey, Marc. Cori and I were sitting here watching a movie and thought you might want to come by. I never gave you your birthday present last night. You busy?"

Of course. The surprise party was at Cori Lambert's house, which was odd. Her house was small. Some might describe it as tiny. Unless the party was in her backyard, there wasn't enough room to invite the entire Montgomery clan and Marc's friends.

"You still there?" Dax asked.

"What? Oh, yeah. Still here. I think I'll head home and get with you guys tomorrow." Marc waited for Dax to give a mandatory reason that Marc had to stop at Cori's house on the way home.

"Okay, then," Dax said. "Dinner tomorrow night work for you? Cori's a good cook."

"Sure," he replied, more confused than ever. The town gossip vine was rarely wrong. He was sure he'd heard rumors of a surprise party for him.

"Great," Dax said. "Let's say about six. That work?"

"Um, sure. Six tomorrow. See you then."

Marc slapped his hat on and started toward the side entrance. Leo waved goodbye as he took a to-go order over the phone.

His cell went off just as he unlocked the SUV. "Singer," he answered.

"Sheriff? This is Robert Troutman at the club. Some kids broke into the office and made a mess of things. I need you over here right now."

Troutman was the Executive Director of the Whispering Springs chapter of the Texas Cattlemen's Club. He was a no-nonsense manager who took his job seriously. The recent cattle thefts had him on the phone daily with both the sheriff and police departments, demanding to know what was being done about the rustling.

"Robert, I'm headed home. I can send an on-duty deputy to take the report."

"No, sir, Sheriff. I want you. I caught one troublemaker red-handed. I think you're going to want to handle this quietly. Influential family, you know?"

Marc wanted to groan. What a crappy way to end his birthday. He hoped it wasn't one of the Montgomery kids. The Montgomerys weren't the only family with money and influence in the area. There were others, and yes, Robert was probably right. He should handle this himself.

"Okay," Marc said with a long exhale. "I'm on the way."

On the outskirts of town, the Whispering Springs Cattle Club had recently moved into a new building. The grand opening had been only two weeks prior, which was

CYNTHIA D'ALBA

probably what had drawn the attention of the trouble-some teens.

The lot around the building was empty, save for one car that Marc assumed belonged to Robert. He slid from his SUV with a sigh and slapped his hat back on his head. The heels of his boots knocked on the concrete steps as he climbed onto the porch. When he pulled on the front door, it opened easily.

"Robert," he said to the man pacing in the hall.

"Sheriff. It's about time you got here," the older man chastised.

"Sorry, Bob. I used the siren and everything," Marc said, stifling a grin. "Now, where's the teen you caught?"

"I tied him up," Robert said. "I left him in there." He pointed to the party room. "I wanted him out of my office."

Marc nodded. "Okay. I'll go talk to him."

"You do that." The Executive Director crossed his arms over his chest. "I want to see some action on your part." The last statement was shouted loudly at Marc.

Marc's brow furrowed. "Okay, Robert. Calm down. I said I'd take care of it." He whirled on his heel and headed toward the closed door of the party room. No light seeped under or around the doors, which was odd. How inconsiderate of Robert to leave this poor kid in the dark.

As he pulled one of the doors open, bright lights flashed on.

"Surprise!" a million people yelled.

Okay, not a million, but it felt like it as Marc stumbled back at the sudden brightness and loud yelling. He blinked and glanced around.

"Surprise, bro," Dax said, draping his arm over Marc's shoulder.

"Surprise, honey." His mother brushed a kiss on his cheek. "You're a tough man to fool," she said with a laugh.

Then he was engulfed in a crowd of family and friends, wishing him a happy birthday and laughing about all the false leads they'd thrown his way.

Tiffany Yeats hugged his neck with a laugh. "You should've seen your face this afternoon," she said. "It was all I could do not to laugh."

"Yeah, well, what would you have done if I'd taken you up on your offer?" he asked with a grin.

"I knew you wouldn't," she replied with a shrug. "But if you had, well, we'd be having dinner, I guess." With another kiss on his cheek, she said, "Better get back to my date before he finds out I asked another man out tonight."

Marc was chuckling as she hurried off into the crowd.

"Happy birthday, handsome," Angel Winns said as she wrapped her arms around his neck and kissed him.

"Thanks, Angel." He wiggled his way out of her arms. "Save me a dance." He didn't want to encourage her, as he'd stopped dating her a little while back, but one dance couldn't hurt, right?

For the next couple of hours, drinks flowed freely, and guests ate and danced to the live country band. At close to eleven, he sagged into a chair, having just finished dancing with his mother.

"Come on, old man," a gaggle of Montgomery wives said. "Dance with us."

Marc's eyes opened wide. "With all five of you at once?"

"Sure," Lydia Montgomery said. "You can handle five women at once, right?"

Marc grinned. "At one time, maybe."

But he allowed himself to be pulled back to the dance floor. The five women danced around him as he moved to the music. Magda Montgomery twirled him around. Porchia Montgomery caught him at the end of the twirl and stood him upright.

"Whew," he said to Porchia. "Thanks. I don't think I'm as young as I used to be."

She laughed as Caroline Montgomery moved in to take his hands.

The music suddenly screeched to a halt. The sound of a hand pounding on the microphone echoed through the hall.

"Hello? This thing on?"

The crowd turned toward the stage. A girl, maybe fourteen or fifteen, stood at the mic stand, looking over the crowd. Dressed in cut-off jean shorts, a T-shirt that proclaimed DAD JOKES ARE HUMERUS, and a pair of bright yellow flip-flops, there was something about her face that seemed familiar, but Marc was sure he'd never met this girl.

Marc started forward. His gut, which rarely wrong, warned him she was going to be a problem.

"Hello!" She hit on the mic again. "Can you hear me? Can someone point out a sonofabitch named Marc Singer?"

Marc frowned. What the heck? He glanced around

the room, wondering if someone was playing an extremely poor joke on him.

Stepping to the edge of the stage, he said, "I'm Marc Singer."

The girl spread her arms wide. "Congratulations, Dad. I'm a girl."

Two

Her words confused him. Obviously, she was a girl, but *Dad*? What the heck was she talking about?

"Honey?" His mother rested her hand on his shoulder. "Do you know this person?"

Marc shook his head and stepped closer to the stage. "You want to come down from there and tell me what this is all about?"

Around him, the room was mostly silent. The other partygoers listened, absorbed in the drama taking place on the stage.

The girl shook her head. "I think all these people should know what a liar you are." She aimed her next words toward the party guests. "Did you all know your sheriff has a daughter he doesn't recognize?" She tapped her chest. "Me."

As the girl continued to address the room, one of his part-time deputies, Cash Montgomery, took a position on the left stage wing. Cash's brother, Travis, took up a position on the right wing. His brother Dax and his parents stepped up alongside Marc in support. The rest of the large Montgomery family moved in close behind Marc.

Marc frowned and said harshly, "You can come down on your own, or Cash or Travis will escort you down."

At Marc's words, the two Montgomery men moved toward the teen.

"Geesh, Dad, chill out. I'm coming." With an exaggerated eye-roll, the girl jumped off the four-foot-high stage and landed in front of him.

"Who are you?" Marc demanded.

"Chloe Tate."

At Marc's gesture toward the band, the music resumed.

Cash lifted his chin to Marc, then turned to the party guests. "Come on, everybody! Let's dance," he shouted into the mic before leaping off the stage and pulling his wife onto the dance floor.

The rest of the Montgomery clan quickly followed suit, leaving Marc, Dax, Dax's girlfriend, Cori, and his parents standing in a huddle around Chloe.

"Let's move over to the side so we can talk," said Cora, Marc's mother.

The group walked across the room away from the loud music and dancers. However, Marc noticed that while moving with the rhythm of the music, most of the dancers' attention remained on his "daughter drama."

"Now, let's state this again," Marc said, his voice harsher than typical. "Chloe Tate, you said? Part of the Tate family one county over?"

She laughed. "Not hardly." The girl circled her face with her hand. "Don't I look familiar?"

Marc studied her. His mother took the girl's chin between her thumb and finger and turned Chloe's face side-to-side.

"You look like your mother," Cora said. "Do you see the resemblance, Lon?"

Her husband, Lon Cooper, slowly nodded his head. "Jenny Winslow."

Chloe grinned. "Bingo."

Marc frowned. "What am I missing?"

"Honey," Cora said, "This is Jenny's daughter."

At the mention of Jenny's name, Marc's heart skipped a beat. A long time ago, he and Jenny Winslow had married as soon as they'd turned eighteen. That'd been over twenty years ago. The marriage had lasted only four years and had certainly not produced any children. And even if he and Jenny had had a daughter from that marriage...

He began doing calculations in his head.

"Hi, Chloe," Dax said, extending his hand. "How old are you?"

Thank goodness Dax had asked. Marc's brain was too overloaded right now to do math gymnastics.

"Fifteen," Chloe said.

"Does your mother know you're here?" Cora Cooper asked.

The teen's face flamed scarlet.

"I'm going to take that as a no," Marc replied. "Where's Jenny?"

"Amsterdam."

"In the Netherlands?!" his mother exclaimed. "How long has she been gone?"

"Guys, I'm not sure this is the best place to have this discussion," Dax said. "I suggest we adjourn to Marc's house."

"Agreed." Marc gestured toward the stage. "How long is the band contracted to play? Would it be rude to leave early from my own surprise party?"

"Another thirty minutes, but I think everyone would understand," Dax answered.

"I'll say my thanks and goodnights. Then, we can head out." He looked at the teen girl who'd just thrown a twist into his party. "You." He pointed at Chloe. "Don't move."

Marc climbed the stairs to the stage, then using Chloe's example of tapping the microphone, he drew the guests' attention to him. "Thank you all for coming. It's been years since I've had a surprise birthday party, and you did a great job of fooling me this year." He pointed at the group and laughed. "Good job fooling this old man, but I'm calling it a night for me and my family. The band will be here another thirty minutes, so stay and eat up all the food. Thanks again. I'll see you around town."

He jumped down and waved as he hurried back to where his family waited. To his surprise, his sister, Samantha, had joined the group.

"Hey, Sami." He pulled her in for a hug. "When did you get here?"

"Happy birthday, bro. Just walked in. Had to work late. Sorry to miss all the excitement."

"We're headed back to the house. You coming?"

Her wide-eyed gaze shifted to Chloe and back to him. "Wouldn't miss it."

Marc turned toward the teen. "How did you get here?"

"Duh. How do you think? I drove. I sure didn't walk."

Marc wiggled his fingers, palm up. "Hand over the keys. You're an underage driver, meaning in my county, you're too young to drive."

Chloe sighed dramatically but pulled a key fob from her front pocket. "I can follow you."

He shook his head. "No, ma'am. You're riding with me. Cori? You're in Dax's truck, right? Will you bring Chloe's car to my house?"

"Sure," she said and held out her hand. "I'm a very safe driver," she said to the teen. "I promise."

Marc shook his head. "Wait, that reminds me. Where are your vehicles? The lot was empty."

"Everyone parked at Leo's or on the street close to there," Dax said. "There was a bus that dropped everyone off." He looked at his girlfriend. "But by now, it should've started taking folks back to their cars, right?"

Cori nodded. "Yes. It started return runs about an hour ago."

"Great. Let's move this party to my house. Chloe? The keys?" Marc arched a brow at her.

Chloe handed over the key fob. "She's new. Don't scratch her."

Cori smiled as she dragged her hand across her chest in an X. "I swear."

For the first time, Marc saw the teen smile.

"I'll drive Mom and Lon back to Leo's in my truck," Marc said. "Cori, can you take Dax to his truck?" He frowned. "Did you leave your car at Leo's too?" he asked Sami.

She shook her head. "I was so late, I just parked outside. I can drive the folks."

"I'll do it" Marc insisted. "Can you go to my house and unlock the doors? And put your dog in the backyard?"

She saluted. "Aye, aye, Captain."

Twenty minutes later, Marc pulled into his drive and parked behind Sami's truck. A new Bronco with Michigan tags was parked on the curb. His mom and Lon pulled behind that SUV and parked. Dax was parking across the street when Marc exited his vehicle.

"Where does Jenny think you are right now?" Marc asked Chloe as they walked toward his house.

"At a friend's house."

"I have so many questions."

She nodded. "I understand because I do too—how did you not know Mom was pregnant?"

Marc's answer was a sigh.

His family gathered in the living room. Extra chairs dragged from the kitchen gave everyone somewhere to sit. Chloe sat in one of those chairs, her long, curly, auburn hair hanging around her face.

"I think before we do anything else, we need to call Jenny and tell her you're here," Marc said. He glanced at his phone. "What's the time difference between Texas and Amsterdam? Anyone know?"

19

"Seven hours," Chloe said. "The Netherlands is seven hours ahead of central time."

"Great. It's after seven-thirty in the morning. I'm sure she's awake. I need her phone number, Chloe." When the teen hesitated, he said, "Procrastination will not make this go away. I'm going to call her, even if my mom has to call your grandparents to get the number."

His mom held up her phone. "It's kind of late to call Adele in Maine, but I will."

"Mom and your grandmother have been friends for years. She *will* call her," Marc warned.

"Fine," Chloe snapped. She passed over her phone and crossed her arms.

He found the number in her directory under "Mom." After copying the number into his phone, he pressed send, his heart racing. He hadn't spoken to his ex-wife in sixteen years.

"By the way," Chloe said. "She goes by Jennifer now."

Marc nodded as a female voice answered, "Hello?"

Yeah, it'd been over a decade, but he'd know that voice anywhere.

"Jenny. It's Marc. Marc Singer."

Her soft chuckle filled his ear. "Yes, Marc. I remember your last name. I did use it for a while. After so many years of no contact, this call has me alarmed and curious. It's after midnight back there, isn't it?"

"It's late." He felt his family's heavy stares. "Hold on. I'm moving to where we can talk privately."

Sami booed and hissed as he carried his phone to his kitchen. He grinned at his sister as he left the room.

TEXAS BOMBSHELL

"Okay, I'm back. So, Jenny, Chloe tells me you go by Jennifer now."

She quietly gasped. "Excuse me," she said as an aside to someone else. "I need to take this call."

Marc heard people in the background. Then a door closed and the background noise vanished.

"Yes, Marc," she said with a terse tone. "I use Jennifer now. How did you meet my daughter?"

"Well, funny story. She crashed my birthday party tonight and announced to my friends and family that she was my daughter. Is there something you need to tell me?"

"Chloe's in Maine? With my parents?"

"Nope. In Texas."

"Texas! Are you serious?" Jenny went silent and then, with a long sigh, asked, "How did she get to Texas? If you tell me she drove a new Bronco there, she is so grounded."

"Well then, she's grounded because a new baby-blue Bronco is parked at my house, but you're ignoring her claim that I'm her father. Jenny, is she mine?"

"No. Of course not. I was married to David Tate when she was born."

"Then why is she here telling me—and my family, I might add—that she's my daughter?"

Jenny sighed. "I'm sorry she bothered you, Marc. She's been stressed out lately with school and all the traveling for my job. I'll get a flight out of Amsterdam as soon as I can and come get her. Where in Texas are you living?"

"Whispering Springs, near Dallas. You can fly into DFW. What about her father...David? Can't he come get her?"

21

"He died when Chloe was ten, so it's just me and her. I'm sorry. I hate to ask this, but is there someone she can stay with until I get there?"

"She can stay here, and before you freak out, Sami's here, as are my mom and Lon, so she'll be properly chaperoned."

"I'll let you know as soon as I get a flight booked. Is this your cell number?"

"Yes."

"Okay. I'm sorry for the inconvenience."

"I'll see you soon."

He clicked off and walked back into the living room in time to hear his brother ask, "So, you're pretty smart?"

Chloe nodded. "I am. Mom says I got all the smart genes."

Sami frowned. "And you're in college at fifteen?"

With a laugh, the teen said, "Yeah. Technically, I finished all my high school requirements years ago. Mom won't let me go to Harvard until I'm seventeen, so I finished a college degree at a local university. Right now, I'm taking graduate-level classes online."

Marc retook his chair. "Chloe, I talked to your mom."

"Bet she was pissed off. Did she go ballistic on the phone?"

"Pissed, yes, but she didn't blow up too badly." He sighed and leaned his elbows on his knees. "Here's the thing. She said you aren't my daughter. Your father was David Tate, who passed away years ago, so I'm confused. Why are you here telling these lies?"

"It's not a lie," she protested. "I have proof."

"Chloe, your mom and I were divorced before...well..."

"I was conceived," she said, crossing her arms over her chest. "I know all about sex and how babies are made." She waved her hand as though shooing away the idea. "Doesn't matter if you weren't married then. That doesn't make you any less my bio dad." Chloe's voice rose higher and louder with her protests.

"Everyone's tired," his mother said. "Nothing is going to change overnight. Why don't we all get some rest and we can talk about this in the morning?"

Marc had questions—lots of questions—but it was almost one in the morning. The drive from Michigan had to be exhausting. Chloe had yawned a few times on the drive to his house. Right now, her shoulders were slumped, suggesting to him that she was tired. He knew he certainly was. Maybe his mother was right about letting this rest until morning. Whatever this proof was Chloe claimed to have wouldn't disappear overnight.

"Sami, can you put fresh sheets on your bed and let Chloe have your room? You can take the couch in my office. Dax, can you give Mom and Lon your room? Maybe Cori can put you up for the night."

Dax grinned at his brother while wrapping his arm around Cori's shoulders. "I think we can make that happen."

His mother stood. "I'll help with those sheets, Samantha. Show me where the linens are kept."

"I can help, too." Chloe stood. "Just point the way."

"I think Cori and I will head out," Dax said. "But

we'll be back tomorrow, right, babe? I want to hear the rest of the story. Is Jenny coming to town too?"

"She's getting a flight out of the Netherlands as soon as she can, but I don't think she'll be here today. Sunday is my guess."

Dax studied Marc. "Is it going to be weird to see her after so many years?"

Marc shrugged. "Naw. It'll be fine."

However, his words didn't match the waves of nervous anxiety rolling through his gut. They'd been so in love on the day they'd married. But Jenn had a brilliant mind and was much too smart for him. She'd taken college courses while she'd been in high school. As soon as they'd graduated, she'd started college. She'd had enough credits to start as a sophomore.

Not him. He'd gotten a minimum-wage job. That was all he'd been qualified to do with a high school diploma.

With some financial support from her parents, and a few scholarships and grants, their financial situation had still forced Jenn to hold down a job while putting herself through college. He'd never believed he had the potential for college, and it had become crystal clear to him that he was the anchor holding his wife back from fulfilling her potential.

"Dax and I will be back tomorrow, or rather later today. Let me know what I can do to help." Dax's girl-friend, Cora Bell Lambert, PhD, had an active child psychology practice. She was the ideal person to help Chloe come to terms with Marc not being her biological father.

"So, dinner at your house tomorrow is out?" Marc asked Cori with a grin.

"Not necessarily. Let's see how things go around here in the morning." She kissed Marc's cheek. "It'll all work out. Don't worry."

"I know." He looked at his brother. "She's a keeper."

Dax's arm tightened around Cori. "I know, bro."

Cori shook her head with a chuckle. "He is too, Marc."

"We're all set," his mother announced. "Come on, Lon. You look like you're asleep."

"Not as young as I once was," Marc's stepfather said, rising to stand. "We'll see you guys in the morning."

"Where's Chloe?" Marc asked his sister.

"Bathroom. I told her I'd help bring in her suitcase from the car as soon as she's out. You know, Marc, I can go back to my apartment in Dallas tonight. I don't have to stay here."

His sister, Sami, had recently been hired by the Whispering Springs Police Department. As part of her training, she was living in a temporary Dallas apartment and attending the police academy. Having been an MP in the Army, her physical condition was already at the top of the class. She was primarily focused on gaining an understanding of the Texas laws she'd be enforcing.

"If you don't mind, I'd feel better with you in the house. I want Chloe to feel comfortable, and even with Mom and Lon staying, I think it would be beneficial if you were also here."

She snickered. "Worried about appearances, Sheriff?"

"Elections are in the fall. I don't want to have to

defend having an underage, unrelated teen girl sleeping at my house."

"I'm here," Chloe said, entering the room.

"Come on then," Sami said as she started toward the front door. "I can't wait to see the inside of your car. Looks new. Is it?" His sister was still talking as they walked out the door to the Bronco.

Marc scrubbed his hand down his face. *Happy birthday to me.*

Three

Sleep did not come easily for Sheriff Singer that night. When he could sleep, his dreams were filled with his ex-wife. He relived their lives together, their long nights of hot sex, their loud and vicious fights followed, by days of her silent treatment. With maturity, he could see all the ways he'd been wrong...and right. While he'd never have admitted it back then, her brain had intimidated him, and he'd truly believed he was holding her back from her full potential.

Rolling over, he stared at the ceiling and thought about the teen sleeping in his guest room. It was true that he and Jenn had been divorced during the time Chloe would have been conceived. However, it was also true that there had been that one-night stand the day their divorce had been finalized. Their way of saying goodbye, or that's what they'd assured each other. He'd boarded the next plane out of the country with the Army, something that'd been a huge point of contention with her. She'd told him she would not be a grieving military wife left at home. Since their celebratory night, they'd not said another word to each other for sixteen years.

Neither of them had attended their tenth high school reunion. He'd assumed that, like him, she hadn't wanted to answer questions about the failure of their marriage or why the golden couple from the class had split.

That didn't mean he never thought of her. He did.

That didn't mean she didn't infiltrate his dreams at night when he let his guard down. She did.

That also didn't mean he wasn't still pissed off at himself for all the mistakes he'd made with her.

The sweet aroma of coffee made his brain disengage from dragging old memories to the surface. He glanced at the clock. Six a.m. He hadn't slept this late in years. He stretched, and the previous evening slammed into his consciousness. For a second, he wondered if it had all been a dream, but no. Jenny Winslow's daughter really had shown up in Whispering Springs, claiming he was her bio dad.

And then there was actually hearing Jenny's voice again. It'd been the same, but not. There was a mature, sexy, confident quality that hadn't been there in her twenties.

Coffee. He needed a jolt of caffeine. He wasn't expected at the station today, but his showing up every day was more the norm than not. He should probably let the weekend staff know not to expect him. For the first time in forever, his personal life took precedence over work.

After stuffing himself into jeans, a T-shirt, and a pair of joggers, he followed the coffee aroma to his kitchen.

His mom and sister occupied chairs at the table, each cradling a cup of coffee between their hands.

"Where's Lon?" Marc pulled down a mug from the cabinet and poured himself a large black coffee. "He still asleep?"

"He and Chloe have gone to get donuts. He met Porchia last night, and she told him she'd save a dozen of her best pastries for him this morning," Cora replied. "You know Lon. Someone could lure him into a paneled van with the offer of fresh pastries."

Sami laughed. "Dad has always had such a sweet tooth."

"Speaking of Chloe, how did she seem this morning?" Marc took a sip of the hot brew.

His mother shrugged. "Good, I think, didn't you, Sami?"

With a nod, Sami said, "Yeah. Dreading seeing her mother, I think." She glanced over at Cora. "I know I would."

Cora chuckled. "If you'd pulled a stunt like this, you wouldn't have been able to sit down for a week."

Sami grinned. "No doubt."

Marc pulled out a chair and sat. "Everybody sleep okay? Sami? Personally, I think that couch sleeps better than a bed."

She swallowed the coffee in her mouth. "Yep. Slept like a log. But I swear I could hear Dad snoring." She looked at her mother with an arched eyebrow.

"You probably did. He was exhausted."

"Did Chloe add any more to her story this morning?"

Both women shook their heads.

"Not to me," Sami said.

"Nor me," his mom added. "Maybe Lon can get more out of her while they're gone. How was talking to Jenn again? Been a while, right?"

"It was...odd. It's been a very long time, but you and her mom are still close, right?"

"Of course. I see her every Monday and Thursday for Mahjong at the country club. She says Jenn is doing great. I told you she left her medical practice, right?"

"Yeah. Took some job with a medical company or something?"

"Executive Vice President for Research and Development for Stroker Medical."

"Probably why she was in Europe," Sami said.

Marc scratched his chin. "She didn't say." As he lifted his coffee mug, he watched the baby-blue-colored Bronco pull into his drive. His brother's truck stopped and parked along the curb. "Lon and Chloe are back, and it looks like Dax and Cori are with them."

"Good morning," Cori called as the front door opened. "We come bearing fresh donuts and pastries."

"Great," Sami yelled. "I'm starving to death."

Marc sighed, but a thrill of pleasure settled in his gut. Until very recently, his house had always been quiet and empty. Now, it seemed as though the walls were bursting at the seams with family and noise. He found it oddly comforting.

Cori set a large white box on the table. "We ran into these two at Porchia's. Since we were coming here, she made sure the pastry boxes held different things."

"Yum," Sami said.

"I promise you will all be spoiled when you leave here," Marc said with a laugh. He opened the box Lon had added to the table and drew in a deep breath full of the delicious aromas of sugar, dough, and oil. "I promise that nobody is a better baker than Porchia."

Dax threw his arm around Cori. "You haven't tasted Cori's pies."

Marc pointed an almond croissant at his brother. "I'll look forward to it." He noticed Chloe standing in the doorway, looking a little overwhelmed, not that he could blame her. His family could be a little loud and rowdy when they were all together. He used the croissant to point to a chair. "Have a seat, Chloe. Want something to drink?"

"Coffee, please."

"I'll get it," Sami said, jumping up from her chair.

"I bet you didn't expect to face my entire family when you decided to drive to Texas, did you?" Marc asked with a smile. "They can be hard to take in one swoop, especially that one." He pointed to his sister.

"Hey, I resemble that remark," Sami said, setting the coffee in front of Chloe. "Milk and sugar are in front of you."

The teen chuckled. "I hadn't given meeting anyone other than you much thought."

Each family member found a place around the table, some in chairs, others perched on stools.

"Chloe, when I talked to your mom last night, she assured me you are not my daughter."

The teen bit into a bear claw and shrugged. "Well, she's wrong. You are."

Marc held back a sigh. Were all teens so stubborn?

"I don't believe your mother would've lied to Marc," his mother said.

"She's not lying," Chloe said. "She's just wrong. DNA doesn't lie."

Marc ran his hand down his face. "DNA."

"That's right. DNA," Chloe said.

He blew out a breath. "I think I'm going to need you to explain."

She swallowed the last bit of her bear claw and reached for a chocolate donut. "Like I said last night, I'm smart."

"And humble, too," Sami said.

The teen shrugged. "It is what it is. I took a biology class at the university last semester. The course curriculum included a segment on genetics. As part of a class project, each of us did our own DNA test. We had to fill a tube with spit. It was easy but kind of gross. Anyway, I got Mom's sample to send with mine. Since the man I believed to be my father, David Tate, is deceased, I couldn't get his but he had a twin. I got Uncle Paul to give me a sample of his spit." She looked at the group. "Not all identical twins share identical DNA material since gene mutations can occur after the fertilized egg splits, but it was the best thing I could do at the time."

"And then?" Cora prompted.

"The results came back in a couple of months. Obviously, Mom came back as my parent, but my test reported no DNA match with my uncle. None. It's impossible for David to be my biological father when I share no common DNA with his twin brother. But I had all these first cousins and first-cousins-once-removed popping up. All of them shared the last name of Montgomery or Landry. I knew I had this whole group of Montgomerys I was related to, but I didn't know a single Montgomery. I was stymied for a while, not sure where to go with these results."

"Why didn't you just ask your mother?" Marc asked.

"I did," she said with teen disdain. "She handed me my birth certificate, and I guess that was supposed to be the end of it."

"Are you telling us that you told Jenny that your DNA tests didn't show David Tate as your biological parent, and her response was to hand you a piece of paper? That doesn't sound like the girl I knew growing up," Cora said.

"Well," Chloe said, "maybe I didn't exactly tell her that, but I did ask if she was dating anyone other than Dad during that time. She said no. She met him, knew he was the one, and married him within two months after they met."

Marc's stomach cramped with her words. David Tate was the love of Jenny's life, not him. That hurt. He'd always had a faint dream that she'd held a secret flame for him burning in her heart. Obviously not.

"Anyway," Chloe continued, "I decided I needed to find out who all these Montgomerys were. I reached out via email and got a response from Olivia Montgomery Landry. When I asked about the Montgomery family, she explained they were in Texas. She was kind enough to run through who each Montgomery was and how they were related to her. There was also a Noah Graham, who she explained was related to her brother's wife. He was the one who collected all their samples and sent them in. Like me, it was some type of school project." The corner of her mouth twisted up, and she shrugged. "I guess I need to find him and thank him. Without him, I'd never have found you guys."

"I'm not following," Marc said. "Olivia had no idea I was related to her, or that Dax and Sami even existed."

"Yeah, she knew. She told me about the missing sister. I think that must be you, Mrs. Cooper."

"Call me Cora, and yes, that would be me."

"I did a ton of online research on the Montgomery family. You also have a distant branch in Wyoming, in case you didn't know." She looked at Marc's mother. "You have a nice teaching profile, Cora."

His mother blushed. "Thank you, dear."

"If we have time, I'd love to discuss some advanced calculus concepts I've been working on."

Cora beamed. "I'd love to."

"Back to the story," Marc said.

"Ah, well, you are my mother's age. You went to school together. Your high school annual shows you and Mom as a couple. Once while she was gone, I dug through some boxes in the attic and found your marriage license and wedding pictures." She looked at Dax. "I'm pretty sure you were out of the country when I was conceived, so I didn't think you could be my father. And Sami?" She looked at his sister. "You weren't even in the running."

Sami laughed. "Oh yeah. I lack the necessary equipment."

Chloe turned her gaze to Marc. "So that left you, Marc."

"We'd broken up and divorced by then," Marc insisted, choosing to ignore that one time he and Jenny had been together after the divorce. They'd had sex for years without a pregnancy. He found it hard to believe that that one time had led to this.

She shrugged. "Give me some spit, and in a couple of months, we'll know if you're my father or not. On the other hand, give me a vial of blood, and we'll know a lot quicker."

Marc pulled his arm off the table. "Yeah, well, I like all my blood."

"I'll give you my blood," Dax said. "I want to know if I have a niece."

Marc glared at him. "No, you will not."

Chloe frowned. "Look, Marc, either I'm your kid or I'm not. I think I am. Don't you want to know for sure?"

Marc rubbed the back of his neck. "Let's get your mom here and see what she has to say." He hated to admit that the teen presented a strong argument for his parentage, and he wasn't sure how he felt about that. Her arrival and news left him flat-footed when it came to responding.

Chloe shrugged. "She's not going to be pleasant to be around. You've been warned."

"I've been warned," Marc agreed.

Cori leaned around Dax. "Cora, when are you and Lon headed back to Maine?"

"Yeah," Dax said. "I swear you told me you were teaching this summer."

Cora wrinkled her nose. "Unfortunately, we have to leave tomorrow. Classes start on Monday."

"How long is this summer session?" Marc asked, suddenly wanting his mother to stay longer. He might be almost forty, but he needed his family around him right now. Thank God Dax hadn't died overseas. He felt the same way about Sami—glad she'd completed her military years—but she hadn't been blown up in Afghanistan as Dax had.

"Only three weeks. I'm not teaching again until the fall session, so we'll be back before you know it." She looked at Chloe. "I'm afraid our discussion about advanced calculus might have to wait."

"Or we can talk by phone," the teen said.

"Or we can talk on the phone, or email, or text," his mother agreed with a smile. "I'm also on all the social media sites."

"I know," Chloe said. "I stalk you there."

His mother laughed.

"Have you heard from my mom?" Chloe asked Marc.

"I haven't looked," Marc confessed. "I'm not used to waking up to company and talking in the mornings. Hold on. I'll check." He retrieved his phone from the charger and opened his text messages. Sure enough, there was a flight number and estimated arrival. "Jenny will be in this afternoon about one."

Cori stood. "Dax and I have a few things we need to get done today. You're still invited to dinner tonight." She looked around the table. "All of you are."

"That's sweet of you, Cori, but we don't want to inconvenience you," Cora said.

"I wish I could, but I don't think it'll happen," Sami said. "So, unless something changes, don't expect me." She looked at her phone and stood. "I've got to get going now. Thanks for the donuts," she said to Cori and Chloe. "And the couch, bro." She hugged her parents. "Love you guys. Sorry, I have to go."

"We'll be back, honey," her mother said.

"Call me when you get home," Sami said. "Sorry I'm tied up the rest of the weekend."

"We understand," her dad said as he hugged her.

The door slammed behind Sami as she left.

"Dax and I should get a move on too," Cori said. "Please come for dinner. I love to cook. Come at six, and we'll have drinks. Okay? Please?"

"Of course we will," Cora replied. "Lon and I will enjoy it. What can we bring?"

"Just your appetites," Cori said with a smile.

Cora patted her husband's stomach. "Never a problem with this one."

"See you tonight, too, Marc? Bring Chloe and her mom."

"We'll see," Marc said. "Jenn and I have a lot to discuss tonight."

"Understood."

"I'd love to come over for dinner," Chloe said. "Text me the address and—"

"And she won't be driving over," Marc said. "Not legal."

Chloe crossed her arms in a defiant stance and glared.

Marc shrugged. "Glaring doesn't change the fact you're an underage driver in a county where I'm the sheriff." He looked at Cori. "I'll be in contact about dinner later."

"Good enough," Dax said, "Let's go, honey. We've got those errands."

"Why don't Lon and I take Chloe with us for a while?" his mother said. "That'll give you a chance to check in with the station or do whatever you normally do on Saturdays."

"Yeah, you might want to clean the house," Chloe said. "Mom's a stickler for things like that."

Cora burst out laughing.

"Gee, thanks, kid." Marc frowned. "Who said I was bringing your mom here?"

Chloe tapped the side of her head. "I'm smart, remember?" She looked at Cora and Lon. "Your car or mine?"

Marc just sighed. He wasn't ready to have a teen girl.

Even though all evidence pointed to him being her bio dad, it wasn't a sure thing. No reason to get the cart before the horse.

Chloe left with his mom and Lon. The sudden silence in his house was unnerving, as was the emptiness. He could see the fork in the road of his life. Things were going to change.

As Chloe had suggested, he did need to do a little housecleaning. It wasn't horrible, but it wasn't company-ready either. He spent the rest of the morning scrubbing toilets and vacuuming floors.

Another thing Chloe was right about was bringing

his ex-wife to his house. They needed to talk privately, and that was something he couldn't do in any restaurant or hotel in Whispering Springs. Marc, with an unknown woman, would fire up the gossip vine like a forest fire, especially if they appeared to be having a heated discussion. Yeah, his house was the only place they could talk.

Whispering Springs had a lot of positive aspects, one of which was an international airport within a reasonable drive—as long as one considered ninety minutes to be reasonable, and he did. He'd sent Jenny a reply text that he would be at the airport to pick her up. He assumed she would get his message when she landed.

Using his position as sheriff to get favors was something he did not do, and he would fire any of his staff who used their position in such a fashion. However, rules were made to be broken sometimes, right?

He drove his shiny white, Whispering Springs Sheriff's SUV to the arrival area of Dallas-Fort Worth Airport and whipped into an open space along the curb. He hoped the branding would keep the local airport cops from running him off from parking at the arrival doors to wait for Jenny.

He arrived at one, expecting her plane to land within minutes. To his surprise, Jenny stood curbside, her luggage parked beside her leg. Initially, she didn't see him, which gave him time to covertly observe his ex.

At seeing her for the first time in sixteen years, his heart pounded painfully against his chest. The air rushed from his lungs. His stomach twisted in his gut. A bead of nervous sweat rolled down his spine.

Damn, how could she be more beautiful now? Her

long hair—auburn like her daughter's—hung in waves over her shoulders and down her back. Dressed in gray slacks and a white blouse, she held herself tall, her shoulders back. She wore an air of confidence that, frankly, would intimidate most people from approaching her. She had to be tired after flying such a long distance, but there wasn't a wrinkle in her clothes or on her still gorgeous face.

He hit his emergency flashers and slid from the vehicle. "Jenny?" he called. "Over here."

Her head snapped toward him. She nodded but did not smile. Grabbing the handle of her luggage, she started toward his SUV.

Marc hurried toward her. "Here. Let me get this," he said as he reached for her suitcase.

"I've got it," she replied in a sharp tone.

He pulled his hand back. "Okay, then. Over here."

After leading her to his SUV, he opened the rear door for her luggage. "Can I help you put it in?" He heard his words and wanted to snicker. Being around the girl of his youth apparently brought out the thirteen-year-old still living inside.

She, however, did not look amused. "No. I'm fine." She jerked the luggage off the concrete and into the rear seat. Afterward, she slid into the front passenger seat as he held the door open.

It was possible she could have given him a chillier reception, but he wasn't sure how. And besides, what put a stick up her ass? It was his life being disrupted by her daughter. He hadn't asked for this.

A spicy, sexy scent assaulted his nose when he retook

the driver's seat. As nice as it was, he would not let it influence him. He was the injured party here, not her.

He fired up his SUV and pulled back into the traffic.

"So, you have a daughter, huh?"

Her head turned toward him. "It would seem you do also."

Four

Dr. Jennifer Tate settled into the front seat of the SUV with a sigh. Curses! Marc looked good. Heck, better than good. Why do men age into silver foxes and women age into crones? More evidence that God was a man. No woman would be that cruel to another woman.

Her first glance at her ex in over a decade had shaken her. She knew he'd become a cop. She didn't know he was a sheriff. Or at least that was what was stenciled on the SUV. *Whispering Springs Sheriff*.

When he'd called her name, her heart had leapt at the sound of his voice. He'd always had a deep voice, but now, there was a gravelly quality that made her insides quake.

They say the eyes are the windows to the soul, but his were covered with a pair of mirrored sunglasses that protected the outside world from looking in. How had she looked to him? Did her eyes expose her nervousness? Did he see the slight shake of her hand as she'd lifted her luggage into the back? Was he sneering inside at her obvious discomfort at being in his presence again?

His face, with its angles sharper and more defined than they'd been in his youth, had aged exceptionally well. His high cheekbones were more prominent. Sure, there were some lines, but those gave the impression of wisdom and experience, not stress and worry. The afternoon scruff suggested he was a man more concerned with his life than trying to impress.

She was so glad her fatalistic view of him joining the military had been wrong. He'd come home strong and in one piece, and for that, she'd been relieved and thankful.

As he walked around the SUV, she fought the urge to pull down the passenger-side sun visor and check for a mirror. She'd done the best she could in the plane's bathroom, but the Texas heat and humidity had hit her in the face the second she'd walked outside the terminal. How did people live like this?

Growing up in Maine, then doing medical school, residency, and work in New York, followed by settling in upper Michigan with Stroker had continued her coolish weather life. But this? Whew. She hoped her deodorant was doing its job.

Marc climbed behind the wheel and fired up the SUV. As he pulled into the line of traffic, he glanced over at her and said, "So you have a daughter, huh?"

Well then. Let's jump right to the subject. No small talk for him.

"It would seem you do also," she said.

His gaze, which had been focused forward out the windshield, snapped toward her.

She held up a hand. "Kidding...maybe...I think." She brushed her hair off her face. "Chloe is, well, *sometimes*, too driven. She's too smart and too grown up for her age. When she gets her mind set on something, it can be hard to convince her she could be wrong."

"Is she wrong?" he asked, flipping on the turn signal to merge onto the interstate.

"Yes, of course, she's wrong." Her stomach clenched with nerves because now she wasn't sure. She'd thought it impossible, but the determined set of his lips was so much like her daughter's. At seven-thirty this morning, her life had jumped on a Tilt-A-Whirl ride, and she wanted off before she got sick.

"She ran through all her research this morning." He glanced over and shrugged. "She makes a convincing case."

"That damn DNA project." She shook her head. "There has to have been an error at the lab. Or maybe with her sample collection. That's possible, especially with home DNA tests like she used. Seems like I read somewhere that up to forty percent of these home DNA tests can give a false positive, so we know it happens from time to time."

"Does it? I know very little about the mechanics of DNA testing, but I've always thought they were closer to one hundred percent accurate."

"If the sample is collected professionally and run in a reputable lab, then yes, the results are close to ninety-nine-point-nine percent accurate."

"Chloe wants for her and me to have blood drawn to get a definitive answer."

"Hmm. I don't know that I want that."

"Why not? Do you think she might have inherited my dumb genes?"

She startled and jerked her gaze toward him, a deep frown forming on her brow. "What? That's crazy, Marc. You're not dumb. Why would you say that?"

He rubbed his face and changed lanes. "You always made me feel so, I don't know, less intelligent." Glancing toward her, he smiled. "You were always such a brain."

"I worked hard," she said. "Everything didn't come easy for me, but for Chloe?" She sighed. "She can grasp ideas and concepts like a sponge in water. I held her back from graduating high school until she was ten. She would probably have completed all the requirements by eight otherwise."

"Did you home-school?"

"I wish, but no. My job didn't allow me to be home all day. That was one of the great things about David." Her heart ached at the thought of the man who'd saved her life back then, but she wasn't ready to tell that story. "David worked from home, so he was the one who did all kinds of learning activities with her."

"Was your husband a brainiac like you?"

She chuckled. "I'm not a brainiac. Neither was David. I have no idea where Chloe got those smart genes. I mean, sure, I'm bright, but I'm not in her league."

"Chloe said your husband died. I'm sorry."

"He did, and thank you. It's been a few years ago. Chloe and I have moved on."

"Do you want to talk about it?"

"No, I don't. There's nothing to tell. He's gone and

left me with a brilliant child whose mind can be scary one minute and incredible the next."

"I noticed that. She seems...driven."

Jenn laughed. "Driven is a nice word. She can also be stubborn, obstinate, irrational, and hormonal." She tucked one leg under her. "I spent years dreading the arrival of teen hormones. Remember those days?"

He grinned. "I do, and I wouldn't go back for any sum of money. Wait, maybe for a couple of million bucks and knowing everything I know now might convince me."

She shook her head. "Wouldn't be the same."

"I know."

"Mom tells me you never remarried."

"True. Thought about it, but I couldn't find another woman with the ability to nag me like you did."

She slugged his arm playfully. "Asshole."

He huffed out a laugh.

The area around her navel tugged at the sound. The low, rough sound of his laugh shot fireworks of happiness off in her belly. Always had, and it appeared she still wasn't immune. For just a second, all the years and all the pain fell away, and they were eighteen again. Deeply in love and unable to keep their hands off each other.

She forced her mind back to the present day. They were mature adults. No longer a couple. No longer lovers. She wasn't even sure they were still friends, but that was yet to be seen. How ironic would it be if it turned out they did share a child?

"This isn't funny, Marc. I mean, my underage daughter drove a long way— illegally, I might add. All the way here, I tried to decide what punishment she should get, but nothing else would have an impact other than taking away her books. Grounding her wouldn't phase her. She'd only read more college textbooks for classes she hasn't taken yet, and the last thing I want to do is encourage her to eschew neighborhood girls of her age who have befriended her." She blew out a long breath.

"Take away her car?"

"Sure, I can do that, but she'll be sixteen soon enough. She has a hardship license restricted to daytime hours, and she's legally only supposed to use it to travel between home and school. With my work schedule, driving her to and from the university was impossible, and I don't want her taking Ubers."

He exited the interstate onto the highway for Whispering Springs. "She sounds like my mom. Mom is teaching some advanced calculus class this summer, and Chloe wants to ask her some questions."

"Where is Chloe? I guess I expected her to be with you."

"With my parents." When she shot a questioning look his way, he grinned. "A lot has happened in the past sixteen years. Dax and Sami are with me in Texas. Mom and Lon came down so Mom could make up with her brothers."

"Still calling him Lon, huh?"

"Yeah. Once I started, it seemed easier to continue that rather than backtrack to calling him Dad."

"You never wanted to talk about what happened between the two of you."

The muscles in Marc's jaw visibly tightened. "Still don't."

"Okay, then. How are Dax and Sami?"

He told her about Dax losing part of his leg during the Afghanistan withdrawal. Being trained as an orthopedic surgeon and now working for a medical device company, she was fascinated.

"How's he doing with the artificial leg? We've got some impressive new improvements on the near horizon," she said.

"Actually, he's doing great. He has a serious girlfriend who's been incredible in helping him get back to normal. Heck, she's got him riding horses again."

"I look forward to meeting her if I have time while I'm here. And Sami?"

"She hired on at the Whispering Springs Police Department. She's in the police academy right now, but she'll be a good fit for that department."

"Wait. You're driving a county sheriff's car, and she went to work at the police department?"

"Well, I'm driving a sheriff's car because I'm the sheriff."

"I wondered about that. Marc, that's awesome. Good for you. You like the job?"

"Love it most of the time. Some of the job sucks, like domestic abuse or child abuse calls, but I like serving the community. I've worked hard to get the department staffing up to par in numbers and training."

"Why didn't you hire Sami?"

"Can you imagine me telling Sami what to do?" He

shook his head. "No, thank you. I have enough headaches without adding her to the mix."

Jenn laughed. "Remember the time you forbid her from following us on a date, and she did anyway? Then she wrecked her bicycle trying to ride up the mountain and we had to take her to the ER for stitches?"

He chuckled, and damn. That sound was as sexy as his laugh.

"I remember." He nodded. "She and I were both grounded for two weeks."

"Not that that stopped you from going out the window at night."

He looked at her with a sexy grin. "No ma'am. I had a woman waitin'. I had to go."

This time, with a shake of her head, she laughed.

As they drove, she began to see signs advertising various businesses in Whispering Springs, Texas. She gestured toward the next one they passed. "Are we getting close?"

"Just outside of town."

"How large is Whispering Springs?"

"About twenty-thousand people, as of the last census report, but I wouldn't be surprised if we've grown since then."

"Are you here for good?"

"I think so. I love the area. The people are pretty nice, and I have tons of cousins and extended family in the area, so I'm pretty happy."

"At some point, I want the whole story on your mom and her brothers, but right now, I need to focus on Chloe."

"Sure." He paused then glanced her way. "Jenny?"

"Yeah?"

"Is there *any* way I could be her father?"

Jenn chewed on her bottom lip.

"I mean, we were together that one time," Marc said. "And we didn't bother with a condom."

"Yes, I remember." She sighed. The night was burned into her memory like a brand. There'd been no way to remove it.

"So, it's possible?"

"I suppose, but I don't think so."

"Let me ask you a delicate question."

Jenn looked at him. "Don't bother. I slept with David fairly quickly. When I discovered I was pregnant, he was thrilled. I mean, like over the moon happy. He wanted me, and he wanted the baby." She averted her gaze away from him. "You were gone, Marc. Out of the country and out of my life. Standing beside me was a man who adored me and wanted to support me emotionally and financially through med school and residency." She glanced toward him. "He handed me a lifeline, and I took it. No questions asked." She looked away. "Besides, you didn't want children, remember? You told me if I got pregnant, I should abort."

Her stomach ached at the memory.

"I was such a fuck-up back then," Marc said. "I didn't mean it." He reached over. and for the first time, touched her shoulder. "I am so sorry. That was a horrible thing to say to my wife, especially since I only said it to hurt you."

"It's the past," she said. "Water under the bridge." She

didn't mention that the memory of that night, those words, that fight still caused her so much pain.

"Is it?" Marc shook his head. "I was lost, Jenny. You knew what you wanted to do with your life. I was an immature fool who was jealous of his wife. I hope you can forgive me, and we can be friends."

She arched a brow. "Friends? That's what you want?"

"That's what I want."

His voice held such conviction that she believed him.

"Okay. We can try being friends."

He turned into a residential area. "We're almost to my house. I think we should decide how we want to handle this father situation before we get there. The last thing I want to do is show a divided front to Chloe." He pulled over to a curb and stopped. "Would it be so horrible if I were her father?"

Her palms began to sweat at his words. She slid her hands down her slacks covering her thighs. "I don't know, Marc." She looked at him. "I'm very conflicted on this."

"You've never questioned if I could be her father?"

Her eyes closed, and her shoulders slumped. "Of course, I've wondered. I never saw a piece of David in her, but ..." She looked at him. "She laughs like you. She has a freckle birthmark on her upper thigh that matches yours. And frankly, her advanced intelligence reminds me of your mother."

He inhaled deeply and blew out a long breath. "I think we should do the blood tests on Monday. If she's mine, I want to know. If she's not, she needs to know that. We can't let her go through life with such a huge question mark."

"You're right, but it's hard for me to talk about that time in my life."

"I know David had a family. She told me about her Uncle Paul. How will they take the news if the tests say I'm her father?"

"I'm not sure. Paul and his family adore Chloe, and she loves them. Paul's children are much younger than Chloe, but she's close to them. She used to babysit for them from time to time. She loved doing that, so maybe we don't tell them...?"

The look of skepticism he tossed her way made her squirm in her seat.

"I know. I'd have to tell them, but I don't think it would change how they feel. I hope not, at least." She didn't mention David's parents. Now wasn't the time.

"One step at a time, I guess. Bloodwork and then decisions."

She nodded. "Bloodwork and then decisions."

Within the next block, he pulled into a driveway and parked behind Chloe's blue Bronco.

"There's Baby Blue," she said. "Chloe named her car," she explained at the question on his face.

"It's a nice truck," he said.

"Fully loaded, and yes, I know I've spoiled her a tad, but damn, Marc. I am so proud of that girl. This is seriously the first thing she's ever done like this. Usually, I have to bribe her to get her away from her computer and out of the house."

Marc gestured toward the backseat. "Want me to get your luggage?"

"Don't worry about it. Once I get a hotel reservation

for Chloe and me somewhere, you won't have to haul everything back out."

He stopped walking and looked at her. "Hotel? I assumed you'd stay here."

"I can't put you out like that. I mean, you've got your folks here, plus your sister and brother." She looked toward the craftsman-style house. "I'm sure you have no room left."

"Mom and Dad are leaving tomorrow and staying with her brother tonight. Dax spends all his time with his girlfriend, and Sami is staying in Dallas while attending the academy. Chloe is settled in one guest room. I'd like to get to know her better even if it turns out she isn't my child. She's your daughter, so I'd love both of you to stay. It would be odd for Chloe to be here with me with you in a hotel."

"Well, when you put it that way, I'll stay. But let's worry about the luggage later."

And right now, the location of her luggage was the least of her worries.

Five

The front door opened, and a wide-eyed Chloe stepped onto the porch. "Hi, Mom."

Jenn narrowed her eyes into a glare. "Don't *hi mom* me. You've got some explaining to do."

The teen's shoulders slumped. "You would never have let me come to Texas if I'd asked."

"So, you're operating on the ask for forgiveness instead of permission theory?" Jenn climbed the steps and faced her errant daughter. "Not a good operating theory. Trust me on this. We'll discuss the repercussions of your actions later."

"Hey, kiddo," Marc said from beside her. "You have fun with my folks?"

"You bet. Your mom and I have been working on designing a software program. She's awesome. So's your dad. He made me laugh all day."

"That's great. C'mon on. Let's go in. Your mom's been traveling all day, and I bet she'd like to freshen up."

"I'll get your suitcase," Chloe said and bounded off the porch.

"Guess she'll get my luggage," she said under her breath to Marc.

"Shooting for brownie points?"

"Oh, yeah."

Marc's parents welcomed her warmly with cheek kisses and tight hugs, which, now that she thought about it, was more than he'd done. Chloe hauled in Jenn's heavy suitcase and sat it in the living room.

"You want me to put this in my room?"

Jenn's eyebrows rose. "Your room? You have your own room, do you?"

Her daughter blushed. "You know what I mean."

"Put it in the other guest room," Marc said.

"But Cora and Lon..." Chloe started.

"Are staying with my brother, Lane," Cora said. "The room's all ready for you, Jennifer."

"Thank you, Cora. You look wonderful."

"So do you, dear." She looked at Marc. "Lon and I are going to head to Lane's to get ready for dinner tonight. I thought we could take Chloe with us so Jennifer can have some time to relax before tonight."

Jenn frowned. "What's tonight?"

"We're going to Cori's for dinner. She's doing a shrimp boil in my honor." Chloe's face shone with the excitement reflected in her voice.

"Who's Cori?" Jenn asked Marc.

"Dax's girlfriend. I told you about her in the car."

"Right. Sorry."

"We don't have to go if you don't want to," Marc said to Jenn. "We can stay here and chill."

"Aw, Mom. Come on. Cori's cool. She's a child psychologist. You'll love her. She's smart, like you."

Marc grinned at her. "She is. Dax is dating way out of his league."

Jenn looked at her daughter. "We'll see. It depends on how I feel later."

"If you're too tired, don't worry about going," Cora said. "We'll take Chloe with us and bring her back later." She walked over and hugged Jenn, then whispered, "You and Marc need to talk and make some decisions. Take some time with him, and let me enjoy meeting my grandchild."

When Jenn pulled back and gave Cora a questioning look, Cora said, "I know what I know."

"What does that mean?" Chloe asked.

"Adult talk," Jenn answered. "You have everything you need for tonight?"

"Totally," Chloe said. "I'll take your luggage to your room. Marc, would you move your car so Lon can drive Baby Blue?"

"Sure."

Chloe hefted the weighty suitcase and headed toward the rear of the house.

"It'll all work out," Cora told Jenn. "Life has a way of tossing us a few curves, as I well know." She shook her head. "Don't be stubborn like me. I didn't talk to my brothers for decades and mostly punished myself by missing out on so much. Take those curves at full speed, and never let fear of the unknown slow you down. Got it?"

Jenn nodded. "Got it. I'll keep that in mind."

Her daughter raced back into the room with a small bag.

"What's with the bag?" Jenn asked.

Chloe lifted it. "Swim suit and beach towel that Cora and Lon bought me. Lane has a pool."

"Ah. Okay. I'll see you later. Give me a hug."

Her daughter wrapped her arms around Jenn and hugged her tightly. "I'm glad you're back. Don't be too mad at me."

Jenn took her daughter's face between her hands. "I love you too much to be mad for long, but we *will* be having a very long talk in the very near future."

Chloe scrunched her nose. "I know." She stepped out of Jenn's reach and turned toward Cora. "I'm ready."

With everyone else outside, the only noise was the quiet hum of the refrigerator from the next room. Jenn wrapped her arms around herself. She shouldn't be here. She should toss her daughter in Baby Blue and hightail it out of Texas and back to the safety of her life, her world. After all the years of not seeing him, she had to admit that the power Marc held over her hadn't dimmed. She still wanted him, and she didn't dare risk it. She couldn't face him walking away again, only this time with their daughter. She'd never survive. Not this time. She's barely survived the first time. If David hadn't come into her life when he had....

Yes, she'd suspected Chloe hadn't been David's child, but she'd always shoved that thought to the back of her brain. She wouldn't allow herself to even think about it. But she and David had always, *always* used condoms. She and Marc hadn't. David had been older, mature, and stable. Marc had been wild and untamed. Being with him had been like trying to ride a tiger...thrilling with threats of danger.

She couldn't allow danger and uncertainty into her life now. She was the Executive VP of Stroker. People looked up to her. She had responsibilities and people to answer to. She wasn't a young girl any longer. She was closing in quickly on forty. Crazy passion and out-of-control lust should be left to the young, right?

"Well, they're off," Marc said as he closed the door. "I don't know who was more excited. My mom or Chloe. Hey, you okay? You have a strange expression on your face."

"I'm fine. Just tired," she lied.

"Sure. I get it. C'mon on. I'll show you where you're staying, and you can lay down if you want."

She stopped him with a hand on his arm. "Can I get something to drink?"

"Of course. Coffee? Coke? Tea?"

"Coffee, please. I have a headache, and I think the caffeine will help."

She took a seat at the kitchen bar as he brewed two cups of coffee.

"Milk? Sugar?"

She shook her head. "Black is fine." Her fingers curled around the yellow mug. "We should talk."

"We've been talking. I thought we'd said everything." He sat next to her at the bar.

"If you really want to do DNA blood tests, I'll give my permission."

"I do."

"If it comes back that she is your daughter—"

"And it will," he interjected.

"If it comes back that she is your daughter," she began again, "I don't expect anything from you."

He frowned. "What do you mean?"

"I won't be looking for child support or anything," she said. "You won't have any obligations to her."

His face turned red with anger. "You think I wouldn't or couldn't support my own child?" He slammed his chair backward and stood. "Just how low is your opinion of me?"

Six

Marc's hands rolled into fists. Once again, Jennifer Winslow Singer Tate had told him in not so many words that he wasn't good enough...that she was the smart one, the one who had all the answers.

"That's not what I meant, Marc," she said coolly. "Sit down and stop overreacting."

"Like always, isn't that what you mean?"

"No, and stop putting words in my mouth. Sit down."

Instead, he paced around the kitchen. "I want that test. I want to definitively know. And if she's mine, and I'm beginning to think even you think she's my kid, then I want to get to know her. I want her to stay here in Whispering Springs for the summer."

She raised her chin. "That's not happening. I can't stay here for months. I have a job,"

"I didn't ask you to stay, did I? I said I wanted Chloe to stay."

Her lips pressed into a firm line, "I'm still her mother,

no matter what the test says. I have the final say on what happens with my daughter."

His back straightened. "We'll see about that."

Following his example, she raked the legs of her chair along the tiled floor and jumped to her feet.

His cell phone rang with the station's designated tone. He snatched it out of his pocket and snarled, "Sheriff Singer."

"Sorry to bother you on a Saturday, Sheriff, but there's been an explosion at the Butcher place. Looks like the kids built themselves a moonshine still out in their barn. The danged still blew up and set the barn and fields around it on fire."

"Damn it, Nate. Didn't we warn them last time about making their own moonshine?"

"Yes, sir, but we've had so much rain that Bubba Butcher thought it'd be okay, but then Archie lit a cigarette, and wham! The whole place went up."

"Anybody dead?"

"No, sir. The boys got burned, but it's not that bad. Their pa's pretty mad, though."

"Is the fire department there?"

"Yes, sir, as well as a bunch of other ranchers trying to help get the fire under control. Chief Gruber asked if you could come out to the ranch since it's technically out of their jurisdiction and in yours."

Marc rubbed his hand down his face. Those damn Butcher boys and their love of moonshine. "Fine. I'll be out shortly." Shoving the phone back into his pocket, he said, "I've gotta go. We aren't done talking," he warned.

She gave him a casual shrug. "I don't know what else

needs to be said."

In a gruff tone, he said, "Make yourself at home. I'll be back as soon as I can."

Two hours later, Marc pulled back into his drive. Was he calmer? Not fucking hardly. Those Butcher boys were going to be in jail or dead before they hit eighteen.

Was he still pissed off at Jenny? A little. Maybe he'd overreacted a tad, but what if Chloe was his kid? Jenn had had fifteen years with her, and he was just now finding out she existed. However, he didn't want a legal battle over parental rights.

Whoa, cowboy. Hold your horses. You don't even know if Chloe is yours.

But deep down, he felt a connection to the kid. Could be his imagination, he supposed. Still...

He let himself into his house. All was quiet and still. He began to call Jenn's name but stopped. She'd said she was exhausted. He didn't want to wake her if she was sleeping.

The fire had left his clothes smelling smokey, an odor he abhorred. As he made his way to his room, he noticed the door to the guest room was closed. Fine. She was sleeping. He'd leave her alone.

He stopped short when he walked into his bedroom. His stomach fell to his knees as his breath caught in his throat. The vision in front of him hit as though he'd run into a brick wall. Jenn was curled on his bed, his comforter wrapped around her, leaving only her brightly painted red toes showing. Her long auburn hair spread along his pillow, and he knew her scent would be imprinted on it. He'd have to change the pillowcase if he didn't want to sleep with an erection all night.

Her lips were slightly parted as though waiting for her lover's kiss. She was as beautiful as he remembered.

He swallowed against the lump of lust lodged in his throat. Fuck. He'd thrown so much away with that divorce. But look at how fabulous she was doing, just like he'd known she was destined to be. He would have held her back. She would have settled for less of a life with him.

The first time he'd laid eyes on Jenny had been in Mrs. Matthews's fifth-grade class. She'd transferred in when her parents moved to town. Every boy in the class had fallen in love with her on sight. Every single one. He most of all. So, he'd pulled her hair. He'd teased her with frogs. Then, in the ultimate flirt, he'd snapped her bra, which had really pissed her off. She'd chased him across the playground until she could pull the loop off the back of his shirt. She'd held the material high over her head while the other girls cheered her daring. That evening, he'd had to explain to his mother what had happened to the back of his shirt and why there was now a hole near the collar.

In eighth grade, she'd gone steady with Otis Cranberry. Marc had told himself she was only seeing Otis because his parents had a pool, and she and her friends could use it. Whether that had been true or not, he hadn't a clue, but her unavailability had made her all the more desirable to his hormonal teen self.

Finally, he'd asked her out in tenth grade to the football homecoming dance. She'd turned him down. She'd had a date with a senior that night. So, he'd asked out Jenn's best friend, Anita, in an attempt to get Jenn's attention and make her jealous. It must have worked because Jenn had asked him to give her a ride home in his car not long afterward. And that had been it. They'd been like magnets stuck together...until they'd reached twenty-two and been married for four years.

Oh, their fights had been legendary, but the makeup sex had been hot, and steamy. Their last argument had been filled with accusations and hurtful words from both sides.

"Marc?" Jenn said softy, her eyes opening slowly.

"Yeah, it's me."

"I didn't want to miss you when you got home, so I thought I'd wait in here. I guess I fell asleep." She struggled to a sitting position. "What happened?" She patted on the bed.

Shaking his head with disgust, he perched on the edge of his bed. "Those damn Butcher boys built another moonshine still. This time, it was in the barn. Damn thing blew and caught the barn on fire." He scrubbed his face, the smell of burned wood on his fingers.

"You could've been hurt."

He laughed. "Not really. Most of the time, my job entails speeding tickets, cattle on the road, and underage teen drinking parties, with the occasional blowing up of a still."

"A real-life Andy of Mayberry."

With a snort, he said, "Not too far from true. There's nothing dangerous about this job."

"I like these silver streaks," she said, touching the side

of his head. She frowned. "You smell like smoke."

"Sorry." He stood. "We're due at Cori's in an hour. I need to shower."

"What should I wear?"

"Shorts. Tee. Casual."

"I've been in business meetings and at a professional conference since last Monday. I'm pretty sure I don't have much in the way of casual with me."

"Whatever you wear will be fine, I'm sure."

When she got on her knees to walk to the edge of the bed, his cock took notice.

Down boy. Not appropriate.

She sat and swung her feet to the floor. "Okay then. I'll see what I can drag up."

What she dragged up to wear made him want to stay home and explore how she was able to pull those painted-on jeans up her legs. Then he wondered how hard would it be to get them back over her tight butt and down her shapely legs.

Maybe he'd be the only one who'd see her white silky top and painted-on jeans as sexy. He mentally snorted. Impossible. There wasn't a male alive who wouldn't appreciate her outfit.

She held out her arms and turned in a circle. "Okay?"

His cock jumped. He grinned. "Perfect. I thought you didn't have anything casual."

"Chloe's jeans." She grabbed the waist and tugged. "Maybe a little too tight. You think?"

"Nope." He popped the P. "Looks great."

"I might have to stand all night. Not sure I can sit down."

He chuckled. "I can open the sunroof on the SUV so you can stand in the passenger seat and hang out the top on the way there."

She laughed. "I can only imagine the town talk about that. Do we need to take anything? Wine? Dessert?"

With a head shake, he said, "Cori said just come. She has everything handled."

Luckily, Jenn was able to sit, but not without some complaining, which made him laugh. As long as the subject of paternity didn't come up, they got along great. For tonight, he would let that sleeping dog lie.

Cori's house was a cute, older, two-level Southern home with a covered porch and baluster railing. A couple of dormer windows in the upstairs bedrooms popped from the roof. She'd done a complete renovation a couple of years ago, so even though the structure had some age, the interior was new and up-to-date.

"Cute house," Jenn said as he pulled to the curb.

"Agreed. She'll tell you she watched too many HGTV renovation shows before she bought it and thought the reno would be a quick month." He laughed. "I think it took her almost a year of bugging her contractors to get all the work done, but they finally finished late last year. It might have taken a while, but the inside look great." He looked at her. "What does your house in Michigan look like?" He wasn't sure why he asked, but suddenly it felt important that he knew.

She shrugged. "Rock and cedar exterior. Circle drive. Garage. Five bedrooms. Big kitchen. Big yard. Nothing special."

He didn't believe her. Sounded expensive and fancy.

She probably made ten times his salary.

"Gated?"

"The community? Yes. Why?"

"I don't know. You've seen how simple my house is. I just wondered. Let's go."

One time, a buddy of his had married a very wealthy lady. He'd asked the guy if it bothered him that his wife made so much more money than he did. His friend had laughed and slapped Marc on the back, saying, "My definition of a successful man is when his wife makes more money than he does. Based on that, I'm successful indeed."

Maybe his friend had a point.

Dax was holding the door open as they approached the house. "About time you got here," he said as his way of greeting them. "I've been dying to hug this gal." He spread his arms wide. "How are you, Jenny?"

Jenn stepped into his embrace, and they hugged tightly.

He wasn't jealous of his brother. *He wasn't...* right?

Jenn stepped back and studied Dax. "You look great, Daxton."

Dax laughed. "You and my mother are the only two people who get to call me that."

"And me." Cori stepped around Dax. "I'm Cora Bell Lambert. Everyone calls me Cori."

Jenn took Cori's extended hand. "I'm Jennifer Tate. Everyone calls me Jenn except these two."

Cori linked her arm through Jenn's. "Men can be so set in their ways, am I right? Like an old dog. Hard to teach them new tricks."

The two women walked into Cori's house laughing.

Marc looked at his brother and spread his arms wide. "Where's my hug?"

Dax laughed. "How about I trade you a beer instead?"

Marc dropped his arms to his side. "Now, that's a trade I can agree to."

Once inside, Marc found his dad reading the Dallas News, his mother and Chloe with their heads together over a puzzle, and the ladies in the kitchen. Kobi, Dax's PTSD service dog, was sprawled on the floor next to the sofa. The dog wasn't wearing her service vest, meaning she was off-duty and taking advantage of the time off to nap.

Marc followed Dax to the kitchen and took a bottle of beer, twisting off the top and shooting it at the trash can. It bounced off the wall before tumbling into the trash.

"I meant to do that," he said.

"Sure, you did," Cori said. "Now, go wipe that smudge off my wall." She held out a paper towel.

"Yes, ma'am," Marc said with a laugh and wiped the beer residue off the wall.

Cori poured a glass of wine for Jenn and put the bottle back in the refrigerator.

"None for you?" Jenn asked.

Cori shook her head. "I've had an upset stomach for a couple of days, so I'm sticking with water and soft drinks."

"Sorry to hear that."

"Yeah, but it'll pass. I've always had a sensitive stomach. I'm sure I ate something that didn't agree with me."

"Everybody to the living room," Dax announced loudly. "I have something to say."

Marc rolled his eyes at his younger brother. "Still the attention whore," he joked. He found a seat on the sofa. Jenn followed his lead, but he noticed she sat at the other end, not close to him.

"Mom? Chloe? You guys listen up," Dax said.

"Okay," Cora said, sitting back in her chair. "I'm all ears."

Dax and Cori stood in the arched doorway between the kitchen and the family room, hands clasped and wearing identical smiles. Kobi rose and trotted over beside Dax, her head resting on his leg. Whatever was happening had Dax anxious, and Kobi, his service dog, was doing her job to keep him calm.

Dax drew a deep breath and said, "I know Cori and I have only been together for a couple of months, but...." He looked at her, and she smiled up at him. He looked back at his family and said, "Losing my leg was the best and worst thing that has ever happened to me. But it taught me that life is precious and not to be wasted."

Marc saw Cori squeeze Dax's hand in encouragement.

"When you meet the perfect person..." Dax glanced at Cori and then back at the family, "you don't want to waste a second of time apart." His face broke into a wide smile. "Cori and I are getting married."

His mother's hand flew to her mouth as she gasped in surprise. "This is wonderful." She was the first one in the room to reach the couple. She kissed Dax's cheek and hugged Cori tightly.

The rest of the family followed closely behind with hugs and congratulations. Kobi barked at the noise as though joining in all the excitement from the announcement.

Marc slapped Dax's back. "You're lucky sonofabitch. Cori is awesome."

"I am," Dax agreed. "I was afraid she would think I was crazy asking her so soon, but man, when you know, you know."

"Don't let him fool you," Cori said, snuggling next to Dax. "I was onboard from the second date. He's perfect."

Marc coughed. "Not hardly. Maybe you need to rethink this, Cori."

Dax punched Marc's arm with a laugh. It hurt. There'd be a bruise there tomorrow.

"Where's the ring?" Chloe asked. "I want to see."

Cori flashed a large, pear-shaped solitaire on a gold band. "He's got good taste, right?"

The women gathered about Cori to admire the ring while the guys stepped away.

"I'm proud of you, son," their father said. "I like her."

"Me, too," Dax replied with a grin.

"Do you know when you'll be getting the old ball and chain?" Marc asked and followed the question with a snicker.

Their mother popped the back of Marc's head. "Behave."

Dax laughed. "Soon, I hope, right, honey?"

Cori nodded. "Yes. This summer, for sure."

"What did your parents say, Cori?" Marc's mother asked. "Oh! I just realized Clover Jean and I will be related like we always dreamed." She laughed. "Growing up, we would talk about how our kids would marry each other so she and I could be family, and now, you are. I've got to call her."

"Wait, ma," Dax said. "We are having lunch tomorrow with them at the country club. We're going to tell them then, so for tonight, mum's the word."

"Have you told Sami? I hate she couldn't be here tonight," Jenn said.

"She knows," Cori said. "She helped Dax pick out the ring. I was hoping she'd make it tonight for dinner, but she didn't think it was doable."

"I'll eat her portion of shrimp," Marc offered. "I'm helpful like that."

The group moved into the backyard, where a large shrimp boil pot and burner had been set up and was ready to go. Dax lit the flame under the pot filled with water and spices to allow it to come to a boil. Then he picked up a ball and threw it. Kobi ran down the yard until she could find and retrieve her tennis ball.

"Marc, can you get some tunes going? Dad? Give me a hand carrying everything out, okay?"

"I can help," Chloe said.

"Thanks, Shrimp," Dax said. "We've got it. You can join the womenfolk."

Chloe's face pinkened, and she giggled at the nickname.

Chairs had already been set around a large table covered with a plastic red and white checkered tablecloth.

Jenn and Cora found chairs next to each other and began chatting in low tones, too quiet for Marc to eavesdrop. And once he got the music going, discreetly listening in on conversations was impossible. Chloe and Cori pulled up chairs close to Jenn and Cora to add their comments. Kobi circled the women, finally settling beside Cori, who ran her fingers through the dog's thick hair.

Marc sucked down the last of his beer and headed into the kitchen to grab another. Inside, his dad and brother were standing at the table talking.

Marc held up his empty beer bottle. "Anyone need a fresh one?"

"I'll take one," his dad said.

Marc twisted off the tops of two beers and handed one to his father. "What are you two jawing about?"

"The wedding," Dax said. "I want to make sure that they will be able to come back for it."

"I thought you didn't have a date yet." Marc pulled a draw off the cold bottle.

"Not in stone, and certainly not until we talk to Cori's parents." He rubbed the back of his neck. "They may not be as excited as you guys are. I mean, I'm not what one would call a prize catch."

"Bullshit," Marc said. "Besides, who cares what they think? You and Cori are adults. You can do whatever you want."

"I know, but..." Dax glanced at his dad. "You're okay with my marrying, Cori, right? You understand falling quickly for the perfect person. That's what you always told me about mom. When you met her, you just knew."

His dad smiled. "I'm thrilled for you, and yes, I knew

when I met your mom that there'd be no other woman for me. From what I've seen of Cori, she seems like a wonderful woman. I think you'll have a great life together. But, Marc, you know her better than your mom and I do. What do you think?"

"I think Dax got lucky. Cori's a catch. Why the guys in this town never saw that is beyond me."

"Probably blinded by her sisters."

Marc nodded.

Their father frowned. "What's wrong with her sisters?"

"Not a thing," Marc said. "Beautiful women, both of them. It's just that I think Cori has always felt like her lamp didn't shine as bright as theirs. Am I on target, Dax?"

With a nod, he said, "Spot on, which is ridiculous. Cori has more going for her than either of them." Dax looked around. "The water's going to boil soon. Leave the shrimp in the fridge until we're ready. Dad? Grab the plate of corn. Marc, carry out the potatoes."

"What are you going to do?" Marc asked with a chuckle.

"What else?" Dax pulled a beer from the refrigerator. "I'm carrying a beer."

Paper plates and napkins filled a large trash bag as dinner was finished and clean up began. Cora whipped the disposable tablecloth off the table and jammed it into the standing trash bag. Jenn and Chloe folded up the chairs and stashed them in the small storage room Cori indicated. The men carried the dirty platters back into the house.

Dax loaded the dishwasher and leaned against the counter with a wide grin. He patted his stomach. "Anyone leave room for dessert?"

Cora groaned. "I don't know, son. I think I ate my weight in shrimp."

"Would everyone please take a seat in the dining room?" Cori said. "We have another surprise."

Marc led the way from the kitchen to Cori's small dining room, where a dark-wood table gleamed under the ceiling lights. Each person found a chair and sat. As soon as they were settled, Dax and Cori came from the kitchen with Cori carrying a cake covered with thirty-nine flaming candles. They were singing "Happy Birthday" at the top of their lungs. The rest of the family joined in.

Setting the cake in front of Marc, Cori said, "Next year, I'll have to bake a full sheet cake just to have enough room for all the candles. Make a wish."

Marc laughed, thought about what he wanted most in the world, and blew out the thirty-nine candles.

"Whew," Dax said. "I was worried we were going to set off the smoke alarm."

Marc groaned. "You're not that far behind me."

"I know, I know." Dax held up his hands in surrender.

"Am I too late?" a voice called from the living room.

"Sami!" Cora called. "You made it."

Marc's sister rushed into the dining room. She threw her arms around Marc's neck. "Happy birthday, old man."

Marc swatted behind his chair, catching her on her ass.

"Hey!" she protested.

"You deserve it," Marc said, still laughing.

"And you're not too late," Cori said. "We're just now cutting the cake."

"Hey, Sami." Jenn waved from the far end of the table.

"Jenny!" Sami hurried around the table until she could hug her former sister-in-law. "You look fabulous."

Jenn fluffed her hair. "Nothing like a ten-hour flight and a short nap to make a woman look her best."

Sami was laughing as she pulled up a chair next to Jenn. "Hey, Chloe. How's it going?"

The teen grinned. "Good."

"Now, before we cut the cake...." Dax started.

"Ohmygod," Marc moaned loudly. "He's going to give another speech."

"Hush," his mother scolded playfully. "He fixed dinner. He gets the floor."

Marc's eye-roll was accompanied by chuckles around the table.

"We, that is, Cori and I, were going to give Marc his birthday present last night. But..." He arched a brow toward Chloe. "We were upstaged."

"Sorry, not sorry," she called back.

"Anyway, happy birthday, bro." Marc set a thin, white box tied with a blue bow on the table. "You're a hard man to buy for."

"Thanks, Dax. Thanks, Cori." He untied the bow and lifted the lid. Pushing the tissue paper aside revealed a framed watercolor. He lifted the painting out of the box and studied it. The picture was of a driveway that passed between two rock columns and under an arch. He recognized the columns and drive as the entrance to the old Hanson's Ranch. He wanted to buy it, dreamed of having it, but on a sheriff's salary, the price was way out of his financial range.

On the archway over the drive, the words SINGER RANCH had been added. He looked up at Dax. "I love it. My dream in a painting." He held up the print for the others to see.

"Pass it here," Sami said. "I want to see it up close."

As Marc handed the watercolor painting to his mother to pass along, Dax said, "Wait. That's not all. Keep digging, Marc."

"*Oookkaay.*" Marc dragged out the word as he pulled tissue paper from the box. From the bottom, he lifted a plain, number ten envelope with his name typed on the front. "This what I'm looking for?"

Dax and Cori smiled. Dax draped his arm around Cori. "That's it."

"I hope it's a million dollars," Marc said playfully.

Dax just grinned wider.

The envelope flap wasn't sealed, so it was easy for Marc to pull the pages out. His brow furrowed as he read the word "DEED" written across the top in large letters. "I don't understand," he said to Dax.

"Keep reading."

Marc's gaze scanned the document until all the pieces clicked into place. His mouth gaped. "You bought the Hanson Ranch?"

"No. *We*—you and me—bought the Hanson Ranch, just like you wanted."

"But, how?" He knew his eyes were wide with shock as he looked at his brother. "How could you afford this?"

"I came into some money recently, and well, I wanted to do something for my big brother." Dax held out his hands. "You really wanted that ranch, right? The price was right, so, wham, bang! I bought it for us."

Marc stood, shock ringing through his body. He'd meant to walk over to Dax, but his legs refused to move. He grasped the back of his chair to keep himself upright. "You're not kidding? This isn't some type of birthday joke?"

"Nope. Not kidding."

"Why? How? I don't know what to say."

Dax walked over to where Marc stood. "You have always been there for me. Growing up, you were my best friend. You kicked Bill Jenner's ass in the sixth grade when he pushed me off the swings, and I had to get stitches in my chin, remember? When I was gone overseas, you wrote, called, sent packages. You were there with me every step of my recovery. Mom read me all your letters. You took me in here in your house when I showed up unannounced. You asked no questions. You accepted Kobi when I came home with her. You are the brother every man should have. Being able to do something like this for you makes me happy." Dax arched a brow. "As long as you're good with me and Cori building our dream house there too."

"Of course. I love you, man. Thank you." The two men embraced as Marc fought the emotional tears that burned the corner of his eyes. "But I have to know...did you steal part of the money that the U.S. sent to bribe tribe leaders in Afghanistan? I mean, I'll have to arrest you and turn you over to the Feds, but I'll still love ya, man."

Dax laughed loudly. "No. I didn't steal U.S. money. Remember the trip to Arkansas to see my buddy who was dying? The one who gave me Kobi?"

Marc nodded, his brain still on overload.

"He was a trust fund baby with no wife and no kids, He had no cousins or extended family. He was the only child of parents who are only children. His parents are so wealthy, they could light their grill with hundred-dollar bills and never miss the money. There is no family to inherit when his parents die. When he died, he left me a sizable inheritance as his way of saying thanks for being there for him. So," Dax shrugged, "I used part of the money to buy the ranch. And before you ask, I didn't use it all. Cori and I have a nice nest egg to start our life together."

"Son, that is the kindest thing I've ever heard," Lon, their father, said as he stood and hugged both of his sons.

"It is," Cora agreed. "I'm sorry your father and I have to head home tomorrow. I would love to have seen your ranch while we were here. But we'll be back, right, Lon?"

"I heard a rumor we have a wedding to attend later this summer," Lon answered.

The cake was cut and pieces devoured, but Marc remembered very little of the rest of the evening because that's the way it was when a bombshell like being gifted your dream property exploded.

Seven

ᑖᕽᓵ

J enn pulled the covers up to her chin and suppressed a little shiver. She could say one thing...Marc had a hell of a good air conditioner. But then, living in Texas—which, in her opinion, was hell's front porch—required a powerful unit to keep a body from melting all summer like the Wicked Witch of the West. Of course, she'd never lived down south and had no plans to do so. However, it was impossible not to see the personal interest stories on the morning shows about baking cookies inside cars or baking bread in mailboxes to show the rest of the country how high the temperatures could get in the South.

This morning didn't feel like that at all.

She pulled on the robe she'd left on the chair and headed for Marc's kitchen, hoping she wouldn't have trouble figuring out his coffee pot. The caffeine pull was a strong one this morning. Finding a brewed pot had her doing a little tap dance of pleasure and relief. She poured a cup, took a long sip, and smiled. Strong and black. At least they still had that in common.

Through the window over the sink, she saw Marc sitting on the deck. Her belly twisted, and her heart rate climbed. She hated herself for letting him still affect her like this. She was a grown woman. She should control her emotions, and she would.

Opening the French doors, she was met by an unexpected cool breeze. "Can I join you?"

He turned and studied her standing in the doorway. With a nod, he said, "Of course. How did you sleep?"

She sat and blew on the hot coffee. "Like I was a medical resident coming off a non-stop thirty-six-hour shift." When he frowned, she explained, "I died and never turned over once the entire night."

"Good. Flying always leaves me tired, as though I was the one flapping my wings."

She chuckled. "And the time zone changes mess with your clock." Turning toward him, she said, "It's really nice out here this morning."

"You sound surprised."

"From the way the national news shows portray the weather in the south, I was sure my deodorant would be getting a challenge, but this?" She gestured toward the leaves shimmying in the morning breeze. "This is nice."

With a quiet laugh, he said, "Don't get used to it. These aren't typical temperatures. But we enjoy them when we can."

"Last night was memorable."

"I'm still stunned." He shook his head. "I had no idea. None. If that framed watercolor wasn't sitting on my dresser, I'd think it'd all been a dream. I don't know how I'll ever repay Dax's generosity,"

"It's a hell of a great birthday gift, but it sounded as though he was repaying you and not expecting anything in return. Belated happy birthday, by the way."

"Thanks." He arched an eyebrow. "Did you remember?"

"I always remember your birthday. I may have never sent you a card or called, but I always think of you on June the first."

"You've had a night to sleep on it. Have you changed your mind about doing the blood DNA test?"

The change in subject was abrupt enough to be jarring. She supposed it'd been on his mind as much as hers.

"I've thought of little else." She stared at the trees as she spoke. It was easier than looking at her past. "If you are Chloe's biological father..." she turned toward him, "and that is a big if..." she looked away again, "then it's only right that she knows, if for no other reason than she'll have access to your family's medical history. David's family has some issues with genetic diseases. His grandfather and father died from Huntington's disease, and even now, his mother is in a nursing home due to early-onset Alzheimer's. His brother has malignant hypertension controlled with a combination of drugs. I've always worried she would inherit those medical genes from David, but now?" She said the last with a shrug and lifted her coffee to her lips. She tried to play it loose, but she'd spent the last fifteen years concerned about the Tate genetic line.

"And David? What did he die of?"

"Suicide." She looked at him hard. "Chloe doesn't know, and I don't want her to know. He began showing early signs of Huntington's, like memory lapses, lack of concentration, and occasional clumsiness. I set up genetic testing for him to confirm if he carried the gene, but he was so sure he had it. The idea of spending years of his life affected, as had his father and grandfather, was more than he could handle. He never showed for his genetic appointment."

"I'm so sorry." Marc reached over and laid his hand over hers. "Sorry for him, you, and Chloe. What happened?"

When she lifted her coffee to her lips, he retracted his hand back into his lap. The whole suicide situation was hard to think about. She didn't want to remember, but nothing would ever erase that memory. "Physician-assisted death in Oregon. I told Chloe he died in a car accident while he was there on a business trip."

She heard his intake of breath with the explanation, and she supposed she could have continued with the car accident lie, but she never was a great liar when it came to him.

"God, Jenn. That must have been awful for you. Did you know before...well, before his trip?"

She took another long gulp of her rapidly cooling coffee. "No. I didn't. Obviously, I would've tried to talk him out of taking such a non-reversible step." She sighed. "He called to say goodbye and tell me he would always love me. He thanked me for Chloe and asked me to make sure she grew up as strong a woman as I am." She shrugged. "And that's the last time we spoke."

"Fuck. That must have been horrible."

"You have no idea."

They sat quietly with their own thoughts for a few minutes. She allowed herself to get lost in the chirping of birds as they flitted from tree to tree.

"Did you ever think of having Chloe tested for Huntington's?"

"I've thought about it, but I haven't taken any action. Even as brilliant as she is, I worry that finding out she carries the Huntington's disease gene could destroy her life, as it did David's."

"I don't have anything like that in our family. If Chloe is my kid, that removes the risk of her inheriting that gene," he said quietly. "Another reason to rule out David as the father, right?"

"Yes." Her stomach roiled with nerves. She had wanted Chloe to be David's child while at the same time, not wanting her to be his. She'd cared a lot for David and would always be in debt to him for the kindness and care he'd shown her and Chloe. David had adored Chloe and would have done anything for her, including ending his life so she wouldn't suffer watching him die. But the idea that her precious child could carry the genes for such a deadly disease had kept her up at night more times than she wanted to admit.

"But," she continued, "she is still my child. Until she is eighteen, she still follows my rules and my decisions. I don't want you coming in at this late date, throwing around unwanted opinions on my childrearing."

"From what I have seen, you've done a great job with Chloe. It's obvious she's a handful for sure, but she's polite and thoughtful." He chuckled. "With Friday night being the exception, I think."

"And she's so grounded," Jenn added.

"Well, understandable." He snorted as he looked toward her. "If only she knew about the time we took off to Canada to see the Rolling Stones in concert."

She shook her head with a chuckle. "Oh, man. What a night."

"And the time we took Dad's boat out for a midnight cruise without permission."

"Damn your sister. We'd have gotten away with it if she hadn't told on us."

"I sure wasn't taking her along like she wanted." He looked at her and pumped his eyebrows. "I had plans."

Jenn laughed at the memory of that night. A starlit sky. Stolen vodka from her parents' bar. Sexy music from his boombox. She'd every intention of going all the way that night with him, and would have if his parents hadn't sent the lake's police patrol to tell them to come home. "I knew what your plans were, you dirty boy."

"Yeah, the same as yours." He was laughing when the French doors opened, and Chloe walked out, her arms extended over her head in a long stretch.

"Hey, you two," she said through her yawn. "What's all the laughing about?"

Marc and Jenn exchanged looks, and both snorted.

"Reliving our youth," Jenn said. "Sleep good?"

"Yeah. That's a great mattress." She sat on the footstool in front of her mother. "Did you and Marc talk about the DNA test?"

Her daughter looked so mature, yet she was still so young. Her baby was growing up too fast. It wouldn't be long before she was out on her own, and she wouldn't need her mother. As it was, Chloe was more mature than Jenn had been at her age. The realization that she and Marc had started going steady when they'd been fifteen hit her like a blow to the chest.

"Mom? Are you okay? You look weird," Chloe said.

"Gosh, thanks for the morning compliment," Jenn joked. "Marc and I were just talking about the DNA test." She sighed. "Are you sure this is what you want to do?"

"Yes!" Chloe said adamantly. "I want to know." She looked at Marc. "But I already know, Mom. I feel it in here." She placed her hand over her chest. "I know."

"How will you feel if David wasn't your dad?"

"I loved him. I really did, but mom...? I never felt a connection to him. We were so different, he and I. I never saw him, or Uncle Paul, in my face or my walk or whatever. I've wondered for a while."

"You never said anything. I guess I'm surprised you noticed the differences, but I suppose nothing about you should surprise me these days."

Chloe smiled and tapped her finger on her temple. "Mom, I'm smart. Too smart is what Uncle Paul said. So did Dad. You think I didn't notice that I didn't look like any of my cousins?"

Jenn's heart hurt for her child. She'd been advanced in her learning as a toddler. It shouldn't surprise her that

Chlo had noticed the differences between herself and her cousins.

"And Mom?" Chloe's face grew grave. "I know how David died."

Jenn reared back, glanced at Marc, and then at her teen daughter. "What do you mean? He died in a car accident in Oregon."

"I'm not a kid anymore, Mom. I know what happened in Oregon."

Jenn's heart broke for Chloe. Physician-assisted death was tough for adults to handle, but she never wanted Chloe to experience that level of grief. "What do you know?"

"He killed himself because of Huntington's disease. I mean, it was legal and all, but he did."

"How did you find out?"

"I found his death certificate one day while I was looking for my baby pictures."

"When?"

"About a year after he died."

Jenn nodded. "I'm so sorry, Chloe. Why didn't you tell me?"

Chloe shrugged. "I didn't know how."

Jenn pulled her daughter over to her and hugged her. "I'm sorry," she repeated. "That had to be hard."

Chloe nodded. "I cried. I didn't understand why he didn't love us and wanted to die. Then I looked up Huntington's disease. According to what I read, he wasn't anywhere near the final stages. He could have had years left with us. It pissed me off that he took the chicken shit way out instead of fighting."

"Oh no, honey. You have to remember, he'd watched his grandfather and father die from that disease. He didn't want you and me to go through what he had. I know this is hard to understand, but he did it because he loved us so much."

Chloe looked at Marc. "I don't know if Mom told you about Dad's crummy genetic genes."

Marc nodded. His face was so serious. "She did, and even though I didn't know David, I can't imagine him wanting to leave you and your mom. I think Jenn's right. I think everything he did was because he loved you both very much."

"How are your family genes?" Chloe asked him in a concerned tone.

"Mine are excellent," he said with a smile. "But we need to do the paternity test to see if David's genes are something you need to worry about."

"Pfft," she said. "Now that I've met your mother, I think I'm a lot like her. I have to be related to her."

Marc chuckled, then looked at Jenn. "What are your plans?"

"For what?"

"For going back to work."

"Oh. I thought Chloe and I could leave here on Monday or Tuesday and head back to Michigan."

"What?" Chloe said in disbelief. "We have to stay here until we have the test results."

"No, we don't. We can get the results in Michigan as easily as here. Besides, you have classes starting next week." When her daughter wouldn't meet her eyes, and instead tried to stand and leave, Jenn caught her wrist.

"Chloe? What have you done? Or rather, what did you not do?"

"Nothing."

"Then look at me."

Her daughter turned, and Jenn knew that look of obstinacy. "You didn't enroll for the summer session, did you?"

Chloe looked her dead in the eye. "I did not. I prioritized this trip over another class. I can take a couple next session to make it up." She retook her seat with a roll of her eyes. "Besides, these summer classes are so easy."

Jenn wanted to chuckle at her daughter's words. She was taking upper-level calculus classes and finding them not much of a challenge. "You're still going home with me," Jenn said emphatically. "You are not staying here. We'll get the blood drawn before we leave, and wait for the results in Michigan."

Chloe scoffed. "Like we don't know what they'll say, but fine. Whatever."

"I'm starving, "Marc said. "Who's up for breakfast?"

"Me!" Chloe replied. "I'm getting hangry."

He laughed. "Get dressed, and I'll take you to the Sunshine Café. They serve the greasiest, calorie-laden breakfast in town." He winked at Jenn, which made her heart pitter-patter. "You'll love it."

She rolled her eyes and patted her hips. "Yeah, like I need more calories." Standing, she pulled her daughter to her feet too. "You know what they say, when in Rome...."

. . .

They took Marc's Sheriff SUV, with Chloe thrilled to ride g in the back.

"First time in the backseat of a patrol car, huh, Chloe?" Marc asked, glancing at the grinning teen in his rearview mirror.

"Uh-huh."

"And last," Jenn added.

Chloe harumphed. "That will be between me and my arresting officer."

Marc and Jenn exchanged glances and then laughed. How could he love this child any more than he did now? One of the questions he hadn't asked Jenn—mostly because he was afraid of the answer—was if she had slept with anyone other than him or David. He understood rebound sex. Hell, he'd had rebound sex. He couldn't fault her for something he himself had done. Still....

He checked his rearview mirror, again looking for evidence of his paternity one way or the other, but Chloe was a clone of her mother. Beautiful. Tall. Thin. Sharp, knowing eyes in an oval-shaped face with a straight nose. Of course, his nose might have been straight if not for that baseball pitch in high school. So, the nose told him nothing. Her hair was the same auburn as Jenn's. Chloe looked so much like Jenn when he'd asked her to go steady at age fifteen.

"Why are you looking at me?" Chloe asked. "Do I have a booger or something hanging out of my nose?"

"Chloe!" her mother gasped. "Really?"

The teen shrugged with a grin. "Just asking."

Marc laughed. "No. I was thinking how much you look like your mother."

"I might be the first cloned human."

Marc chuckled. He glanced over in time to see Jenn roll her eyes.

"I forgot to mention that Dax called while I was dressing. He and Cori are going to meet us this morning."

"Great," Jenn said. "I really like her."

"Me, too," Chloe said. "Even if she's a child head shrinker."

"Chloe," her mother chastised again. "Be nice."

"I'm always nice," the sarcastic teen replied.

Marc was still grinning as he pulled into the parking lot for Becky's Sunshine Café. He wondered if he should warn them about the interior, but that was half the fun of taking newbies there. "Looks full. Glad Dax and Cori got here early to get us a table."

When they entered, Chloe groaned. "What the f—er, fudge. I need sunglasses."

"I'd scold you for your language, but..." Jenn looked at Marc. "I think my eyes are bleeding."

The café's name was fitting for the design. The booth benches were upholstered in extremely bright yellow faux leather. The laminate-covered tables were white, which coordinated with the yellow and white checkerboard tile floor. Even the stools at the counter wore the signature, blinding yellow seats.

Marc laughed. "You'll get used to it."

A loud wolf whistle split the air, and he saw his brother waving his arm from the back of the room.

"There they are," Marc said to the ladies. "Let's go." He put his hand on the small of Jenn's back. He loved how his hand filled that space perfectly, as though God had designed it just for his hand.

As they weaved through the crowded diner, he shook hands and greeted townspeople who wanted to say good morning. When they finally reached the table held by Dax and Cori, he pulled out a chair for Jenn across from Cori and one for Chloe at the end of the table between the two women. Then, he took a seat across from his brother.

"Thought I was going to have to rescue you from all your fans," Dax said.

"Bite me."

Dax laughed. "Now, is that how someone elected to office speaks to a constituent?"

"Apparently," Marc replied.

"What can I get cha?" their server asked as she pulled a pencil from behind her ear.

"Coffee all around?" Marc asked.

"Not for me," Cori answered with a frown. "Just water, please."

"Are you okay?" Jenn asked.

"I'm fine, but that darn upset stomach of mine. The acid in the coffee gives me heartburn."

"Have you seen a doctor?" Jenn asked.

"Take off your stethoscope, Dr. Tate," Marc said. "We have excellent medical care here."

Jenn lifted her nose in the air. "Can't help it. It's like a reflex."

He nudged her shoulder with his to let her know he was kidding.

"Hey, Dax," Chloe said. "I'm going to have a birthday soon. Can I have a ranch, too?"

"Chloe!" Jenn's face pinkened.

However, everyone else at the table laughed.

"Not this year," Dax said. "Look how long Marc had to wait for his."

"Ugh." The teenager's dramatic eye-roll brought another round of chuckles.

"The painting was lovely, Dax," Jenn said.

"The watercolor doesn't do the place justice," Marc said.

Over eggs, bacon, and pancakes, Marc and Dax took turns describing the old Hanson Ranch.

"Five-hundred acres of some of the prettiest grazing land you've ever seen," Marc told them.

"It abuts my parents' place," Cori said.

"Really? Dax said something about building your dream house. Are you planning on building close to your parents' ranch?" Jenn asked with interest.

"Oh, hell no," Cori said. Her eyes popped wide, and she looked at Chloe. "Sorry. I forgot you were sitting there."

"That's okay. I know lots of cuss words in a variety of languages. Want me to teach you a few?"

Cori and Dax laughed.

"Maybe another time," Cori answered.

Jenn leaned over and whispered in Marc's ear, "Are you sure you want to be kin to her?"

Her hot breath circled his ear and shot chills down his spine. His cock responded quickly, drawing his jeans tight across his lap. He stifled a laugh with a cough.

"I hate that we have to go home tomorrow," Chloe said with a loud sigh. "I want to see Marc's ranch."

Marc grinned. "It's not much to see right now. The house needs a lot of work and..." He looked at Dax. "Want to run out there after breakfast to show them the land?"

Dax looked at Cori. "Do we have time?"

She shook her head. "Not really. Sorry," she said apologetically. "We're meeting my folks at the club for lunch. We haven't told them about this." She wiggled the ring finger of her left hand. Rainbow-colored flashes sparkled on the table as the sun reflected off the large stone.

"Understood," Jenn said. "Priorities."

"No reason the three of us can't go as soon as we're done with breakfast," Marc said.

"I'm done," Chloe announced, shoving her plate forward.

Jenn looked at her empty plate. "I guess we're going to Singer Ranch for a look around."

Eight

The ranch tour left Marc beaming with pride. Jenn and Chloe had said all the right things, admired the potential of the older house, and adored the spot where Dax and Cori were going to build their house...at least, Marc was pretty sure he had the right location. Since they hadn't been able to come, he might have gotten it wrong, but as Jenn had said, "Even if you're off a little, anywhere close to this pond would be great."

"All I can add," Chloe said, "is that you need to put some type of fountain in that pond to keep the mosquito larvae from hatching."

"And what do you know about mosquito larvae?" Marc asked with a chuckle.

"Well, the larvae hang just below the surface. A fountain keeps the water stirred up, which keeps the larvae from coming to the top to breathe, so wham! Dead."

"Don't ask a question unless you want the answer," Jenn told him.

"I'm beginning to understand that." He turned out

of the drive and back onto the road. "Remind me to call Dr. Lydia Montgomery when we get back to my house."

"Okay, why?"

"She's married to Jason, Lane's son. She, along with Caroline Montgomery and Paige Montgomery, runs the town's largest medical practice. I'm sure she can help us with these blood tests."

Jenn nodded but didn't reply. He hoped like hell she wasn't having second thoughts. She'd had Chloe all to herself for five years. Was it possible that the idea of sharing her with Marc, or anyone else, was difficult for her? Could having to share Chloe with another parent explain why she'd never remarried after David's death?

Now that he'd thought about it, he wondered if she had dated or had had any serious relationship since David died. After all, she was gorgeous, smart, and financially stable, or at least that's what he assumed, given the description of her house in a gated community. With their divorce and David's suicide, was it feasible she didn't want to risk allowing another man into her life? Maybe even including him?

Lots of questions and few answers. And the only way he could see to get those answers was to ask Jenn directly, something he put on his to-do list.

On the way home, per Chloe's request, Marc ordered and picked up a Hungry Man All Meat pizza from Leo's Grill. Chloe carried the conversation through dinner, trying to explain why the Riemann hypothesis was so hard to solve, something she and his mother had been discussing the previous day. Marc nodded and hummed so she would think he was following her line of thought, when in reality, he had no earthly idea what she was talking about. However, he'd found when his mother did this, the best thing to do was let her talk and for him to nod in appropriate places. The strategy seemed to work for Chloe also.

Jenn was distracted through dinner. She didn't even pretend to be listening to some mathematical theory.

After loading the dinner dishes into the dishwasher, Chloe headed to her room, saying she was tired and wanted to read. He must have looked confused because Jenn assured him this was nothing to be concerned about. Chloe had an addiction to reading, her preference being true crime and mysteries. Her other obsession was unsolved, true crime podcasts.

Following her daughter's lead, Jenn excused herself to check emails and call her assistant in Michigan. But unlike Chloe, instead of going to her bedroom, Jenn booted up her computer while sitting on his sofa.

Before it got too late, Marc telephoned Dr. Lydia Montgomery. Since she had been at the surprise birthday party only a couple of days ago, he didn't have to go into much detail about what he needed. Fully versed on the situation, she was happy to help. She told him to bring Jenn and Chloe and meet at her office at eight in the morning.

"Okay," he told Jenn as he set his phone on the charger. "We're all set for the blood draw in the morning." He sat on the couch next to her. When she didn't scoot away, he draped his arm over the sofa's back. "You've been quiet all evening, ever since we left the ranch. Have I done something?"

She moved her hand to rest on his thigh. "No. Well, yes, actually. Not recently, but in the past."

"Well, that's cryptic." He placed his hand over hers and squeezed. "Want to elaborate?"

"I'm concerned." She tucked her leg under her bottom and turned to face him. "I've tried to forget it, and I know I told you it was water under the bridge, but you never wanted us to have a baby. You told me if I got pregnant, I should terminate. You can't know how those words affected me."

The pain of her words stabbed his heart. He closed his eyes and shook his head. Then he looked into her eyes. "When you told me yesterday to forget it, and you were past it, I didn't believe you. Your soul is all love and caring. I recognized that even back then, and I picked words I knew would hurt you deep inside."

Lacing his fingers through hers, he continued. "That's what I was trying to do...hurt you so you'd be in as much pain as I was. That was mean and immature, and I am so very sorry, honey. I wish I could take all those horrible words back, plus all the others that I said in anger. It's true I didn't want kids when we were teens. We were both honest about that.

"Then after we married, you were getting every scholarship and grant you could lay your hands on while working at the school library and taking a full load of classes. That construction job I worked didn't pay much, and then only when I could work. We were just barely making ends meet." He shook his head again. "I panicked at the thought of adding a baby. I didn't see how we could stretch our money any further than we were."

He moved his arm off the sofa back and ran his fingers through her long hair. "I was embarrassed by my insecurities and fears. I was frustrated with tons of guilt for not being able to provide for my wife. I didn't want you to leave me when you realized you could do better."

"So, you left me instead."

His hand stopped moving in her hair. "That's not how I saw it. I reached for a job with better potential."

"You fucking joined the Army." While the statement was whispered so Chloe wouldn't hear, her tone was harsh and angry.

"For us," he snapped through clenched teeth. "For you."

She leaned toward him. "After I told you not to. After I begged you not to."

"I wanted to be able to take care of you and my family." His breath was coming fast. His heart raced. "I loved you. I wanted you to love me, too. I wanted you to love that I wanted to take care of you."

"I did love you," she shouted at him and then lowered her voice. "I loved you with every cell in my body." Her shoulders sagged. "But love wasn't enough, was it? I never felt I was enough. I only knew I failed you. I failed at marriage." Her head dropped, her gaze falling to her lap.

He turned her face toward him. "I was the one who failed. Not you. Never you."

He leaned forward. If she didn't stop him, he was going to kiss her. She didn't move. Her gaze held his as he tilted his mouth toward her.

Their lips met. Soft, hesitant at first, as though

waiting for the other to make a decision. Marc didn't want to give her a chance to change her mind. Palming the back of her head, he pushed her toward him, increasing the pressure of their mouths. He swept his tongue along the seam of her mouth, and she opened. Their tongues met, entwining and licking as the kiss deepened.

He pulled her body closer on the sofa, almost onto his lap.

She moaned, and the sound almost broke him.

His fingers tightened in her hair as he slid his other hand to her waist.

She pulled back. "We can't. Chloe could walk in any second. This..." She waved between them. "This would confuse her."

"She's a smart gal. She would understand two adults kissing."

Putting some space between them, she said, "Not just two adults. Her mother and the man she wants to be her biological father."

Her words etched into his brain. He looked at her. "If David wasn't her biological father, and I'm not, was there another man who could be?"

She stood abruptly. "I'm not discussing my sex life with you."

"You mean your sex life now or your rebound sex life sixteen years ago?" he snarled; his lip curled in a sneer. Jealousy ate his gut like acid. He despised the idea of any other man touching her, then or now.

"Fuck you, Marc."

She whirled and walked to her guest room. He

expected to hear the door slam, but it snicked shut quietly.

Damn. That hadn't gone like he'd planned.

Over breakfast, Chloe reminded him of the chittering birds in the backyard, jumping from tree to tree and tweeting out their morning messages. Except in the teen's case, she was excited about the blood tests. She'd spent the evening doing a deep dive into genetics and all the various gene mutations, and she wanted to explain every tiny nuance of gene studies.

Marc and Jenn nodded in response to Chloe's chattering, both wearing matching fake smiles.

He was so sure he was Chloe's father, but what if he wasn't? What if neither he nor David had fathered this amazing girl? Who the fuck else had Jenn, well, fucked? Chloe's test said she was related to Montgomerys. That's how she'd found him, but if he wasn't the Montgomery link, who was?

His brother Dax? No way. Unless Chloe's research was wrong—and he was beginning to think she was rarely wrong—Dax had been out of the country. No. Dax being with Jenn was ridiculous. First, he wouldn't. And second, well, there was no second. His brother wasn't a serious consideration.

No, the genetic link to all his first cousins was too strong. He was the one who'd fathered Jenn's child. The paternal blood test was only a formality.

He thought again of Jenn being with another man

back then and in the future. The notion of any man touching her, being with her, was eating him alive. He'd pushed his possessiveness and jealousy about her into the dark recesses of his mind when she'd sent the divorce papers, and over the years, he'd battled to keep that monster at bay. But last night's kiss had blown open those prison doors and let the beast out. The question of who else had been with his wife had kept him on edge all night.

His cell phone chimed, which was the only thing that quieted Chloe.

Leaning his chair back on two legs, he snagged his phone from the charging cradle. "Sheriff Singer."

"Hey, Sheriff. This is Brody Justice. Just got a call from the D&R. Reno said they're missing some calves. Got cows with engorged udders and no babies."

"Dammit," he muttered as he scrubbed his hand down his face.

Reno was a Montgomery first cousin. He and his twin, Darren, ran the D&R.

"How bad?" he asked.

"Reno says they're missing ten newborns."

"Goddammit." He glanced over at Jenn and Chloe and mouthed, "Sorry."

"Darren saw a truck early this morning, so we've got a lead."

"Finally. I'll come straight to the D&R before I go to the station. I have a little business to take care of, and then I'll be out unless you need me there before nine."

"No rush. Wouldn't make a difference if you were standing beside me," Brody said. "Them babies are long gone and probably impossible to trace. No branding on them yet. Too young."

Marc's jaw tightened. Almost a damned perfect crime. The calves are too young to brand, so even if they are found, it would require genetic testing to trace them back to the cow and sire.

"But you're going to like this," his deputy continued. "One of the bulls didn't take too kindly to having a stranger in the field and let one of the rustlers know it. We've got blood."

"Thank the lord in heaven. We're going to get these bastards, and when we do, I can't wait to tighten the cuffs on them. Thanks for the good and bad news. I'll be out this morning." He ended the call.

"What?" Chloe asked. "What's the D&R? What's bad?"

"Did it ever occur to you, young lady, that it's none of your business?" Jenn said with an arched brow.

"Is it a secret, Marc?" Chloe asked.

He smiled at her. "Not a secret. We've had some trouble with cattle rustlers over the past few months. We might have gotten our first lead."

"Cattle rustlers?" Jenn said, the surprise evident on her face and in her voice. "I thought that only happened in old Western movies."

"I wish, but no. Rustling's more sophisticated today than it was back then, but it still goes on. Any time a crook can make money off of someone else's hard work, the chance for crime is there."

"What's the D&R?" Chloe asked again.

"It's a ranch right on the county line. It belongs to

Darren and Reno Montgomery. They're my first cousins," he explained.

"Is this the first hit on a Montgomery ranch?" Jenn asked. "Seems pretty stupid, given you're the sheriff."

"Not the first, and remember, until recently, no one around here knew there was a familial connection between me and the Montgomerys." He checked the time on his phone. "We need to get a move on. Lydia is doing us a solid. working us in this morning, so I want to be on time. Plus, I want to get on out to the ranch."

"Go brush your teeth," Jenn said to Chloe.

"I've already brushed them," the teen whined.

"Do it again."

Chloe huffed. "If you want to talk secretly with Marc, you could just ask me to leave the room."

"Leave the room then," Jenn said.

With a roll of her eyes and a loud and over-the-top sigh, Chloe stood and slowly pushed in her chair. Then, she carried her breakfast dishes to the dishwasher and loaded them into the rack.

"You can drag around all you like," Jenn said, "but we are leaving today, and if you miss your appointment with Dr. Montgomery, too bad, so sad. No DNA tests."

"Fine. Talk behind my back." She stalked out of the room.

Throughout the entire exchange, Marc bit the inside of his cheek to keep from laughing. Once they were alone, he asked, "What did you want to say?"

"First, thank you for taking Chloe in when she showed up unexpectedly." She lifted one shoulder. "And me too. Second. As soon as we get out of the medical office, I'll come back here, load our bags, and we'll get on the road."

"That's no problem. I'll drive you back here to get Chloe's Bronco."

She shook her head. "No. We've imposed enough. I'll follow you to Dr. Montgomery's office in Chloe's car so you can head on about your business." She frowned. "Do you think we have time to load the Bronco now so we can head out as soon as we're done?"

He didn't like how anxious she was to leave and be done with all this. She seemed almost eager to put some distance between Texas and her Michigan home, or was it distance between her and him?

His mouth pulled into a tight line. "You don't have time. If you'd told me you wanted to leave immediately, maybe we could've made time, but as it is, no. You'll have to come back." He pointed toward the garage door. "There's an electronic keypad on the garage. The code is...." He paused, embarrassed that his sentimental streak would be exposed as soon as he told her the code. With a sigh, he said, "Zero two, zero three, eight, four. The garage door will open. We can leave the kitchen door unlocked so you can get in without a key. Go out the same way, reenter the code, and the garage door will close."

He waited for her to say something. She didn't disappoint.

A wide smile stretched her lips. "My birthday."

"Yeah, well, I figured a Whispering Springs thief probably wouldn't know my ex-wife's birthday. That's the only reason." He lied with conviction, but her wink said she wasn't buying it.

"Can I come back now?" Chloe yelled from the back of the house.

"Yes," Marc called back. "Get a move on. We're going to be late."

Chloe was huffing when she entered the kitchen. "Go away. Come back. Hurry up. What is wrong with you people?"

Jenn lifted an eyebrow at Marc as though asking, "Are you sure you want a piece of that?"

He nodded.

Whispering Springs Medical Clinic was expecting Marc and his party when they arrived. The receptionist ushered them directly from the reception room back to Lydia's office. The three Montgomery women were in the room when Marc, Jenn, and Chloe entered. Lydia sat on the corner of her desk. Her sister-in-law, Caroline Graham Montgomery, occupied the desk chair. Her other sister-in-law, PA Paige Ryan Montgomery, was sitting on the credenza along the wall. Three visitors' chairs had been placed in front of Lydia's desk.

"Good morning, Marc," Lydia said. "Y'all sit." She pointed to the chairs, and the three visitors sat. "I don't think I've had the pleasure of actually meeting the young lady who has the whole town talking." Lydia extended her hand toward Chloe. "Hell of a way to make an entrance. I'm Lydia Montgomery."

Chloe shook her hand. "Chloe Tate. My mom, Dr. Jennifer Tate." She indicated Jenn sitting beside her.

"Nice to meet you, Dr. Tate." Lydia pointed over her shoulder. "That's Caroline in the chair and Paige denting the top of my brand-new credenza."

"Hey," Paige protested. "I'm only a little pregnant. Give me time to get heavier before you worry about me sitting here."

Lydia chuckled. "Okay, gang. Marc explained the situation. I've got the lab set up for testing. I know Marc and Dr. Tate have a complete understanding of the tests, but do you have any questions, Chloe?"

Marc chuckled.

Chloe rolled her eyes. "The last time my IQ was tested, I was at one-eighty-seven. I understand exactly what will happen, here and in the lab."

"Chloe," Jenn warned under her breath.

"Sorry. It's just I get tired of everyone treating me like..."

"A teenager?" Lydia asked.

"Exactly."

"Fair enough," Lydia said. "Any questions, Marc? Dr. Tate?"

Both shook their heads.

"You probably know then that it usually takes about five days, give or take, to get a result."

"I read two days," Chloe said.

"True," Lydia agreed, "but that's after the lab receives the sample. The lab's in Dallas, so I expect we'll know something this week." She reached backward and Caroline put papers in her outstretched hand. "Fill out these forms, and we'll be set."

Fifteen minutes later, they were standing back in the parking lot, Marc and Chloe wearing identical blue stretchy wraps over their puncture wounds. Chloe was nervously pacing.

"Are you okay?" Marc asked.

She looked at him with her mom's green eyes. "I want you to be my bio dad." Tears gathered in the corners of her eyes. "What if you're not?"

"Aww, honey," Marc hugged her. "I'll love you no matter what we find out."

"Promise?" She sniffed.

"Promise."

And if he wasn't this incredible teen's father, he thought his world might end.

Jenn put her arm around Chloe. "You're a smart, smart girl. Your DNA test said you were related to the Montgomerys." She looked at Marc. "I'm a betting woman, myself. My money is on both of you getting what you want."

Nine

After a long two-day drive and a night of aching muscles and tossing, Jenn sat at her breakfast bar and hugged the cup of hot morning coffee between her hands. Her kitchen overlooked her back lawn, which was alive with green grass and flowering shrubs. She loved Michigan in the summer. The greenery. The temperatures. The warm sun. However, she could live without all the pesky biting and stinging insects that seemed to thrive in her backyard. She hated using chemical substances to control them. That had never seemed good for the environment or the birds.

She opened her laptop and signed into her email. She'd been avoiding it for the past two days. She'd expected an overflowing inbox, and she wasn't disappointed. Usually, the ones that required her immediate attention were either from the CEO or her assistant, and while she would never confess this aloud, she always went for her assistant's first.

The first meeting of the day was at ten, followed by

ones at two and three this afternoon. At least she got a break for lunch.

As the thought crossed her mind, an instant message popped up from Kevin Bland.

Kevin: *Hey, babe. Lunch today? I leave out for New York this afternoon, but at least our schedules finally put us in town on the same day. Kismet? I think so. Sorry you had to cancel this weekend and fly home. Hope nothing serious. Want me to get us a room at Radisson Plaza? We could do room service.*

Jenn opened her calendar to make sure her assistant hadn't added something and not sent a message. She sighed when LUNCH WITH KEVIN filled the time slot from eleven to one.

Kevin: *I checked with Yolanda, and she said you were free. I asked her to block off a couple of hours for us. :smiling emoji:*

"Mom?"

Jenn looked to where Chloe stood in the doorway, still dressed in pajamas. Then she checked the time on her computer.

"What are you doing up so early?"

Chloe shrugged and shuffled over to the coffee pot. "Couldn't sleep. What's your excuse?"

"Work," Jenn said.

"You're going in today?"

"Of course. Yolanda has a ton of meetings lined up for me. Being gone a couple of days longer than I planned has thrown my calendar into disarray." She thought about the lunch invitation, feeling conflicted about what she wanted to do.

"Can we talk before you go?"

Jenn nodded. "Let me get a refill, and then you tell me what's on your mind." She refilled her mug with black coffee and joined her daughter at the breakfast table built into a sunny kitchen nook. "What's on your mind?"

"Are you still going to date Kevin?"

Jenn tilted her head. "I am not discussing my personal life with my fifteen-year-old daughter. I believe it falls under *none of your business*."

"I am your child, and as such, any man you date or marry, could play a role in my life. Therefore, in a tangential way, it is my business."

"While I can concede that point, Kevin is a friend, and I enjoy his friendship."

The teen faked gagged. "He is his name, Mom. Could he be any blander and more boring?"

The corners of Jenn's mouth twitched as she fought a laugh. "Well, I'm not agreeing with your assessment. Kevin has his strengths. He's nice and easygoing."

"Please, Mom. That man has no charisma. Even his blond hair is boring. And what about Marc?"

Jenn drew in a breath at the question. Her brow arched. "What about Marc?"

If only she knew the answer to that question. She didn't. Kevin had barely crossed her mind since Marc had called on Friday night, or rather Saturday morning, in Amsterdam. Her conference had scheduled presentations until noon on Saturday. Her plan had been to skip all the Saturday presentations and head to Paris to meet Kevin that morning. He'd been disappointed by her late cancellation.

Kevin was a nice guy. A few years younger than Jenn, he was attentive and responsive to her needs...in bed and out. Perfect for dinner dates or other professional obligations where she needed an escort. He wasn't the first man she'd let into her bed after David had died, but he'd been around the longest. He was a skilled lover, and even if she held him only in high esteem and friendship, she'd enjoyed their times together. He believed himself in love with her, but she'd never led him on with false proclamations of love. She knew what love felt like. What they shared was lust and friendship, and right now, that's all she could handle.

"How do you feel about Marc being my bio dad instead of David?" Chloe asked.

"How do you feel about it?"

"I asked first."

"Yes, well, I'm older and your mother, so you have to answer."

Her daughter rolled her eyes, which was her usual response to Jenn pulling the mother card. "I really loved Dad, but I'm kind of relieved not to have his familial genes." She winced. "Do you think I'm awful?"

Jenn smiled and reached over to squeeze her daughter's hand. "Awful? No. If David was sitting here right now, he would tell you how relieved he is too. Whether he was your biological father or not, he loved you from the second he knew I was pregnant. He would have done anything for you."

"Except stay alive." Chloe's lips tightened.

"You can't think like that," Jenn said. "What he did, he believed he was doing out of love for you, for us."

"What would have happened if you'd told Marc that you were pregnant? Would you have gotten back together?"

Jenn shook her head. Marc's sharp words echoed harshly in her mind. Even though she'd believed him when he'd said he was sorry about them, and that he'd only said them to hurt her, she also knew he didn't want a child back then. They might have gotten back together, but it would never have worked. He hadn't wanted a baby, and she hadn't wanted an Army husband. They'd each drawn their lines in the sand, and neither had been willing to cross to the other side.

"Well, I didn't know Marc was your father, so your question has no answer. The past can't be changed. We can only move forward."

"So, you don't believe in the quantum principle of superposition where time travel is possible?"

Jenn laughed. "Good question, and we could have an excellent discussion, but I have to go to work. In this time period, the purchase of goods and services requires money."

"Do you think we'll hear today?"

Jenn didn't have to wonder what Chloe was asking. "Probably tomorrow. The blood was drawn on Monday. Olivia probably had the samples transported to the lab on the same day. A couple of days of testing, so that'd be yesterday and today."

"I want to spend the summer in Texas getting to know Marc and all my relatives there."

Jenn stood. "That's something we'll have to discuss

when I'm not running out the door." She held out her hand and wiggled her fingers.

Chloe screwed up her face with an unasked question and a shrug of her shoulders.

"The other set of Bronco keys. Hand them over."

"What? You think I'm going to run away?"

Jenn tilted her head and lifted her eyebrow. "The keys. Now."

Chloe huffed and stomped back to her room. Jenn packed her laptop and transferred her coffee to a travel mug, which she topped off. Heavy footsteps on the stairs alerted her to Chloe's return.

"This sucks," Chloe said.

Jenn held out her hand again. "Sure does and will continue to suck until I can trust you again."

"I'm not happy right now." Chloe dropped the keys into Jenn's hand.

"Yeah, well, I wasn't exactly thrilled to get a call in Amsterdam that my underage daughter was wreaking havoc in Texas."

A slow smile crept onto Chloe's face. "Yeah, sorry to mess up your trip to Paris with Mr. Boring, er, I mean Mr. Bland."

She ignored Chloe's comment because she didn't want to know how her daughter knew about her assignation in Paris. "What's on your agenda today?"

"Cora, Marc's mom, is going to let me watch her advanced calculus class. It's streamed live, so that'll be interesting."

"I'm sure it will." Jenn dropped both sets of Bronco keys into her purse. "I love you. You know that, right?"

"Yeah, but..."

"But nothing. No matter who submitted the other half of your genetic makeup, I'll always be your mom, you lucky girl."

"Gag. Go to work."

Jenn laughed. "I'll check in later."

Since her typical days were stuffed full of meetings and phone calls, Jenn liked to work as she drove in.

"Call office," she said to her car.

"Calling office."

The sound of a phone ringing echoed in her car, then, "Dr. Tate's office."

"Good morning, Yolanda," Jenn said.

"I'm so glad you're back," her assistant said.

"Has the office been quiet?"

Yolanda laughed. "You wish, but crazy insane is more the truth. Did you see I scheduled a lunch with Kevin today? He was quite insistent."

"He can be that way. I won't need the whole two hours, but leave it on the books. That way, no one can sneak in a meeting."

"Gotcha. Have a good trip? What's Amsterdam like? Oh, what's Texas like?"

"A good trip would not have required me to retrieve my wayward daughter from another state."

Yolanda snickered. "That girl's too smart, I tell you. Idle hands are the devil's playthings, or at least that's what my grandma said when she wanted me to help her clean house."

"And I've got a clever daughter with too much free time on her hands. The devil will have a field day, I fear."

"She's a good kid, Jenn."

"I know. Now, about Amsterdam versus Texas? They're so different they might as well be different planets. We'll talk when I get there. Anything I need to know for my meetings today?"

Her assistant went over the agendas for each meeting while Jenn navigated the stoplights and heavy traffic. Growing up in Maine hadn't prepared her for crazy drivers and bumper-to-bumper traffic. While it was nice to be home, she hadn't missed not driving for the past few days.

Her boss was waiting in her office when she arrived, wanting to discuss her trip and the management of their Europe-based offices. Her morning didn't get any less busy. When she hurried into her office at eleven-twenty, Kevin was sitting on the corner of Yolanda's desk chatting as though he owned the place. Note, he did not.

He turned when she entered, a smile lighting up his face. "There you are." He stood and gave her a kiss on the cheek. "I was scolding Yolanda for letting you run late for our lunch. Are you ready to go?"

"Come on in my office, will you?" She looked at her assistant. "Forward the phone to reception and go on to lunch."

"You don't have to tell me twice," her assistant replied as she pulled her purse from the bottom drawer. "I'll lock the outer door so you won't be disturbed."

Jenn started to tell Yolanda that wouldn't be necessary, but on further reflection, decided what she had to say to Kevin was best said without being interrupted. "Thank you. Take a long lunch. I'll see you about twelve-fifty."

Yolanda grinned. "You're the boss. The materials for your two o'clock meeting are in a folder on your desk."

She left, and Jenn heard the lock snick into place. Only then did she go into her office and close the door.

"It's about time." Kevin swept her into his arms and lowered his head for a kiss, which landed on her cheek when she turned her head. He frowned. "What's wrong, darling?"

Stepping out of his arms, she said, "We need to talk."

He smiled. "You found out about my Paris plans, didn't you?" He took her hand and pulled her close again. "I don't know how you did it, but you always were smart. Fine. I was going to ask you today during lunch, but you've forced my hand." He laughed as though he hadn't a care in the world. "You know I adore you, love you to distraction." He held up a hand when she started to speak. "Yes, I know what you're going to say, but..." He laced their fingers and pressed their clasped hands to his chest. "You're gun shy about marrying again after David. I get that. I understand. I don't care that you're forty—"

"Thirty-nine."

"It doesn't matter that I'm thirty-five. We have years ahead of us to build our lives, have a family, and do all those things families do. I love you, Jenn." He dropped to one knee, and her heart dropped to the floor beside him.

"Kevin," she started, but he interrupted.

"Marry me, Jenn. Make me the happiest man in the world."

She'd tried to stop him from asking. She didn't want to hear those words from his lips. Pulling back her hand, she turned away. "Kevin, we've talked about this." Looking at him, she continued, "I enjoy our time together, but maybe it was wrong of me to tie up your time when I knew we only had the here and now. I've never lied to you. I've tried never to lead you on, but I don't feel the same way about you as you apparently feel about me. I like you. Adore you as a friend, but beyond that?" She shook her head and turned to face her large windows overlooking a park. "No."

"You'll come to love me," he said, walking up to her from behind. "We have the rest of our lives for me to love you and for you to learn to love me back. I know, deep inside, you're fighting against loving me because you think you don't deserve me, but you do."

His heat radiated her back. His scent whirled about her. His tone was soft and loving. And none of these things could penetrate her heart.

His last words poked through her consciousness. He thought she believed herself unworthy of love? Unworthy of him? *Ego much, Kevin?*

"Yeah, no." She wanted to lambast him about his theory that she was fighting her love for him because she felt unworthy, but why? Let the man walk away with his dignity and pride. Slowly, she turned toward him. "This is it, Kevin—no more. You deserve a woman who loves you and wants the things you want. I am not that woman. Let's part as friends with no hard feelings."

His eyebrows furrowed. "You can't be serious."

"Dead serious." She stared at him, and he took a couple of steps back.

"I...I can't believe you're doing this," he said.

"I'm sorry, Kevin," she said for the millionth time. "I will not marry you. I don't love you. I'll treasure our time and our friendship, but that's all I have to offer. I hope you find a woman who can be for you what you want."

"Bitch."

She sighed. Why did men always go for that word when they didn't like what a female told them?

"Probably so," she agreed. "Goodbye, Kevin."

"You're going to regret this. You're going to miss me."

She nodded. "Maybe so. Good luck."

He glared at her, then stomped to the door, slamming it behind him. The outer door also closed loudly.

She sank into her desk chair and rested her head on her desk. After five minutes, she sat up, ordered a turkey and Swiss cheese sandwich to be delivered, and opened the folder for her first afternoon meeting.

The afternoon passed in meetings, memos, and phone calls. When she finally rolled into her garage at close to seven, exhaustion settled over her like a wet blanket. She sat in the quiet of the car. She could feel the change. She had options, different directions she could take her and Chloe's lives. Go one way and get one result. Go the other way, and possibly get a different result.

Which was the right road? Right for her, and, more importantly, right for Chloe.

Ten

Patience was a virtue, or so his mother had always told him. Unfortunately, patience wasn't one of Marc's strengths. He wanted those test results *now*. He wanted the renovation of the old Hanson place finished *now*. He wanted to move to Singer Ranch *now*.

He had very little doubt that Chloe was his daughter. He wanted to spend time with her, but that would be a little tough given his job in Texas while she lived with Jenn in Michigan. He scrubbed his face with his hands.

"Sheriff?" Tiffany Yeats said from his door. "You've got a visitor."

Marc looked up; his vision was blurry from re-reading the recent reports on missing cattle trying to piece together similarities among the theft reports. To his frustration, the vast majority of cattle rustling had been in his own county. His blurriness had to be due to eye exhaustion. He'd never needed glasses and he refused to start wearing them now. He wasn't old enough for glasses...was he? "Who is it? I'm kind of busy."

She stepped in and lowered her voice. "It's Cash Montgomery. I figured you'd want to see him." Stepping closer to his desk, she asked, "Can I do anything to help? Want me to refile all those reports?"

"No, not yet." He glanced down and sighed. She was right. He should see what Cash wanted. Cash was family, and he wanted always to put family first.

As he had that thought, a vision of Jenn and Chloe flashed in his mind. The weekend had been stressful. He'd never been great at expressing his feelings, and looking back, he'd done a shit job on that front, for sure. He hoped he would be given the chance to make it up to them.

"Send Cash back, Tiffany."

She winked. "You got it, boss."

He liked the girl. He really did, but he might not have hired her if he hadn't owed the judge a favor. Her continued flirting caused him embarrassment and discomfort. But they were of different generations. Maybe the way she acted was within normal boundaries for her age group. He had no clue.

"Cousin Marc," Cash said as he walked into Marc's office, his hand extended. Cash's face held a friendly grin, which was a relief since Marc always worried that Cash would hold it against him that Marc had taken Cash's wife out on a date...before they had married, of course.

Marc chuckled. "Cousin Cash." After shaking Cash's hand, he said, "Have a seat. What can I do for you?"

Cash took the chair in front of Marc's desk and set a notebook in his lap. "I wanted to go over the initial plans for the house renovation. I walked through the place with

Dax, and I can understand why you'd want to save the old homestead. It has great bones. They just don't build houses like that anymore."

Marc frowned in confusion. "I'm sorry. What?"

"Your house. Singer Ranch. Dax hired me as the General Contractor for the project. I confess, I hesitated since I still do some part-time deputy work for you, but I thought...Hey! He's family. Gotta take care of family, am I right?"

Marc's frown deepened. "Do what?"

Cash laughed. "Still a little hungover from this past weekend?"

"Hold on. Wait there. I'm going to call Dax."

"Don't bother," a voice said from outside Marc's door. "I'm here." Dax hurried through and shook hands with Cash. "Sorry I'm late. Cori and I had an appointment this morning, and it ran a little behind schedule."

"No problem," Cash said. "I just got here, and we haven't even started."

Marc's gaze swung from cousin to brother to cousin, and finally, he pointed at his brother. "You. Explain what's going on?"

Dax chuckled. "Yeah, in all the excitement of getting engaged and meeting my new niece—"

"We don't know that for sure," Marc said.

Dax pffted out a breath. "Of course, she is. Tell you what. I'll bet you that she's your daughter. If I'm right, I'm paying for the house renovations. If I'm wrong, I'll pay for the house renovations."

Cash chuckled. "Don't go to Vegas, Dax. I don't think you understand how betting works."

Dax laughed.

"I can't let you do that, Dax. You already bought the land as a gift. I just can't..." Marc's heart raced. He itched to get started on the renovations. In his desk drawer were some of his sketches and notes for what he wanted. He had some money socked away, but not enough to do the entire house at once. His plan had been to do the living room and his bedroom first, move in, and then work on the bathrooms and kitchen. His way would take over a year. Hiring Cash would speed up the process to months.

Plus, Chloe. He wanted to have a room done special for her when she came to visit. He wasn't sure when she would come. He only knew that she would.

"Too late," his brother interrupted. "Already done. I hired Cash to build a house for Cori and me. He tossed in your renovation for a steal, isn't that right, Cash?"

"Um, yeah. A steal."

Marc leaned on his desk. "Lying to a law officer is a big offense."

Dax and Cash exchanged glances and shrugged at each other.

"Look, Marc," Dax started, "I never expected to leave the hospital in Germany. To my surprise, not only did I live, but I have fallen for the most beautiful woman and convinced her to marry me. I can afford to do this. Let me do this for you."

With a long sigh and a scratch on his facial scruff, Marc said, "We will be discussing this more. I'm not comfortable with you doing all this." He looked at Cash. "But to tell you the truth, you're exactly who I had in mind to do the renovations. You will be paid by me, though."

Cash shrugged a shoulder. "I don't care who pays as long as I get paid. My wife spends like there's no tomorrow." He glanced around and lowered his voice. "Don't tell Paige I said that."

Marc and Dax chuckled.

"It'll never leave this room," Marc said. "Now, let's talk about what you saw when you walked through the Hanson house."

Marc knew his attention should be on the stolen cattle. He'd been in touch with the Texas Rangers' division that handled these matters and they would follow up. Deep in his gut, he knew the crooks had some insider information. He just couldn't decide if it was from his office or some other law enforcement office. Still, this was his count, and some of the cattle from his family, and dammit, he wanted it to stop. But he could give Cash thirty minutes or so.

Later that afternoon, he was reviewing the reports from other counties when his personal cell phone rang. "Marc Singer."

"Mr. Singer. This is Raj from Dallas Testing Labs. Is this a good time to talk?"

"Yes." Marc's heart leapt into his throat. He could barely draw in a breath.

"Great. Before we continue, I need your code, please."

He pulled a card from his top drawer, although he'd looked at it often enough that he could have recited it by memory. "125GSHS74."

"Great. The DNA test shows that, with a ninety-nine-point-nine percent accuracy, you are the biological father of Chloe Tate."

Marc's heart skipped. His vision blurred as his eyes teared. He found it impossible to draw in enough breath to reply.

"Mr. Singer?" Raj asked. "Are you still there? Do you understand the results as I have explained them?"

Marc coughed and cleared his throat. "I'm here, and I understand."

"Great. You should receive your results via email today or tomorrow and the print copy by mail next week. Do you have any questions for me?"

Marc shook his head, then realized the poor guy on the phone was waiting for a verbal response. "No questions. I understand."

"Have a great day," Raj said and hung up.

A plethora of emotions poured through Marc. Joy. Nerves. Anger. Happiness. And finally, relief. He now knew beyond a shadow of a doubt that he had a daughter.

"Hey, bro, I wanted—" Dax was saying as he reentered the room. He came to a stop. "What's wrong?"

Marc realized he was still holding his phone in his hand. "That was the lab."

"Yeah?" His brother lifted an eyebrow. "And?"

"Chloe's my daughter."

Dax's face lit with a bright smile. He hurried around the desk to slap his brother on the back. "Congratulations—not that I had much of a doubt. I mean, she looks like Jenny, thank goodness, but she's got our mom's smarts."

Marc shook his head. "I know."

"Are you okay with this? You have a deer-in-the-head-lights expression."

Marc smiled. "I'm a little stunned. Happy and thrilled, but I never thought I'd have a kid, much less a teenager."

"Have you talked to Jenn?" Dax retook the chair he'd sat in earlier.

"I haven't."

"So, you don't know if she and Chloe know yet."

"Right. I don't want to be the one to tell her."

"Send her a text saying something like call me after you hear from the lab. It doesn't have to say anything other than you want to talk."

"I'll do that." Marc frowned. "Why did you come back?"

"To talk about your house."

"Can't let you do it, Dax. I appreciate the offer, but it's too much."

"I've already contracted with Cash for both houses, so I'll pay for the labor, and you'll pay for the materials. That way, you get what you want. Besides, Chloe will need her own room at your house, right?"

Marc narrowed his eyes in a mock glare. "You're using my newly-discovered daughter to get your way."

"Yep, I am. So, get with Cash. He's got an architect he uses for projects like yours."

"I will. I wish I felt better about spending your money."

Dax laughed. "I figured I was a dead man last year. Now, I have a fiancée and a few million dollars to build a life with my wife and whatever children we have." He stood. "I'm going to get out of your hair." He gestured to the papers on Marc's desk. "Besides, you look busy."

"It's the cattle rustling. I've got a meeting in the morning with the division of the Texas Rangers that specializes in these things. Whispering Springs County has been the hardest hit so far." He ran his fingers through his hair. "I can't figure out how they are doing this and leaving no trail."

"Inside job?"

"Meaning?"

"Someone in the law end, someone in the ranching end, someone in the cattle selling business?"

"Maybe."

"Okay, I've gotta run. Having dinner with my lovely fiancée." He stood and headed for the door.

"Dax?"

He turned back. "Yeah?"

"How much money did you get?"

Dax smiled. "Ten million, after taxes. After I spend a couple of million getting settled with my wife, we'll still have a nice nest egg."

Marc whistled.

"Yeah, I know," Dax said. "Later."

After Dax left, Marc picked up his phone to text Jenn. as Dax had suggested.

Dax: *Jenn. Call me when you hear from the lab. Thanks.*

Dots appeared below his message.

Jenn: *Slammed at work. Lab called, but I was in a meeting. I'll call them and call you tonight.*

Too busy to take a call about something as important as

your daughter's parentage? The thought irked him. Did work always come first and their daughter second? Well, that wasn't going to happen on his watch. She'd had Chloe for fifteen years. Maybe it was his turn. Shouldn't he get a chance to know his daughter?

Until they spoke that evening, there wasn't much he could do at this point. He'd wait to hear her reaction and then decide if he needed to see a lawyer about legal rights. In the meantime, he wanted to get ready for tomorrow morning's meeting.

He collected all the reports from the cattle rustling in the four-county area. "Tiffany?" he called.

His young desk clerk hurried to him. "Yes, Sheriff?"

"Make me a copy of all these reports and put them back on my desk. I'm going to head home so I can get some work done."

"I'm on it."

A law enforcement insider. He'd had the same thought as Dax. He'd spend some time looking at the reports from that angle.

Besides, reviewing these reports to prep for tomorrow's meeting would give him something to do while he waited for Jenn to call. The problem with texting was that it was only words. Reading a text couldn't convey any emotion that might be behind the words. There was no tone, no inflection. Cold words. But he knew his ex-wife well enough that she wouldn't be able to hide her feelings when they spoke on the phone.

. . .

Jenn read Marc's text and her heart squeezed. She'd told a little lie. Of course, she'd taken that call from the lab. It wouldn't have mattered what she was doing or who she was meeting with. Nothing was more important than her daughter. *Nothing.*

But she wasn't ready to face what having Marc back in her life meant. They shared a daughter. She wasn't all that surprised. As Chloe had pointed out, she didn't share any physical characteristics with her cousins on the Tate side of the family.

When she'd gotten the paternity results, she'd been swamped with conflicting emotions. The first one was relief that Chloe didn't have the medical genes of the Tate family, followed by guilt for not knowing who Chloe's dad was before today. David had dedicated his life to raising a child he'd loved with all his heart. This news would have been devastating to him.

How did she feel about Marc being back in her life? After the lab call, she'd locked herself in her office to think about all the ramifications. This information could change her and Chloe's lives. What if Marc sued for his paternal rights? What if he sued for custody? How would she share the most precious thing in her life with a man who'd hurt her so badly? So many times, she'd wished she could forget him. Erase him from her memory. But that'd been impossible. Even when she hadn't spoken to him for years, he'd still infiltrated her dreams more nights than she wanted to acknowledge. And then, seeing him this past weekend had been dangerous to the well-constructed wall around her heart and her emotions. He could get past all her barriers. She knew it, and that scared her.

She shut down her computer and packed it into her bag. There was a teen daughter waiting at home for news that would change her life. Jenn hoped the change would be for the better.

Jenn entered a quiet house. No television or music, which wasn't abnormal. Chloe preferred the quiet if she was working. "Chloe? I'm home. Where are you?"

"Hey, Mom," came the shout from upstairs. "I'm in my room."

Jenn set her computer case and purse on the sofa and headed up to Chloe's room. "Hey, honey. The roast smelled delicious when I walked in. Thanks for putting that on to cook. Did you have a good day?" She perched on the edge of the bed.

The teen shrugged. "Okay, I guess. I'm auditing Marc's mom's class and doing some of the homework she assigned. What about you?"

"Good day. Is Cora a good teacher?"

Chloe grinned. "She's really good."

"And you're enjoying her class?"

Her daughter frowned. "Yes, but what's with all the questions? You usually do this when you're avoiding telling me something." Chloe's eyes lit with understanding. "You heard from the lab."

Jenn's heart and stomach tied themselves into knots. There were times in her life when she could look back and clearly see a fork in the road. Chloe would look back on this day as one of those forks in her life.

She nodded. "I heard."

"And Marc's my bio dad," Chloe announced with confidence.

"Yes, Marc is your biological father."

Chloe shot a fist in the air. "I know. I just knew it. I told you so. DNA tests don't lie."

"That's true."

"Fabulous. When are we headed back to Texas?"

"Excuse me?" Jenn frowned. "Back to Texas?"

"Yeah. Of course. I want to spend time with Marc and his family. I can't wait to meet everyone." Chloe's face beamed. "I'm so excited." She rushed to her closet and began flipping through the hangers.

"What are you doing?"

"Packing."

"Slow down," Jenn said. "Take a breath and chill. We aren't headed to Texas any time soon."

Her daughter whirled and stood with her fists on her hips. "The hell you say."

"Hey, watch the language."

Chloe tossed her beautiful auburn-red hair over her shoulder. "I'm going. It's fine if you stay here."

Jenn reached over and pulled her daughter to sit on the bed beside her. "I know you're happy with this news, and I want you to get to know Marc, but honey, you can't go running off to stay with a man you don't really know."

"Are you saying you don't trust Marc?"

The question jarred Jenn. "Of course, I trust Marc. He'd never do anything to hurt you, but he also doesn't know the first thing about having a daughter, much less having a teen. Let's slow down a little. I'll talk to him tonight. See where he is on this."

"I thought about it on the drive home, and I'm not going to Harvard. I'll do my graduate studies at a university in Texas to be closer to him. I've been doing research to figure out which one would have what I need."

Chloe's statement was a dagger to Jenn's heart. She fought to keep her face neutral and not show the crushing pain in her chest.

"You may have the brain of an adult, but you're only fifteen. You are too young to live away on a university campus, so going to a Texas school isn't a sure thing, at least not at this point. But that's getting the horse before the cart. There are a lot of steps between wanting something to happen and having it happen. I'm not saying you can't attend a Texas school at some point. I'm just saying, slow down. We have a lot to discuss, and I don't mean just you and me. Marc will have to be a part of that discussion."

"He'll want me there," she said with a confidence only a teenager can muster.

"I'm sure he will want to get to know you, whether it's by texts and phone conversations or it's face-to-face. I'll call him after we eat. That roast in the oven has my stomach growling." And while she was hungry, and the roast did smell amazing, she also wanted to put off hearing Marc's deep, sexy voice in her ear. She wasn't prepared for the eighteen-ton truck of emotion barreling toward her. She was fully aware that being in Marc's orbit again was going to be dangerous to her heart and self-preservation.

Through dinner, Chloe chatted happily about her online school research, what school had what programs, and which ones she believed she might be interested in. Jenn didn't mind that her daughter had little interest in following in her medical footsteps. Becoming a physician wouldn't be much of an educational challenge for Chloe, but the day-to-day office repetition would drive her insane. Plus, the reality of the job often demanded that family come second or third in priorities.

Jenn and Chloe worked together to clean up after dinner. Once the leftovers were refrigerated and the dishwasher started, the time had come for Jenn to face her fears.

"I'm going to my office to call Marc," she told her daughter.

"I want to listen," Chloe said with a big smile. "I want to hear what he says."

As Jenn nodded, she said, "I know you do, but this time, I need to talk with him privately." When her daughter frowned, Jenn added, "I'm not going to forbid him from seeing you or whatever nonsense you have running through your brain."

"Okay, but you have to tell me everything he says."

"Fair enough."

Sequestered in her office, Jenn placed the call, her hands shaking with nerves.

"Hello, Jenn."

Marc's deep, gravelly voice sent chills down her spine and goosebumps popping up on her arms.

"Hi. Sorry I couldn't talk earlier today. I ran from meeting to meeting all afternoon. Then, when I got home, Chloe had dinner ready, and after all her work, I didn't want the food to get cold or overcooked." She told her lies and hoped he bought them. Usually, her face gave her away when she lied. Her mom said she always knew when Jenn was telling falsehoods, but she was convinced she could pull off lying better with her voice than her face.

"Uh-huh," he said.

She heard the doubt in his voice.

"I think you've spent the entire time since you spoke with the lab trying to decide exactly what you were going to say to me," Marc said. "Honey, you have so many excellent qualities, but being an effective liar isn't one of them."

She sighed, and he chuckled.

"Dammit," she said. "I thought I was getting better."

"Maybe to people who don't know you like I do. Now, let's talk about *our* daughter," Marc said, with an emphasis on *our*.

"How do you feel about that?" she asked.

"Not surprised. You?"

"I would've been if she hadn't laid out all her ancestry research. Marc, you have to know I would never have kept her from you if I'd known."

"I wouldn't have blamed you if you had." He was quiet for a moment and then added, "Thank you for not having an abortion. I know what I said back then, but I was an idiot. I'm sorry I wasn't there for you, for her. I'm sorry you didn't feel like you could tell me you were pregnant."

"To be honest, Marc, I didn't know I was pregnant with your child until we did the lab tests. But no matter. We can't turn back the clock. We can only go forward from here, so no looking back and filling both of us with questions and what-ifs."

"Okay. Agreed. But you know I want to get to know Chloe better."

"I know. She also wants to meet your Montgomery family too, but she's only fifteen."

"Meaning?"

"I don't feel comfortable sending her down to Texas on her own."

"Not a problem. You come too. I have your rooms ready."

She chuckled. "I do have a job, Marc."

"So do I. I'd offer to come there, but I'm in the middle of an active investigation I need to stay on top of, so leaving town isn't on my radar."

"The cattle thing?"

"Rustling, and yes."

"Chloe wants to come for the summer, but..."

"But what?"

"I'd need to come with her."

"Great. I'd love that. Come on."

"Are you sure, Marc? I mean, we do have some history between us."

He was quiet for a moment and then said, "Come, Jenny. I'd love to spend the summer with you and our daughter."

Her heart raced, her pulse pounding loudly in her ears. Could she do that? Spend months with her ex-husband? And what about after that?

"It'll take some planning on my end," she said.

"I'll be here...waiting."

Eleven

The next morning, Marc headed to Leo's Bar and Grill party room. The men and women gathered there weren't in much of a partying mood. Sheriffs, police chiefs, and representatives from the Texas Rangers' Cattle Rustling Division gathered for coffee, donuts, and information sharing.

Marc was pouring a cup of coffee when someone patted his back. He turned and smiled. "How are you doing, Sheriff Monroe?"

Cody Monroe, Diamond Lakes County Sheriff, extended his hand for a shake. "Doing good, Marc. Heard about your birthday party last week." His eyebrows lifted. "That was quite the surprise ending."

Marc shook his hand with a chuckle. "That it was. Fortunately, it all worked out."

"So, the teen did belong to you?"

"Yep. Name's Chloe, and –"

"Morning, gentleman," Shade Gruber said as he reached for an empty mug. Gruber had only recently taken the position of Chief of Whispering Springs Police Department, and Marc didn't know him well. However, their interactions had all been good. He had an intelligent mind and a good head on his shoulders.

"Morning, Chief," Marc said. "Do you know Sheriff Cody Monroe from Diamond Lakes?"

The two shook hands and said good morning.

"Marc here was just telling me about his surprise daughter," Cody said.

Gruber chuckled as he filled his mug with the black liquid gold. "I was there. It was quite the show."

"Well, you'll get a chance to meet her and her mother," Marc told them. "They're coming for the summer."

"So, what grade's she in?" Gruber asked.

With a proud grin, Marc said, "Senior...in college." When the surprise showed on their faces, he added, "She's got quite the brain. Graduated high school a few years ago. She's been doing college-level studies." The corner of his mouth quirked. "Now that I think about it, I'm not sure what degree she's working on."

"I'll look forward to meeting her and her mother," Gruber said. "Vivi and I will have you guys over for dinner while they're here."

"Gentlemen and ladies," a voice called loudly, "if you'd find a seat, we can get started. I'm Texas Ranger Harvey Cole, head of the Rustling Investigation Division. I thought we could get together and compare some notes and theories and see if we can get this multi-county rustling ring busted, once and for all."

Ninety minutes later, the group broke up to go their separate ways. Marc was stacking his papers and saying his goodbyes when Harvey Cole asked him to stay behind.

As soon as the room was empty, Marc asked, "What's going on?"

"I wanted to ask you about one of your employees—Tiffany Yeats." Harvey Cole leaned on a table and crossed his arms. "You know who I'm talking about?"

"Sure." Marc mimicked Cole's position. "Granddaughter of the county judge. She's been with me for a few months. Why?"

Instead of answering Marc's question, Harvey asked, "Had any problems with her? Absenteeism? Illnesses? No show for work?"

Marc thought through the past couple of months and shook his head. "None. Model employee, and again I ask, why are you asking about Tiffany?"

"She used to run with a rough crowd."

Marc nodded. "Yes, and got into some trouble. I know all about those days, but she finished college, with a useless degree I might add, and came to work for me. She's always on time or early. Competent at her job. No complaints from other staff or deputies. You got her in your crosshairs?"

"Ex of hers showed up in an emergency room with an injury to his thigh. He happens to work on the Triple F ranch a couple of counties over. Said he was hurt on the job by a cranky bull. The ranch foreman confirmed the incident, but it seemed a little odd, given the rustling at the D&R and the blood that was collected."

"You test for a match?"

"We did, but no match. Still, it raises questions. Is it

possible that your employee has a connection to these thefts and is getting inside information from your office?"

Marc frowned. "I hope not, but I can keep an eye on her comings and goings. I'll let you know if I see or hear anything that raises my suspicions."

"That's perfect." Harvey extended his hand. "Good to meet you, Sheriff. I hope next time is under better circumstances."

Back at the station, Marc headed for his office, the Texas Ranger's warning about Tiffany ringing in his ears. She'd been nothing but helpful, and he hadn't seen anything that would set off his alarms, but he'd keep his eyes open. He still believed there was some inside help somewhere.

Late that afternoon, the desk clerk knocked on his door. "Sheriff? Judge Yeats to see you. You available?"

Marc set his pen down. "For the judge? Of course. Send him on back."

Judge Darrel Yeats walked in dressed in jeans, a pearl snap-button shirt, boots, and a cowboy hat. "Good afternoon, Marc."

Marc stood and extended his hand. "Afternoon, Darrel. You look like a proper Texas cowboy," he said with a chuckle.

Judge Yeats shook Marc's hand and sat. "I'm headed out to look at some cattle. Got me a small hobby ranch in Diamond Lakes County. Heard about your new place. Congratulations."

Marc smiled. "Thanks, Judge. I'm pretty excited. There's still a lot of work to do before my brother and I can start raising cattle."

The judge rubbed his face and looked ill at ease. "I need to ask you something, and I confess, this is an uncomfortable situation, but I need you to be honest with me."

"Of course. What can I do for you?"

"The cattle rustling. I'm getting angry calls from ranchers in the area. They're all upset that they don't see anything happening, and the cattle thefts continue. Then today, I got an anonymous email about your very expensive ranch, the value of the missing cattle, and questioning if there was a relationship between the two. Now, your compensation package is public knowledge. Most people don't care enough to look it up unless their taxes go up or crime does. On your current salary, how did you afford to buy a ranch that should have listed in the multimillions? And why didn't the family put that ranch on the open market for sale?"

Marc leaned back in his chair and steepled his fingers, a spark of irritation igniting in his gut. "So, you're here questioning if I'm stealing cattle from ranches, including my own family's, and selling said cattle to raise money? Have I got that about right, Judge?" He leaned forward and studied the judge. "Or maybe I'm taking bribes to look the other way."

"Now, Marc," the judge started, "don't get smart with me. You have to admit it looks a little suspicious for an admittedly underpaid sheriff to own a prime piece of property like the Hanson Ranch."

Had the judge had his eyes set on that choice piece of property, ready to swoop in and buy it, only to be undercut by Marc and his brother? Was this what all the questions were about? While the judge's logic made sense, having his honesty and integrity challenged was infuriating. Regardless, he refused to let the boiling anger inside get out.

Stiffly, Marc nodded once. "It was a birthday present. To me, from my brother. And before you ask, he inherited some money and used some of it to buy the ranch. The family didn't put it on the market because we bought it and preempted a listing. The family gave me a sale price and first right of refusal because I helped their parents for years. Does that answer your question, Judge?"

"No reason to be snippy," Judge Yeats said. "Only your brother got an inheritance from family, and you didn't?"

Marc felt his spine stiffen. "I understand your curiosity, but the money was a gift to my brother. It was legal and above board. All taxes have been paid, and unless you need anything else, I'm busy." He stood. "Have a safe drive to your ranch. Diamond Lakes County, you say? I guess I didn't know about that."

The judge stood, his cowboy hat clutched tightly in his hands. "Have a nice weekend, Sheriff."

"Judge."

Marc admitted that he hadn't given much thought to appearances. On the other hand, was it really anyone's business how the ranch was purchased?

The conversation left a bad taste in his mouth and put him in a nasty mood. He packed up and headed home, ready for a beer and to sleep late in the morning, like until seven.

He pulled his cruiser into the garage and shut the door. Throughout the drive home, his conversation with Judge Yeats reran in his brain. Maybe he should take out a full-page ad in the local newspaper thanking his brother for the birthday present. He snorted at the idea. Honestly, the best way to handle this was to get the correct information filtered into the gossip vine. The word would spread faster that way anyway.

Stepping into his kitchen, he immediately pulled a beer from his refrigerator. With a quick twist of his wrist, the beer cap separated from the bottle. He flipped it expertly into the trash can on his first try. *Take that, Cori.*

As he sipped and thought about Judge Yeats's visit, the more curious he became about who else had been interested in the Hanson property. Who had Dax bought it out from under? Hillary Hillerman had been the agent who'd handled the deal, but there might be a better information source. After scrolling through his contacts, he dialed a number.

"This is Angel." Angel was a local real estate agent he'd dated for a while. She was in her early thirties, cute, and on the husband prowl. When he'd made it clear that he wasn't looking for a wife, she'd moved on, but they'd stayed friendly. More importantly, she was wired into the local gossip mill, especially if the gossip nugget was real-estate-related.

"Hi, Angel. It's Marc Singer."

"Hello, handsome. It's a little late to be calling for a date tonight," she said with a soft teasing chuckle. "But I can check my calendar for other days."

He laughed but opted to ignore the date comment.

They hadn't been out in six weeks, and he had no plans to reopen that door. "I have a question for you."

"Shoot."

"You may have heard that my brother and I bought the Hanson place."

"I did hear that, and shame on you for not letting me handle it for you."

"Well, of course I would've come to you," he lied, "but Dax bought it as a surprise, so I didn't know until after the fact."

She giggled. "I know. Hillary told me everything. I was just pulling your chain. Congratulations. We really should find a time and celebrate—you know, christen the house properly."

He ignored her not-so-veiled suggestion that they get together. "I know you and Hillary are close."

"She's like a mother to me."

Marc knew Angel well, and when it came to closing a real estate deal, she'd cut off her own mother to get there first, so he wasn't sure how much affection was accurately reflected in her comment.

"I was wondering if there were other people interested in buying that ranch?"

"I can't really disclose that information. It wouldn't be professional."

"I'm not asking for names..." *Yet.* "I'm simply wondering if there were others who were interested."

"Well," she said, drawing out the word, "it is a prime piece of property with its gently rolling hills and spring-fed ponds. The demand for something like that so close to Dallas makes it highly desirable."

"You don't have to sell me on the place, Angel. I own it." He chuckled, and so did she.

"Sorry. Every agent in town was trying to get that listing. The next thing we knew, it was sold. I'll confess there were some disappointed buyers."

"Anyone I might know?"

"Now, Sheriff, a gal doesn't share all her secrets until the pillow talk after dinner."

Marc rolled his eyes but chuckled politely. "Hypothetically, if someone, like the local county judge, for example, wanted to buy it, do you think he, or anyone else who'd been interested, would be upset that it sold without going on the market?"

He heard her quick inhale of breath.

"Well, *hypothetically*, if our local judge wanted to spend a couple of million on a ranch in this county, he would, *hypothetically*, have to sell the ranch he owns in Diamond Lakes County. Now, I'm not saying he was specifically interested in the Hanson place, but I did hear a rumor that an agent at Diamond Lakes Realty has a pocket listing for his ranch over there."

Marc frowned. "Pocket listing? Explain."

"It means there's no formal paperwork in place for a listing, but should the agent run across a buyer who is interested in a smaller ranch, for example, like the judge's place, then the agent has the owner's permission to show it and discuss a sales price. So, it's an off-market listing handled through private channels rather than through a multiple listing service, sort of like you did with the Hanson place. Hillary had a pocket listing from the Hanson family until you accepted or declined the purchase. Once you made a decision, if you'd opted not to buy, Hillary would've listed the property."

"Or maybe reached out privately to other interested parties?"

"Yes, that too. Like I said, everyone wanted to get their hands on that property."

"Thanks, Angel. You've been a load of help."

"You can make it up to me with dinner this week."

"I thought you were seeing the new lawyer in town."

She pffted. "Not anymore."

"We'll get together soon," he promised, and they would, just not alone.

He ended the call and pulled another beer from the fridge. While she hadn't outright said the judge had been trying to buy the Hanson place, he felt sure that was the case, which probably explained his snippiness this afternoon. Still, being on Judge Yeats's bad side could make his job much harder.

His phone chirped with a text.

Chloe: *Is this a good time to talk?*

His heart swelled and filled his chest. There was no fighting the smile that came to his lips. Fuck. He had a daughter.

Instead of replying by text, he pressed the phone icon of her message. In a couple of seconds, a phone began to ring.

"Marc?"

"Hi, Chloe. I thought I'd call you to answer your question. You can call me anytime, any day, for any reason. Got it?"

"Thanks, Marc."

"What's up?"

"Nothing. We hadn't spoken since, well...since you got the lab results. Are you pissed off?"

"What? Why in the world would I be upset? I'm thrilled you're my daughter, even if you did upstage my party."

"Yeah, not sorry," she said in a cheeky reply.

"How do you feel about it? You've spent your life believing David was your dad, and now, you find he wasn't."

"It's a little weird," she admitted. "But I've been working on this DNA project for months, so I've had more time to process the situation than you and Mom have."

"How's your mom doing?"

"She's good. I think she's relieved to stop worrying that I might have Huntington's or something."

"I never knew David, obviously, but he sounds like he loved you very much."

"I think he did."

"Tell me about him."

Marc settled on his sofa and let his daughter talk. They went from David, to her brain, to school, to his mom, and back to David. He asked questions and listened as she talked for an hour.

His house didn't feel so empty anymore, and neither did his heart.

Twelve

Marc spent Saturday and Sunday at the Hanson house with Cash Montgomery. Cash took notes on changes Marc wanted as they walked through each room.

Sunday evening, Marc was watching the evening news when Jenn called.

"Hey, lady," he said. "Did you have a good weekend?"

"Well, I've worked both days, setting up my office for distance working."

"Distance?" He smiled but didn't want to jump to conclusions. Still...

"Chloe has talked about you all weekend."

"That's nice."

"You say that now, but wait until she's underfoot asking questions and making a mess in your kitchen."

"You're coming." It wasn't a question but a statement he hoped like hell was true.

"We're coming. Stroker is going to let me work from Texas for a few weeks, but I'll still have to go back to the office a few days a month. Plus, I do have vacation days that have piled up over the years, so I'll use some of those too."

His heart flipped at her news. "No problem. I'm sure Chloe and I can manage when you're away. Any idea when you'll be here?" Mentally, he started a list of all the things he needed to do in the house before they arrived. He had sheets for their beds, but he should probably get some new ones, some with a higher thread count. He wanted them to be comfortable. And food. He'd need to get to the grocery store and get his fridge and pantry restocked. Frankly, with Dax staying with Cori and Samantha living in Dallas, he'd let things slide. Should he repaint their rooms? No, he probably didn't have time for that.

"Did you hear me?" Jenn's question jarred him out of his thoughts.

"Sorry, what'd you say?"

"We'll head out on Tuesday. We'll be there on Thursday. Is that okay?"

"Perfect."

"And please, Marc, do not go out of your way to accommodate us. I don't want to disrupt your life...well, not any more than we already have. I want you to spend time with Chloe, and I didn't feel comfortable letting her come alone. I know the tests showed you are her father, but until you two get to know each other better, I feel like I need to be around. But, like I said, I want you to go about your normal activities too."

"Like what? Going to work?"

"Well, no. I expect you to go to work. I meant, you

know, if you have a date or something, we'll be fine while you're out." She sounded embarrassed addressing his dating habits, maybe even a little frustrated that she might have to sit home while he went out with another woman...as if that was going to happen. He couldn't remember if she'd asked if he was dating someone—he wasn't—but if the idea bugged her that he might be, well, that could play in his favor.

"No problem."

"Oh, and one more thing. Do you have a home office?"

"I do."

"Can I use it while I'm there? I'll need somewhere to work, take meetings, and so forth."

He put cleaning his office on his to-do list. "That won't be a problem."

"Okay, then, I guess we're set. Thank you again for doing this for Chloe."

"I'm doing it for me as much as for her. She's an incredible person, Jenny. I want to know her better."

He didn't even try to do all the cleaning. He hired a local cleaning team to come in and make his house sparkle inside and out. He didn't think his windows had ever been so spotless. The exterior received the power wash it'd needed for a while. Once the black grunge had been cleaned off his porch, sidewalks, drive, and patio, the fresh white concrete was blinding in the sunlight. He wanted Chloe—and Jenn—to believe his house usually looked like that, and that their previous surprise visit had simply come at a time when he hadn't had ample time to clean.

Wednesday, he was standing in his kitchen when Dax knocked once on the front door and walked in with Cori.

"Good lord," Dax said, looking around. "Haven't you been busy! My eyes are burning from the sun reflecting off your windows."

"Ha ha," Marc said. "Good thing you became a soldier and not a comedian. Hello, Cori."

"Hi, Marc. Your house looks and..." she sniffed the air, "smells amazing. I'm glad the housekeepers I recommended worked out for you."

Their comments made him wonder if his house had been in worse shape than he'd realized. Had he become nose-blind to odors? The idea was appalling. "Yeah, thanks for that. I've hired them for the summer. I don't want Jenn and Chloe thinking I expect them to clean."

"That's very thoughtful," Cori said.

"So, what brings you two to my humble abode?" Marc asked. "Want a beer?"

"I'll take one," Dax said.

"You know where they are. Cori?"

She held up a to-go mug. "I'm good."

Once Dax had his beer, he and Cori followed Marc to the living room. "What can I do for you two?" Marc asked.

Dax and Cori exchanged glances.

"What?" Marc said. "Spit it out."

Dax cleared his throat. "I'd planned to ask you to be my best man—"

"Ah, man. I'd love to."

"Let me finish," Dax said. "As I was saying, I'd

planned to ask you, but Cori wanted you to be more involved than that."

Marc frowned, "Other than being the groom—and no offense, Cori, but no—or giving the bride away—again, no—then what do you want me to do?"

"Marry us," Cori said.

He sat back in surprise. "Marry you? Sheriffs don't have that authority in Texas."

"I know," Dax said, "I checked, but you can become an ordained minister online, and it's legal."

Marc chuckled. "Are you serious?"

"Dead serious," Dax said. He took Cori's hand. "This would mean the world to us, Marc. You wouldn't be just standing there. You'd be an integral part of our ceremony."

"Do I have time? I mean, I don't even know when you're getting married."

"July the sixth," Cori said.

Surprised at their response, Marc's eyes opened wide. "Wow. That's three weeks from now. Are you sure that's what you want?"

Cori shrugged. "If I left it up to my mom, it'd take a minimum of eighteen months to plan. I'd be dressed in a ballgown with a ten-foot train. There'd be hundreds of people at the wedding and at the reception." She shook her head. "I don't want that. I want family and friends only. I don't want Mom and Dad's business associates, some of whom I don't know. I don't want my wedding to be a gift grab." When Marc frowned, she added, "You know, those brides who invite every living person they possibly can to snap up the more wedding gifts. That's not me." She looked at Dax. "And that's not Dax. We have everything we want, and that's each other."

Marc smiled. "That's sweet. Are you sure you're talking about my brother?"

Dax slugged Marc's arm with a laugh.

"I haven't even asked how your parents took the news of the engagement, and now, you're springing a quickie wedding." Marc gave them a side-eye. "Dax, did you knock up your bride?"

Cori's face pinkened. Dax coughed and looked away.

"Ohmigod," Marc said. "You're pregnant."

"Shhh," Cori said. "That's not why we're having a quickie wedding. I honestly don't want all the brouhaha. I would go to the courthouse, but my mother would kill me for that."

"So, what's the plan?"

"We want to get married at the ranch."

"Your parents' ranch?"

"No, our ranch," Dax said.

"Outdoor wedding," Cori said, her hands waving. "Tents. Artificial grass covering the area. Twinkle lights."

"It sounds lovely. Can you get it done in such a short time?" Marc held up his hand. "I'm not saying don't do it. I'm just saying to do it. If it takes another week or two, or even a month, I know Dax. He'll want this perfect for you."

Cori's eyes glistened. "I just want to marry him. I don't care if we marry in a barn."

"We're not getting married in a barn," Dax stated firmly. "This is our one and only wedding. Let's do it right. I hate to admit it, but Marc is right on that point. It doesn't matter if we marry on July the sixth or September the sixth. I want some great pictures to show our kids." He pulled a handkerchief from his pocket and handed it to her. "Here."

"What are you? Sixty-five? When did you start carrying handkerchiefs?" Marc asked.

"When Cori needed something for her tears, and she had to use the country club napkin."

"Step one, then," Marc said. "I'll do the online minister thing and be ready. What else can I do?"

"For now, keep this under your hat," Dax said. "I'm not sure how we're going to pull this off around Cori's mother, but we will."

"Oh!" Marc said as he realized what Dax was saying. "A surprise wedding?"

"Maybe. Possibly. Probably," Dax admitted. "We're still working out the details."

"When's Chloe coming back?" Cori asked. "Is Jenn coming too?"

Marc had called his family last week as soon as the DNA tests had been finalized. His family had been thrilled with the news.

"I expect them tomorrow."

Dax nodded slowly. "And that explains the freshly scrubbed concrete and house. They're staying here."

"They are."

"So...might there be some extracurricular ex-wife activity?" Dax pumped his eyebrows.

Marc scoffed. "This visit is for Chloe."

"Uh-huh." Dax elbowed him.

"That's enough, Dax," Cori scolded. "After a man

reaches a certain age in life, sex just isn't as important, and friendship is enough." She patted Marc's arm. "We understand the difficulties that, um, some older men might face."

"What?!" Marc jumped to his feet. "I'll have you know that...that..." His words faded as Dax and Cori howled with laughter. He retook his seat. "You two deserve each other."

Cori laughed and dabbed at her eyes. "I'm sorry, Marc, but you should have seen your face." She laughed again and rocked.

Dax slapped Marc's back. "Let me know if you need any pointers, old man."

"If you weren't my brother, I'd..." He was interrupted by his doorbell. He frowned. People did not usually just show up uninvited to his house. "Excuse me."

He opened the door and grinned.

"Surprise!" Chloe shouted. "We're here."

Thirteen

The proposed departure time of seven a.m. on Tuesday hadn't worked as well as Jenn had hoped. Because of some last-minute issues that had to be dealt with before vacating their home for a couple of months and a couple of pressing issues at the office, it had been well after three in the afternoon before they'd gotten on the road. Jenn had insisted on taking her Toyota Land Cruiser, leaving Chloe bummed to part with her beloved Bronco. But one of the last-minute details Jenn had to handled was making arrangements to have Chloe's Bronco shipped to Texas as a surprise for her upcoming birthday. Even thought she'd already given Chloe the Bronco, it was still the big present for her sixteenth birthday. If everything went as planned, the truck should arrive in Texas before the big event.

However, the late start had meant stopping at midnight to sleep. Chloe had offered to drive, but Jenn had been exhausted, and while her daughter had driven herself to Texas, Jenn knew she'd be more relaxed if she were awake while Chloe drove.

Getting Chloe to sleep the previous evening had been like trying to put a rambunctious toddler to bed. Her daughter had been too excited to sleep. Plus, Jenn had suspected her mind was running at full steam about what would happen in Texas and how Marc would treat her. The hotel room was finally quiet by one. However, at five, Chloe had woken up and shoved a cup of mediocre coffee under Jenn's nose to get her up and going.

Chloe drove the first leg since she—Jenn—hadn't been fully awake, and Chloe appeared to be on a stimulant—she wasn't, but still, she'd been raring to go.

Jenn's original travel plan had included stopping outside of Dallas, grabbing a hotel, and getting a good night's sleep, followed by a morning shower and makeup. Vanity wasn't her issue, but she didn't want to show up at Marc's house looking like an unkept bag lady. However, her daughter wouldn't even consider stopping. No delay was acceptable to her. Full speed ahead seemed to be Chloe's motto.

So, here she sat in Marc's drive, hair limp, no makeup, and breath similar to a garage on a hot day as her daughter sprinted to the door. Oh, to have that confidence and energy.

Marc greeted Chloe with a surprised expression, then pulled her in for a hug.

Since hiding in her SUV wasn't an option, Jenn slid from the driver's seat and waved. "We're early," she called to Marc. "Sorry."

"I'm not. Come on in. Leave your luggage. I'll get it in a minute."

She pushed her long hair over her shoulders, worked up a smile, and headed up the sidewalk to where Marc waited on his porch, and damn him, he looked good. His shirt was wrinkled, and his hair tousled, but he still looked better than most men who spent time primping. Her heart thumped loudly in her ears while butterflies danced in her belly to the drum beat.

"Welcome to Casa de Singer." He held out his arms, and she stepped into his warm embrace. Hugging her tightly, he whispered into her ear, "Thank you for coming. Dax and Cori are here. I'll tell you everything about their visit later." He released her and smiled. "Come on in. How can you look so good after being on the road all day?"

While she wasn't buying his words, they made her feel somewhat less repugnant. "You're such a liar, but thanks."

In the living room, Chloe was regaling Dax and Cori with a story that included wide arm gestures and a frustrated facial expression. As they entered, she was saying, "And I can't believe all the questions. I mean, follow the formulas, am I right?"

From the glazed appearances on Dax and Cori's faces, Jenn was sure her daughter was regaling them with stories from Dax's mom's class.

"Oh, right," Cori said. "Totally."

"Enough, Chloe," Jenn said with a laugh. "Let's leave the math in the classroom."

Dax and Cori both stood.

"So good to see you again," Cori said and moved in for a hug.

"Looking good, Jenn," Dax said. While he hugged her, he also kissed her on the cheek. "I guess this is welcome back to the family?"

His words flipped Jenn's stomach. She hadn't thought about the situation that way, but he was kind of on point. She grinned as she pulled back. "I guess so. I didn't mean to interrupt your visit." She turned a mock glare toward Chloe. "This one refuses to stop when she has a targeted goal."

Chuckles went around the room.

Chloe shrugged. "Life's short. Why sleep?"

Marc groaned. "Only a teen would think that. Just wait. That lack of sleep will catch up with you," he warned Chloe with a smile.

"We need to get moving. Have you and Chloe had dinner?" Dax asked Jenn.

She shook her head. "Refused to stop, remember?"

"Why don't we bring something back? That way, you three can get settled rather than spend time in the kitchen." Cori said. "I'm thinking thick burgers, fries, and milkshakes. Good travel food."

"Yum," Chloe said before Jenn could tell them she didn't want to be any trouble.

"That'd be great," Marc said.

"We'll run back by in about thirty or forty minutes," Cori said. "That gives you time to unload and settle in a little."

She and Dax left, and a quiet fell over the room.

"Well," Jenn said. "Cori had a point. Come on, Chloe, Let's get our stuff from the car."

"Show me what you need moved inside," Marc said.

Dax and Cori returned forty-five minutes later, bringing the mouth-watering aroma of hamburgers.

"Leo's?" Marc asked, taking a couple of sacks from Cori.

"Food from Leo's. Shakes from Sir Creamery."

Marc groaned. "You know I can't resist a shake from there."

Chloe frowned. "Sir Creamery? Are they good?"

Dax laughed. "Too good. Y'all eat up before the food gets cold. Cori and I are headed home." He hugged Jenn and then Chloe. "Welcome to town."

The next day, Jenn was a little confused by her surroundings. It took her a minute to recognize Marc's guest room. The sun was up and shining brightly through her window. She'd forgotten to pull down the shade when she'd hit the bed last night. Basically, she could have slept standing up she'd been so exhausted. A long stretch of her arms over her head and her legs straight down the mattress, and she was ready to face the day.

As she pushed her arms into her robe, she realized how quiet everything was. Checking the time on her phone, she saw it was six a.m. Chloe wasn't known to be an early riser. Jenn assumed she was probably dead in the bed next door, so she was a little surprised when she opened her bedroom door and heard murmuring voices coming from either the living room or the kitchen. She couldn't tell, but she could differentiate the voices. One was Marc, and the other was Chloe. How long had they been awake and talking? She hated to interrupt their first private time as father and daughter, but her morning routine demanded a bathroom and then coffee. They'd hear the toilet flush and know she was headed their way.

They were sitting at the kitchen table when she entered. Dirty breakfast plates sat in front of each of them. Chloe wore her pajamas and a robe. Marc was dressed in jeans, an oxford shirt, and boots. The shirt was a little tight across the shoulders, not like it was too small, but more like highlighting luscious muscles that wanted to pop out everywhere. The wave in his hair was more evident this morning as though he hadn't taken time to properly dry it. His cheeks sported a slight scruff that made her mouth water. She sort of hated that everything about him made her mouth water, but time marched forward. There was no going back.

"Good morning," she said. "Looks like I missed breakfast."

Chloe sprang to her feet. "I'll fix pancakes for you. That's what we had."

Gosh, it was nice to have a teenager in debt to her. "Thanks, honey. You don't have to do that, but they would be nice."

"I've got it." Chloe turned toward the stove.

Marc winked at Jenn with a smile. "Nice going," he mouthed. "You remember where the mugs are?"

She nodded. Once she had her coffee, she joined him at the table. "How long have you two been up?"

"About an hour," Marc said. "I don't usually have company for breakfast, so this was nice."

She wondered if that was his way of telling her he didn't usually have women spending the night, not that it was any of her business.

"I was just telling Chloe that I'll be going to the office today and tomorrow, but then I'm taking some time off."

"Oh, Marc, you don't have to use up vacation time just because we're here," Jenn insisted.

"Here you go, Mom." Chloe set a stack of five pancakes in front of Jenn.

"I'll never be able to eat all those," Jenn said. "But they look fabulous." She slathered on butter and doused the stack in syrup. It'd been a long time since she'd allowed herself such a luxury.

"I think it's great Marc's taking off," Chloe said. "I can't wait to tear up stuff."

With her mouth full of pancakes, Jenn frowned. She took a sip of coffee to wash the food down her throat before she could speak. "I'm sorry, but tear stuff up? What are you talking about?"

Marc chuckled. "Monday, we start demolition in the kitchen of my house at Singer Ranch. Just about everything is going. Chloe asked if she could help, and I thought, why not? You okay with that?"

Ah. That's why he was taking off. His vacation didn't have anything to do with their visit. Oddly, that realization wasn't as comforting as it should've been. She'd never admit it, but she'd been a tad flattered he'd taken time off to be with them—with Chloe, she meant. Not her.

"I have a confession," she started.

"Too late," Marc said. "Chloe already spilled your crush on the guy from HGTV."

Jenn laughed. "Well, Ben is cute, but what I was going to say is that I have always wanted to do a demo like I've watched on those shows. Get in there. Break up stuff and not worry about damage. I want to help."

"Well, it's more a controlled chaos than craziness, or so Cash assured me, but heck yeah. I'd love to have you along."

"Great."

"Mom, we'll need to go shopping."

Jenn gave her daughter the side-eye. "Shopping? For a demolition?"

"Yes!" Chloe's eyes gleamed with excitement. "I need work gloves and goggles."

Jenn nodded. "Right. I'm sure there's a hardware store, right, Marc?"

"I'll text you the name and address." As he was sending her the text, he said, "Look at the time. I've got to get going." He stood and snapped his fingers. "I was expecting you today, so I have dinner in the freezer. Lasagna and garlic bread. There's a salad in the fridge. Chloe, would you mind putting the lasagna in to cook about four-thirty? It takes a long time."

Chloe's face brightened. "Sure."

Jenn loved that Marc was doing his best to make Chloe feel like a vital part of his life. She couldn't imagine what her reaction would be to having a teen dropped into her life unexpectedly. Marc's response to the situation reminded her of the boy she'd fallen in love with so many years ago. He was the guy who was friends with everyone. He was the one who made sure to include others and made them feel valuable. The Marc she knew then, and the one she was dealing with now, shared very little in common with the Marc at the time of their divorce. Self-confidence oozed from him. His smiles and laughter came quickly and easily. He was the type of man most women would love to have in their lives, so that begged the question...why had no woman snapped him up? Was there a fault or problem she was blind to?

She'd ponder those questions later. "I have a surprise for you tonight," Jenn said.

Marc looked at her with a sexy grin. "Oh? Want to give me a hint?"

"Nope, then it wouldn't be a surprise."

Chloe groaned. "She always does this. She tells you there's a surprise and then lets you suffer all day."

He nodded. "You know what? She used to do this to me back in the day. She's evil."

"Yes!" Chloe said, adding a rap of her knuckles on the table for emphasis. "I'm glad to know I'm not the only one who sees this."

Jenn shrugged. "You say evil. I say fun-loving."

Marc chuckled. "See you ladies tonight."

For the first half of the day, Jenn commandeered Marc's office for phone calls, meetings, and answering emails. Chloe hung in the living room, watching Cora's graduate-level advanced calculus class. When noon rolled around, Jenn was more than ready to get away from the computer.

"Chloe? Want to go shopping?" When her daughter didn't answer, she headed to the living room. "Chloe?"

"Shhh," she said and added a derisive snort. "Cora's having to explain the Cantor ternary function for the fourth time to these guys." She rolled her eyes. "It's so obvious, right?"

"Uh, right." Jenn had no idea what the Cantor ternary function was, what it did, or even if it was important for some reason. She was glad she had a smart daughter, but there were times, like right now, when she worried she was holding Chloe back from her full potential. She was ready for more advanced graduate education, maybe even some doctoral classes. Sure, she was only fifteen in chronological years, but her mind was way beyond.

Chloe closed her laptop and stretched. "Good class."

"Good to hear. Want to grab some lunch and do a little home demo shopping?"

"Yep. I need to change my clothes, and I'll be ready."

"Whatcha hungry for?" Jenn called to Chloe's retreating back.

"Pizza."

Her brain might be mature, but her daughter had the tastebuds of a typical teen.

Following a meal of an all-meat pizza from Leo's Bar and Grill, Jenn and Chloe walked to the local hardware store. They could have driven, but after all that salt and fat of the pizza, Jenn felt the need to walk some of it off, not that this short five-minute trek would do that.

"What do you think about these?" Chloe asked, holding up a pair of cute, flowered gloves.

"I think they would be perfect for yardwork, but we're tearing out a kitchen. Marc's note said leather."

"Excuse me," a man standing beside her said. "Are you by any chance Jennifer and Chloe Tate?"

Jenn's head whipped toward the man. Tall, muscular, and attractive, the man wore dirty jeans with a few earned holes and a sweaty T-shirt. She took a step back. Marc had joked about the Whispering Springs gossip grapevine being active, but she'd only been in this town twice—coming to get Chloe and then her arrival yesterday. How insane was it that someone might know who she was?

"Uh..." Jenn's mind worked to come up with a better response.

"Yep," Chloe said from behind her. "That's us."

Jenn made a mental note to review stranger-danger with her daughter.

The man chuckled. "Don't mean to startle you. I'm Cash Montgomery, Marc's first cousin on the Montgomery side. You figured that Montgomery side out, didn't you?" He extended his hand. "I'll be working with you ladies on Monday."

Jenn took his hand. "Nice to meet you." She tossed her head toward her daughter. "She can't wait to tear up stuff."

Cash laughed. "Demo is the fun part. No rules except be careful and don't get hurt. I heard you talking about gloves. Come on. The gloves you want are a little further down the aisle. Plus, you two will need goggles to protect your eyes. I'll show you."

With Cash's help, they left with two pairs of leather gloves each and goggles. He'd warned them to wear appropriate footwear, preferring they had steel-toed boots but settled for them wearing close-toed shoes with a hard sole.

As Chloe was stashing the hardware store purchases in the backseat, she said, "I have sneakers with me, but that's all. What about you?"

"Sandals, a pair of running shoes, and heels." Jenn arched a brow. "Shoe shopping?"

"Yes!"

Jenn smiled. Advanced brain, teen appetite, and teen shopping gene. She might be doing all right raising Chloe.

It was close to four when they got back to Marc's house. The back of Jenn's SUV was loaded with purchases, everything from the leather gloves and goggles to work jeans and appropriate footwear to protect delicate toes.

As they lugged in their sacks, Chloe said, "I'm going to start the lasagna. I checked the directions this morning, and Marc was right. It will take a while to cook. If it gets done and we aren't ready to eat, I can leave it in the oven."

"Sounds perfect." She looked at her daughter. "You rock. You know that, right?"

"Mom," she said with roll of her eyes, "no one says rock anymore."

Jenn bumped her hip against Chloe's. "Are you saying I'm old?"

"Well, not in those words, but..."

Jenn laughed.

After they unpacked all the sacks, Jenn decided to throw their stiff jeans and T-shirts into the laundry to make everything a little looser come Monday. Since Chloe was already going on dinner prep, Jenn decided to check her emails. She headed for Marc's office and rolled his chair up to the desk to boot up her computer. After opening her email program and waiting while over one hundred messages loaded, she regretted her decision. With a sigh, she opened the first one and dropped her mind back into work mode.

"Why the deep frown?"

Jenn startled at the deep, rough voice. "How long have you been standing there?" she asked Marc. She took a moment to study him. Even though his face wore a mask of exhaustion, and his lines were a little more evident this evening, he was still the most attractive man she'd ever known, bar none. When he smiled and those brackets around his mouth deepened, her stomach fell to her knees.

"Not long." He stepped into her office and perched on the corner of the desk. "Why the frown?" he asked again.

"Work stuff." She shook her head. "Nothing important."

"It was nice to come home to the aroma of dinner cooking."

She chuckled. "I know. I love when she gets into the mood to cook, but I warn you. She's a teen, and her moods can change on a whim. Right now, she's trying to impress you, so don't get too accustomed to it."

"Why, I thought you'd take over dinner duties when she didn't."

She arched her eyebrow, which made him snicker.

"I'm going to run and take a shower before dinner," Marc said. "I meant to tell you that if you want to use the shower in my bath, make yourself at home. Also, the whirlpool tub, but I so rarely use the tub, you'll need to clean out the dust first."

She snorted a chuckle. "I used your shower today, as a matter of fact. I saw your bath when I fell asleep in your room waiting for you the last time I was here. I had that subject on my list to ask you."

"Happy to share." He pushed off the desk and stood. "See you in a bit."

Jenn tried to get her mind back on the new project development emails, but all she could think about was a naked Marc, the water from the shower sluicing down his body, sliding over each ridge in his abdomen. She leaned back in the chair and let her mind drift...This was so much better than a boring project development.

Fourteen

After a day from hell, the shower was heaven. Marc let the warm water roll over his head and down his body. The only thing that would make this better was a naked Jenn was in here with him. But, as they'd both agreed, their past should probably remain there. Mistakes had been made, more on his part than hers, so leaving them—the mistakes and their relationship—back there was probably the right decision.

Mother Nature had decided to turn up the Texas thermostat today, blasting the area with one-hundred-degree temperatures. Then he'd had to endure a second visit from Judge Yeats, pushing for information from the morning meeting with area law enforcement and the Texas Rangers. Marc hadn't told him everything, especially about the judge's granddaughter possibly playing a part in the thefts. For once, Marc felt compelled to play his cards close to the chest with the judge.

Coming home today had been sweet. Walking into a house full of Chloe's music, his daughter dancing in the kitchen, the aroma of a dinner he didn't have to cook, and the vision of Jenn sitting in his office made him want to stop time. A sense of happiness and perfection had filled his soul, and that was something he hadn't felt in a long time.

His phone chimed with a text while he was dressing.

Angel: *You free for that dinner you owe me?"*

Marc groaned. While he hated to admit it, he'd been relieved when the rumor mill had confirmed Angel was dating the new lawyer at Montgomery and Montgomery. Too bad it hadn't lasted because she'd reset Marc as her husband target. He hated to be rude to the woman. She was nice, and truth be told, he needed every vote when he ran for reelection next year. He couldn't afford to antagonize her.

Marc: *Sorry, Angel. I've got company here, so I'm tied up all weekend.*

There. Short and sweet with no promise of the future.

Angel: *Well, boo. I'm bored. Maybe you could sneak away later tonight and bring your handcuffs. *winking emoji**

He winced at the memory. Her name certainly did not describe what she wanted in the bedroom. She had a kinky streak she kept well hidden from the general public. Not that he hadn't had fun, but he had no interest in doing it again.

Marc: *No can do. I'm sure I'll run into you later around town. Need to run.*

He put his phone on vibrate and dropped it into his

shorts pocket. He wanted a nice dinner with his daughter and his ex without constant interruptions.

He found Jenn sitting in the living room with two wine glasses and a bottle of red wine.

"I was ordered out of the kitchen," she explained. "Apparently, I was getting on her nerves."

Marc snorted. "Sorry about the banishment. Share your wine?"

"Of course." She filled the second wine glass. Once he had it, they tinked glasses and drank.

"This is good." His voice held amazement.

Jenn grinned. "You sound surprised."

"I'm not much of a wine drinker, much less red wine, but if they all tasted like this, I could develop a new habit."

"It's a late harvest Cab. Grapes stayed on the vine longer, so they're much sweeter. Once I discovered this brand, there was no going back."

He sipped and nodded. "I can see that. How was your day?"

"I met an interesting person."

"Let me guess—Cash Montgomery."

Her mouth dropped open. "How did you know? Wait. I know. The gossip vine."

He chuckled. "Usually, yes, but this time, I got it from the horse's mouth. Cash dropped by to tell me he'd met you two. He mentioned how pretty Chloe was. I told him Chloe was a clone of her mother. He'd laughed and said that with our history, he'd been nervous to make that observation."

She frowned. "What does that mean?"

Marc explained about moving to town and going around meeting the townspeople and how he'd been set up on a date with Paige Ryan, now Paige Montgomery, Cash's wife. "I found out later that the whole date had been a trick on Cash to get him off his butt when it came to Paige."

Jenn chuckled. "The old date-someone-else-to-make-him-jealous ploy."

"Exactly, and it worked." He rubbed his chin. "Maybe a little too well."

"Hey, Old People," Chloe called from the kitchen. "Grab your walkers. Dinner's ready."

The two adults exchanged glances.

"Old people?" Marc said.

"Oh, we're ancient, according to my daughter. Apparently, nobody says things rock any longer." She gestured with her wine glass. "I think I left my walker in the bedroom. Think you can help this old woman stand?" There was a playful twinkle in Jenn's eye, and he loved it.

"I don't know. My back and sciatica have been giving me fits all day." With a long groan, he stood and then extended his hand toward her. "Come on, old woman. Did you bring your teeth this time?"

Jenn took his hand and let him pull her to standing. "Yep. Got 'em out of the denture cup before I came down."

He chuckled. "Good, because gumming hot lasagna ain't never gonna work."

They were both laughing as they joined Chloe in the

kitchen. She'd set the table with the fresh flowers he'd brought home for her today.

"Wow, honey, this looks great," Jenn said. "It rocks."

Marc bit the inside of his cheek to keep from laughing. "Totally rocks," he agreed.

Chloe rolled her eyes. "God, y'all are so old,"

Frozen lasagna and frozen garlic bread had never tasted better, and Marc was sure Chloe had simply followed the directions on the boxes. Still, this was his daughter...*his daughter*. Wrapping his head around that fact was still hard at times. He'd missed so much of her life, and he promised himself that things would be different going forward.

After dinner was done, the leftovers had been stored, and the dishes in the dishwasher, Jenn said, "Ready for your surprise?" Her smile lit up her face, and he couldn't help but return her grin.

"I am," he said. "Ice cream?"

"Better. Follow me to the living room."

The three of them settled on the furniture, then Chloe and Marc looked at her.

"Well?" Chloe asked with a snark. "We're waiting."

"Okay, okay. Give me a minute. I'll be right back." Jenn hurried up to the room she was using and opened the box of memorabilia she'd thrown in as a last-second thought. Finding what she was looking for, she went back to the living room and presented four picture albums that documented her pregnancy and Chloe's birth through the first eight years of her life. "Ta-da!" She presented the albums. "Chloe's life up to age eight."

"Mom! I haven't looked at those in ages." Chloe's happy face made Jenn glad she'd gone to the trouble to retrieve these before they'd left.

"I thought you might like to look through these with Marc."

"That's great, Jenn. Thanks." Marc patted the space beside him on the sofa. "Come explain what's going on in the pictures."

Chloe took the albums and sat on Marc's other side. "Let's do them in order."

He nodded.

As they opened the first album, Jenn's cell phone rang. She glanced at the readout to decide whether to answer or let it go to voice mail. She smiled when she saw her mother's name.

"I need to take this," she said to Chloe and Marc.

They were so engrossed in the pictures she doubted they heard her.

"Hi, Mom," Jenn answered as she walked to her guest room. She closed the door for privacy.

"Hi, honey. How's the trip going?"

"Chloe and Marc are getting along great, but both of them are on their best behavior to impress the other."

Her mother chuckled. "I'm sure that's true. But I'm more concerned about you. How are you doing?"

"Me? I'm doing okay."

"And the working from a distance? How's that going?"

"Stressful," Jenn confided. "But it's only been a couple of days. Ask me next week."

"And how are you and Marc getting along? Has he changed much?"

Jenn pictured teenage Marc and then adult Marc. Adult Marc was brawnier with more muscles, broader shoulders, a few ingrained smile and sun wrinkles, a deeper, raspier voice, and a little bit of facial scruff that made her mouth water.

"Jennifer? Honey? You still there? Did we lose connection?"

Jenn cleared her throat. "No, I'm still here. Marc? Well, he's pretty much the same, except a little more chilled out."

"Oh, that's good," her mother said, then added, "Don't get any thoughts in your head about playing house with him again. You're doing so well in Michigan. Chloe's happy. You're happy. You have a fabulous job, an incredible house...I mean, there's nothing you want for."

Except the feeling of being held in the arms of a man you love. The feeling of being loved and cherished by the man you love. The thrill of coming home knowing the man you love is waiting for you and anxious to be with you.

"I know, Mom."

"I hate to bring this up, but honey, when he left, you crashed. I thank God every day that David came into your life when he did. I don't know how you would've made it without him."

"I know, Mom," she said again.

"To change the subject, Chloe's birthday is coming up."

"Two weeks. Hard to believe sixteen years old." She sighed. "She's growing up, Mom."

"That's why your father and I thought we might come to Texas for her birthday this year. It's a big one."

Jenn smiled. "Sixteen *is* a big one."

Her mother sighed. "How can my baby be sixteen?"

Jenn chuckled. "Seems like she should be starting grade school instead of grad school."

"She's such a darling child."

Jenn rolled her eyes. According to her mother, Chloe could do no wrong, even going so far as to make excuses for Chloe's illegal jaunt to Texas.

"Uh-huh. Do you know when you'll be here? I can make hotel reservations for you. Marc's house isn't big enough for everyone."

"Oh, we never thought about staying there." Her mother tittered and said, "Yes, please. Check out the hotels and make us a reservation. Our flight lands at DFW at ten in the morning on June thirtieth. I thought we'd rent a car and drive to Whispering Springs. How far is it?"

"About ninety minutes, but it's mostly interstate, so it's not horrible, but why are you coming on her birthday? Why not come the day before?"

"We didn't want to be in the way, dear. Plus, your father wants to surprise her."

"Okay. Then I won't tell her. I suspect Marc will want to do something like a party since this will be the first time he gets to celebrate her birthday after finding out he's her father."

"Of course. We'll go with whatever you have planned."

"Works for me. I'll talk to you before then."

She ended the call, not sure if she should rejoin Marc and Chloe or give them time. That question was solved when Chloe called, "Mom! Come here."

"What's up?" she asked, walking back into the living room.

"You're not going to believe this." Chloe turned the album around. The picture was from Jenn's medical school graduation.

"Yeah, so? It's my graduation."

"Not that. Look here." Chloe drew a circle around an area in the crowd of family and friend spectators.

Jenn took the book and studied the picture closer. Her eyes widened, and her gaze leapt to Marc's face. He shrugged and gave her a sheepish grin.

"You were at my graduation?" she asked in astonishment. Her heart galloped with the realization.

"Yeah. I was proud of you."

"Why didn't you speak to me?"

"You were introduced as Dr. Tate, not Singer and not Winslow. New last name, so I assumed…"

"I never knew," she said.

"That was fun." Chloe closed the album with a snap. "I'm headed to my room. I started a really good thriller, and I think I'll go read. Night." With that, she set the albums on the coffee table and headed to her room.

Jenn remained standing, locked into place.

"Sit," Marc said and patted the sofa cushion.

She dropped heavily down beside him. "I can't believe I never saw you that day or in the picture."

"I was a tiny head in a sea of heads. I'm not surprised," he said with a chuckle. "When I saw the picture tonight, I looked for me. Otherwise, I doubt either you or Chloe would have seen me." He stretched his arm along the back of the couch. "I was proud of you. Graduating medical school was hell of an accomplishment."

"Thanks." She looked at him. "I couldn't have done it without David."

He winced. "You must've loved him a lot. I'm sorry you lost him."

She looked over her shoulder and then scooted closer to him so she could lower her voice. "I loved him, but I think he loved me more." She sighed. "If I hadn't been pregnant, I don't know where our relationship might have gone. Don't get me wrong. David was a wonderful, kind person, and I would never, *never* utter a harsh word about him, especially to Chloe. He threw me a lifeline, and I took it. I'm not ashamed of that. He was an amazing and supportive husband. I couldn't have asked for more."

"But was there passion like we had?"

Her gut clenched at his question. She glanced over her shoulder again and made her voice even quieter. "Passion like ours? Honey, that kind of passion and crazy hunger for another person is something only teens feel, I think." She rested her head on the back of the sofa. "You and I could hardly keep our hands to ourselves." She sighed. "David and I were nothing like that. He was sweet and kind, and frankly...." She glanced over. "After our years of epic fights followed by lust-filled, hardly-leave-the-bedroom make-up sessions, I needed the calm he offered."

"You had a good marriage then?"

"Yes, but Chloe was our glue. He adored her."

"I'm glad he was there for her and..." He twisted his fingers through her long hair. "I'm happy your time together was good, but I'm elated you're here with me now."

"Are you?"

He smiled. "Yes."

"That was my mother on the phone earlier. She's worried."

"About me?"

"About us." She placed her hand on his thigh. Since he'd put on shorts, her hand touched his warm skin. A shiver shook her for a second. "You hurt me...a lot."

He covered her hand with his. "I know, and God, I'm sorry. I wish there was a way to make it up to you." With a gentle squeeze on her fingers, he added, "I would do anything to take back my words and actions. I can't change the past, but I can promise you that I'm a better man now. I'll never hurt you again. I swear. Please give me a chance. I've..." He paused and drew in a breath. "I've never gotten over you, Jenny, and I fear I never will." With a shake of his head and a self-depreciating chuckle, he said, "I've found I'm a one-woman man, though I'm not saying I've been chaste since we divorced."

She grinned. "With your sex drive, I would've accused

you of lying if you'd said you'd never been with another woman."

"There might have been one or two."

She arched an eyebrow.

"Okay, maybe a couple more than that, but those women knew the score. I told none of them that I loved them. I didn't give them any promises for the future. I couldn't." He scooted until their hips touched. "I never dreamed I'd see you again or have the feelings I'm having." He caught her chin between his thumb and index finger and turned her head until their gazes met. "I'll back off if you tell me that's what you want. You're in the driver's seat, but Jenny...? I still want you. I still have strong feelings for you."

Her vision blurred as tears formed. "I'm confused, Marc. I didn't expect...I..." She sniffed.

"Oh, honey, don't cry." He wiped a tear from her cheek with his thumb. "I didn't mean to put you in a bad spot. I'll back off. I'm sorry."

"No." She caught his hand. "I thought I'd killed and buried any feelings I had for you, but..." She shrugged. "My heart is so full of emotion I can barely breathe."

He smiled and leaned forward to kiss her. Just a simple pressing of soft lips to lips. No move to deepen the kiss or move beyond the kiss.

"Just think about giving us a chance while you're here. That's all I'm asking. Can you do that?"

She nodded. "Yes, I can do that." Especially since his job was safer than when he'd been in the military. She wouldn't have to worry about burying another husband.

"Good."

He kissed her gently again. "Now, go to bed before I push for more than you're ready to give."

She grinned and stood. "I'll see you in the morning. Sweet dreams."

She knew his loving words would ensure she'd have some sweet, sweet dreams tonight.

Fifteen

S weet dreams? Who was she kidding? Her dreams had been sexy, erotic, and downright kinky that night. As with most dream recollections, trying to piece together the whole dream was impossible with scenes that were jumbled and hazy. The dream's story, if there was one, remained fuzzy, but she remembered a washboard abdomen and running her tongue down the ridges. There was also a cowboy hat, a sheriff's star, and a pair of handcuffs involved, but she didn't try very hard to reconstruct that one. All she knew was that sometime early in the morning, she sat straight up in bed, her hand between her leg, and an intense orgasm rocking through her body. Her breaths were rapid and ragged as she'd rode wave after wave of erotic tension.

After coming fully awake from the powerful orgasm, going back to sleep was out of the question. Quietly, she dressed and headed to the kitchen to make coffee. Other than the dripping of the coffee, the rest of the house was dark and silent. After setting up her computer on the kitchen table, she glared at the coffee maker, willing it to brew faster. Frustrated at waiting for the glass carafe to fill, she stuck a cup directly under the drip, which gave her a mug of coffee strong enough to grow hair on her chest. One sip and a long sigh flowed from her lips. She booted her computer and dug into the emails that'd arrived overnight.

"Good morning."

Startled at the greeting, her hand slammed to her chest. Her heart shot up to dangerous rates and slammed violently against her ribs. "You scared me to death."

Marc smiled and kissed the top of her head. "Sorry. How long have you been up?" He reached for a mug. "Thanks for making coffee."

"What time is it?"

"About six."

"I've been up about an hour."

He took the chair next to her. "Sleep good?"

"Crazy dreams."

He sipped on his coffee. "Really? Tell me about them."

She felt heat rush to her cheeks as she remembered some of the more erotic scenes. "Oh, you know. Cowboy hats and boots sort of stuff. Probably because I'm in Texas." She chuckled. "I can't remember much," she lied. "And even if I tried to explain the dreams, they never make any sense."

"Cowboy hats and boots?" He smirked. "Maybe a sheriff's star in there?"

She rolled her eyes. "You wish."

"I do, but I know what you mean. I usually

remember some of mine, but trying to piece them together is impossible."

"Exactly. What's on your agenda today?" She threw out the question to change the subject.

"I've got to head out shortly. I'm meeting Judge Yeats, Police Chief Gruber, and a couple of other town officials for breakfast. We try to do this every month to head off any problems before they get rolling." He scrubbed his hand down his face. "If only we could get a handle on the cattle rustling situation."

"You will."

"What about you?"

"Work. I've worked at Stroker for about four years, and you can count the number of vacation days I've used on one hand. If I can get things wrapped up today, I thought I'd take off a couple of weeks and just see Texas. Plus, if we're going to help at your house for a few days, I sure won't get any work done."

"You don't have to use your vacation time for my house," he insisted. "Save it for you and Chloe."

She smiled. "I'll be with Chloe. She wants to help, and so do I."

"You want to swing a maul at a wall, don't you?"

Her smile stretched into a wide grin. "You betcha."

He laughed. "I'm going to have to watch you. You're going to be dangerous."

"I can't wait to get destructive." She rubbed her hands together and gave an evil laugh.

"If you haven't made plans for tomorrow night, I thought I'd invite Dax, Cori, and Sami over for dinner and game night. They've all mentioned, not too subtly, that they want to spend time with Chloe."

"What? They don't want to spend time with me?" she joked.

"Sorry, honey. Chloe is the new, shiny person."

She chuckled. "I don't blame them. She's awesome."

He reached over and took her hand. "Yes, yes, she is, and it's because of her mother."

She dipped her head. "Thank you."

"Plus, I need to see how serious they are about getting married."

"Um, you were there when they announced their engagement. They seemed serious."

"Right, you don't know their latest craziness. They want to get married ASAP and at Singer Ranch."

"Seriously?" She frowned. "How soon are they talking about? Best I remember, and don't take this the wrong way, the ranch wasn't ready for a party."

"Exactly. And, to make it a little more insane, I think they want to hold an engagement party and surprise everyone with a wedding."

Arching her eyebrows, she said, "Yeah, that'd be interesting."

He sighed. "I think they need to move the setting."

"Maybe, but what if—now hear me out--what if we cleared an area out there? Maybe where they want to build their house? People could park in the field near your house. We could put off renovations, maybe? Or start renovations in areas other than the kitchen? I don't know. I'm thinking out loud. I don't really have a plan."

"One of the things I always loved about you was your

ability to go with the flow and think on your feet." He checked the time. "I've gotta run. Don't say anything to Chloe about the wedding. Think about it, though. Maybe you'll have some clever idea. You usually do." He stood and looked at her. "Did you think about our conversation last night?"

"Barely thought of anything else."

"And?"

"And we'll talk tonight." It was a stall tactic at best. She hadn't lied about thinking about him, their past, and her feelings. However, she was conflicted about what would be the best for her and Chloe, and Chloe had precedence over all other aspects.

He nodded. "Think about this then." Putting the knuckle of his index finger under her chin, he lifted her face, leaned over, and kissed her.

A quiet moan rattled up her throat and out. He tasted like a warm night with a cool breeze. Like a hot shower after playing in deep snow. Like a man who could wreck her carefully constructed world.

When he ended the kiss, his face wore a cocky smirk as if he could read every thought that went through her mind. "See you tonight," he said, his voice deep and raspy. "Oh, and one more thing. Start a grocery list of the things you and Chloe like to eat. I want to make sure you both have whatever you need while you're here. Later."

Her heart refused to calm down until after he drove away. She laid both hands over her chest and drew in deep breaths. Other than Marc, no man had ever rattled her like he could and apparently still did.

"What's for breakfast, Mom?"

Jenn glanced at her sleepy daughter and smiled. She made everything Jenn had ever been through worth it and then some.

Later that afternoon, Jenn moved her computer from the kitchen to Marc's private office. She had an upcoming presentation to the board and needed it to go smoothly. Public speaking was not her forte, so she liked to practice in front of a camera to look for hesitations and misspeaks. Plus, after all that practice, she knew her talk well enough to rarely need her notes. But for this first run-through, she needed quiet and privacy.

Initially, she wanted to sit and read her talk into the camera. Then, for the second run-through, she'd stand and watch her hand motions.

Hitting the record button on her computer, she cleared her voice. "Good morning. I'm happy to be here—"

A knock on the office door stopped her.

"Yes?"

The door opened, and a petite, attractive blonde stepped into the office, closing the door behind her.

"Can I help you?"

"I'm Angel Winns," the woman said.

Jenn frowned. "Okay. Have we met?"

Angel leaned against the door. "We haven't, but I thought I'd introduce myself to you. I'm Marc's girl-friend." She tittered. "Well, almost fiancée." She leaned menacingly toward Jenn and narrowed her eyes. "Marc belongs to me, and if you think I'm going to let you swoop in and mess up our lives, you've got another think coming."

Jenn leaned back in her chair. "Is that so?"

"It is. To show you what a good person I am and to make Marc's daughter feel welcome, I've left a casserole in the kitchen." Angel smiled, but there was no warmth behind those eyes. "You don't want me for an enemy, but I see no reason for that. Just keep your hands off my guy, and we'll get along famously."

Jenn nodded. "I see."

Angel straightened. "I thought you would. When are you planning on leaving? The sooner, the better." She chuckled. "I'm sure you understand. You had your chance with him. You blew it. Now, he's mine. I'm glad we understand each other. Enjoy the casserole." She opened the door and put her finger to her lips. "This conversation is our little secret, right?"

When the door closed, Jenn wasn't sure whether to laugh or scream. Was it even possible that there was a shred of truth to what she'd just been told? Had Marc been dating this woman? Or was she a stalker?

Whether Angel-the-girlfriend was telling the truth or not, Marc needed to know about the visit. As she struggled to find the words to describe the encounter, she closed her eyes with a smile. Words weren't necessary. She could simply show him the recording on her computer.

She stopped and saved the recording. First things first. She wanted to make sure that woman was out of the house, and second, she had every intention of tossing out that casserole. Who knew what was in there? She'd lived in New York for years and seen some strange things come through the Emergency Department. Self-preservation suggested no one eat that dish, whatever it was.

At five-fifteen, the garage door opened and closed, followed by the kitchen door opening. "Where's everyone?" Marc called.

"In the living room," Jenn answered.

She couldn't miss his exhausted expression. His face was drawn, the lines deeper. He flopped onto the sofa next to her. With a loud sigh, he dropped his head on the back cushion.

"Good Lord," Jenn said. "You sound like you climbed Mount Everest today."

He rolled his head to the side until their gazes met. "It would've been easier."

"What in the world happened? But, if it's secret, you don't have to tell me."

"Nothing like that. I had two deputies out with flu-like symptoms and another one who left early throwing up. It's been a while since I had to answer that many calls."

"Poor Sheriff Singer," she cooed. "You need a beer and bed?" Her eyes popped wide, and she added. "Um, I didn't mean it like you're going to take it."

He chuckled. "Thanks. I needed that."

"Hey, Marc," Chloe said as she joined them. "You look like death warmed over."

"Chloe!" Jenn scolded

"It's true," Chloe insisted.

Marc grinned. "I can't wait until you're forty and have had a hard day at work. Let's see how you look then."

"Still young and fabulous," Chloe replied. "I'm starving, Mom. What's for dinner? Are we going to eat that casserole?"

"No. I'll go make something."

"What casserole?" Marc asked.

"Some lady left you a casserole today," Chloe said,

"Who?"

Chloe shrugged. "I don't know. Mom, you talked to her. What was her name?"

"Angel Winns."

"Angel was here today?" Marc asked. "What'd she want?"

"To drop off a casserole, I guess," Chloe said. "I'm going to die of starvation if I have to wait for you to cook something."

"I doubt it," Jenn said with a laugh. "What sounds good?"

"Pizza."

Jenn gave her daughter an incredulous look. "No. No pizza, no hamburgers, no fries, and no milkshakes. You need some vegetables. You've eaten junk food for a week."

Her daughter groaned with a dramatic roll of her eyes. "If it were up to you, I'd eat Brussels sprouts, broccoli, and carrots every day."

"Yum," Jenn said with a grin. "Sounds delicious. Besides, as your mother, I have an obligation to make you eat vegetables."

Chloe pretended she was gagging, which made Marc snort.

"Well, I could take my favorite ladies to Rick's on the River. Beautiful setting. Fabulous food. They're known for their Chateaubriand, but anything you ordered will be delicious."

"Sounds fancy." Chloe shook her head and sneered. "That sounds like a date place. It is, isn't it?"

Marc shrugged. "It might be better for a date. How about the Home Diner? Casual place with fried chicken, meatloaf, catfish, buttermilk biscuits, and tons of vegetable options. What would you think about that?"

"Fried chicken? I'm in," Chloe said.

"Great. I need to grab a quick shower and change clothes, and then we can go." Marc stood.

"Marc, can I have a word with you before we go?"

"Of course."

Jenn looked at Chloe with an arched brow.

Chloe sighed dramatically. "I know. Go away, Chloe. The adults need to talk." She stomped out of the room, and in a minute, Jenn heard the bedroom door close.

"So, what's up?"

"Not here. In your office. I have something to show you on my computer."

In his office, she closed the door behind them and pointed to the desk chair. "Have a seat."

He sat and waited.

She leaned over his shoulder to pull up the recording from earlier. His sexy, male scent surrounded her and had her stomach quivering. Damn it was hard to concentrate with a quivering stomach. She couldn't identify the aroma, and she didn't care. All she knew was that she liked it...a lot. With a self-control she didn't realize she possessed, she restrained herself from sniffing his neck.

She found the video and launched it. "Ignore the

beginning," she said. "I was practicing a talk I have to give to the Stroker Board of Directors."

He tilted his head back until their gazes met. "You're looking cute."

"Thanks, but not what I wanted you to see. Now, watch."

She started the video, watched herself, cringed a little at her voice—which she always did—then came the knock at the door. When she turned the chair toward the sound, the arm of the chair hit the corner of her computer, which twisted the camera toward the door—an accident, but a fortuitous one because describing this encounter would have been weird and uncomfortable.

On the video, the door opened, and Angel stepped in. Marc glanced back with a questioning expression.

"Watch." She pointed at the screen.

He refocused his attention onto the video, even leaning a little closer for a better view.

When it was over, she pressed the pause button. "Now, I want to say—"

"Stop," he said, interrupting her. "Don't say anything else. I want to say something."

She nodded and crossed her arms to still her shaking hands.

"This may be hard to explain, and I'm not sure you're going to believe this, but I'm not dating this woman."

"Well, according to her, she believes you are." Jenn tossed her hands up in the air. "So, what's the truth?"

He sighed and shook his head. "We had a couple of dates earlier this year, but we wanted different things. She wanted a husband, and I didn't want to apply for the job.

She moved on to a lawyer with Montgomery and Montgomery, but I heard that was over. She and I were never in love or even close enough to consider marriage."

"Did you stop seeing her, or did she break it off with you?"

"I broke it off." He wore a chagrined expression. "I was finding bridal magazines all over her house whenever I was there. It didn't matter what room we were in there'd always a bridal magazine. I got the strong impression that she was looking for the husband, white picket fence, and two-point-five kids life plan." Closing his eyes, he shook his head. "When it became clear what she desired from a relationship, and I knew we were never going to be on the same page, I told her we couldn't see each other anymore."

"I'm confused then. What's with her visit today?"

"Honestly, I have no idea what was going on in her head. None." He stood and faced Jenn. "Don't give her another second of thought. She isn't a part of my life like that. I stay friends with her because I try to maintain an approachable and friendly manner with the citizens of Whispering Springs. It makes my job easier if I'm not fighting with townspeople right and left. You don't have to worry about her."

Jenn leaned against the closed office door and recrossed her arms. "I'm not worried about her or any other female in town. I'm not going to try to tie you down and force a relationship with you because we have a child."

When he walked toward her, he reminded her of a large, predatory cat approaching its prey. He placed his hands flat on the door, effectively trapping her between his muscular arms. His biceps flexed, stretching the material of his shirt. He leaned close until his mouth was millimeters from her lips.

"What if I want to trap you into something? Did you ever think about that?" His warm breath caressed her mouth as he spoke.

Lust pooled in her belly. Her heart rate and breathing ramped up. She could feel the artery in her neck pulsing with desire and need.

"Marc." Her word was a groan, a plea. If only she knew exactly what she was pleading for. A kiss? More?

He slammed his mouth to hers. Their teeth clashed and tongues dueled as she pulled his taste into her mouth. He caught her face between his large hands. His thick fingers spread on both sides of her face as he changed the angle of her head to take the kiss deeper. Fireworks exploded in her belly. Arousal flooded her panties. When she arched her head to give him better access, he moved his mouth down her neck. She sighed a groan.

Bam! Bam! Bam!

"Are you still in there? Come on! Let's go. My stomach is eating itself," Chloe shouted.

Marc kissed his way up her neck to a sensitive area behind her ear. "I am hungry," he whispered into her ear, "but not for food." He ran his tongue along the rim of her ear, sending an army of goosebumps marching down her spine.

She sighed. "Cool it, Cassanova. Welcome to parenthood, Daddy."

Sixteen

⤜⤛

The food at Home Café was known for its consistency. Because of that, Marc was positive everything they'd ordered had been delicious because they 'd left three clean plates on the table. However, his only craving was for another taste of Jenn's skin under his lips.

On the ride back home, Chloe wanted to see the ranches of the other Montgomerys. Driving around with his semi-erection was the last thing he wanted to do, but Jenn thought it was a great idea. Being late June, the sun didn't set until much later, so there was plenty of daylight left for sightseeing.

Jenn twisted in her seat to say something to her —*their*—daughter. A sense of peace and happiness swelled his heart to overflowing. This, tonight, was what his life had been missing. The question was how to get Jenn and Chloe to stay.

As they headed home after sightseeing, he hoped—crossed his fingers, actually—that Chloe would give him and Jenn some alone time. Instead, Chloe wanted the three of them to watch a movie together, and in the end, he found himself solo in his bed.

The next evening, Dax, Cori, and Sami came over for dinner and game night. He and Chloe took on the other two teams of Dax and Jenn and Sami and Cori in a hysterical game of charades. When Chloe drew a floral bouquet and dress, and he guessed wedding, their conversations turned to Dax and Cori's upcoming "engagement party" they wanted to hold in the field at Singer Ranch.

"I've thought a lot about this, um, engagement party you're planning," Marc said. "If we were talking about an outdoor party in, say, late October or November, I'd be on board, but Cori, you grew up here. You know what the Texas weather's like in July. This year is even worse. We're having one-hundred-plus days. Even a large tent will be suffocating."

"A party outside?" Chloe gasped. "I'd die."

While Jenn was aware that the engagement party could produce a surprise wedding, they hadn't mentioned anything to Chloe or Sami.

"I have to agree with my brilliant niece," Sami said. "It's like being back in Iraq all over again. This heat is deadly. I'm sprinting from the A/C in my car, to whatever building I'm entering—which had better be air-conditioned—and then back to the A/C in my car."

Marc laughed. "Patrol duty is going to be hell on you."

Sami shrugged. "I'll be fine because I'll be getting paid to be out in the heat, but without someone paying me? Nope. This gal has come to love air conditioning."

Dax and Cori exchanged glances, then Dax said, "I'll

admit, I knew the south could be hot, but I didn't appreciate how sweltering it could get. The last two days have been brutal, and we have been reassessing where to hold our party."

"If you really want to have an indoor engagement party and an outdoor wedding, you could have it somewhere inside now and then set a wedding date for October or November," Jenn suggested. "I read the other day that October is the new hot wedding month."

"We can think about the fall for a wedding," Cori said, "but we really want to have our engagement party now, right, honey?"

Dax put his arm around her. "Right."

"Like, when are you talking about?" Sami asked.

"Around July the fourth," Cori said. "That's a Wednesday this year, so maybe Friday?"

"Oh, I know," Chloe said excitedly. "My birthday is on June the thirtieth. We could have a joint party. Birthday for me and engagement party for you."

Cori chuckled. "That's sweet. Thank you for offering to share your birthday with us, but that's a little too soon to get our party together."

"Cori is right," Jenn said. "That doesn't mean we can't have a party for you."

"Whew," Chloe said. "Now if I only had people my age to invite to it."

Marc wanted to kick himself. Of course, a teen would want to be around people her own age. He should have thought about that. He should have found some teens her age to introduce her to. Getting the hang of thinking like a parent was harder than he'd thought.

"I have a sister your age," Cori said. "Why don't I help Jenn put together a party and you can meet her and Noah Graham, who's also close to your age. I know Annabelle—my sister—would be happy to help you meet people."

"Cori, that is so sweet of you," Jenn said. "And we will talk about it, but what about your situation? The engagement party?"

"I've got some ideas for locations," Cori said, as she looked at Dax. "I'm afraid your family is right about the heat. This summer has been one of the hottest on record, so it's probably not a good idea to use the ranch right now. But come fall, let's do throw a big party."

He nodded.

"Then it's settled," Marc said. "Cori, whatever you need from me to help you get this party arranged, just ask."

"What did you and Mom do?" Chloe looked at Jenn. "We've never talked about when you married Marc. What did you do?"

"Oh, honey, we were so young," Jenn said.

"Too young," Marc added.

"Barely eighteen and fresh out of high school."

"That's just three years older than me," Chloe said. "Wait, I'm almost sixteen, so only two years." She scowled. "I can't imagine getting married right now."

"And you're not," Jenn said firmly.

Chloe's response was a roll of her eyes. "Did you elope? Or what?"

"No, we had the church wedding, but it was extremely small, followed by punch and cake in the basement. There was no elaborate reception or honeymoon. Your grandparents couldn't afford to pay for a big wedding and then help me with school tuition too, so they gave us a choice. We could have a big, fancy wedding, or they could help pay for some of my college."

"So, we did the logical thing," Marc said. "With your mom's smarts, she was destined for college, and I knew she deserved it, so I told her I wanted a small wedding."

"That's what you wanted, though," Jenn said.

He shook his head. "Not really. I would've loved to have seen you in some fancy white dress, but I didn't mind. As long as we got married, I was happy."

"Until we weren't," Jenn muttered.

"What happened?" Chloe asked. "Why did you get a divorce?"

Jenn sighed. "It's a very long story, honey. Suffice it to say, we were too young and too immature. Wouldn't you agree, Marc?"

He nodded. "And that's why you won't be getting married until you're thirty." He grinned.

"You could prohibit her from dating until she's about twenty-five," Sami suggested.

"Thanks a lot for your help," Chloe said to a laughing Sami.

The next day, Cori called and invited Chloe over to her parents' house to meet Annabelle. She told her to pack her swimsuit and a change of clothes.

Cori and Dax picked Chloe up about noon, explaining it'd be after dinner before they brought her home. As soon as Dax's truck pulled away, Marc pulled Jenn into his arms.

"Now, where were we before we were interrupted?"

"I think about here." Jenn wrapped her arms around his neck and pulled him in for a deep kiss.

Their hands roamed over arms and shoulders, then down backs to butts. Jenn's hands slid under his shirt, her nails raking up his abdomen. Reaching over his shoulder, he fisted the T-shirt material and jerked it over his head. Flattening her hands against his chest, she glided them over his nipples and down his abdomen to the waistband of his shorts. He hissed in a breath when she ran one finger under that band of material.

Leaning over, she flicked one nipple with her tongue. His cock, which had been stiff with their first kiss, now grew rigid and demanding.

"Enough," he growled. "We have a perfectly good bed." He laced their fingers and led her to his bedroom. Sex against a door was great when you were twenty, but nothing was better than a soft bed where you could spread out and do it right.

Once inside, he closed the door. Bright sunlight filtered through his window until he unlaced their hands long enough to lower the sun-blocking blinds, leaving the room in dimmed lighting. He turned to look at her. She stood where he'd left her at the room's entrance.

"I'm not going to push you, Jenny. I want you. That's no secret." He waved a hand across the crotch of his shorts which were pulled tight with his erection. "But I don't want to do anything that would make your stay here uncomfortable." His heart raced with nervous tension. He'd stop if she said to, but that was the last thing he wanted.

Her mouth pulled into a smile, and she stepped toward him. "I want this."

He met her at the foot of his bed and pulled her in for a kiss. As he nibbled along her jaw, he slid a hand under her shirt. She broke the kiss long enough to pull the silky material over her head and toss it into his reading chair in the corner. His mouth quirked with a smile. She flicked the front latch, and her breasts spilled out.

"You're so pretty, Jenny. You always were when we were young, but you're more beautiful today. Maturity looks good on you."

He took both breasts into his hands and enjoyed the weight in his palms. When he squeezed her flesh, the nipples tightened into stiff peaks. He pinched the rigid nubs and then rolled them between his fingers.

Her cheeks flushed as she moaned at his touch. "Don't stop now," she said in a whispered groan. "More."

"I'm dying to see you naked," he said. The lust lodged in his throat made it almost impossible to speak.

"No one's stopping you." She smiled. "Especially not me."

He chuckled. "I love when you're bossy."

He unfastened her shorts and began to push them down her legs. "Just shorts, or take the panties too?" He nibbled on her ear as he waited for her answer.

"Everything," she responded with a long sigh.

As he slid her shorts and panties to the floor, he followed them down until he was on his knees. Pressing a kiss to the area above her navel, he tapped her right ankle. She lifted her foot, allowing him to slide her shorts and panties free. He did the same with her left, leaving her standing in front of him fully naked.

"Fuck, Jenny. You smell so good." He pressed his nose against her sex and sighed again. "I want to taste your orgasm on my tongue. It's been too long."

Raking her hands into his hair, she pushed his head back until their gazes met. "Again, there's no one in this room stopping you from taking what you want in any way you want it."

Without breaking their locked gazes, he growled, "Spread your legs for me."

Her stance widened.

He ran his palms up the inside of her legs until he reached the junction of her hip and thigh. "Wider," he ordered. "Much, much wider."

She did as he demanded. Liquid arousal glistened on the lips of her sex. The scent filled his senses. He nosed her pussy before flicking out his tongue to run it through the sweet fluid. Her salty and sweet juice zinged his taste buds as he lapped at her melted core. He groaned his love of her tang. He savored it, wanted to store the sensation forever in his mind.

The tip of his tongue found her rigid clit. He reamed around and around that stiff tissue as her hips moved forward and back with his strokes. The sound of her groans had liquid fire racing through his veins.

He traced the sides of her sex with a fingernail before pushing one finger inside. The walls of her canal clenched his finger. He added a second and then a third, shoving all three inside her, curving the tips to stroke the area he knew drove her crazy. Her hands in his hair tightened into fists as her hips thrust rhythmically forward and back. He knew she was close. Her thighs began to shake and quiver, which encouraged him to drive his fingers harder into her. Within seconds, she groaned loudly and cried his name.

She pulled his hair. "I want to feel you inside me. I need that."

He stood, a self-satisfied feeling swelling his heart. "Good," he said. "We're on the exact same page. Get on the bed," he ordered in a gravelly voice.

As she did, he shoved his shorts and briefs to the floor, his now rigid cock slapping against his abdomen. He wrapped his fingers around the base of his throbbing dick and stroked it a couple of times. Her eyes followed his motion. Her breath quickened. It was only then that he joined her on his bed.

He pushed her hair back over her shoulders and kissed her firmly. She threw her leg over his hip, pulling him over her. Balanced on his forearms, he held his full weight off her, not wanting to give her any displeasure. Their mouths met again, the kisses slow and deep. He wasn't sure if the message of his continued love penetrated her consciousness, but he vowed to keep trying until she fully understood what he was trying to say.

"I think you've misunderstood what I was saying," Jenn said as she kissed her way down his throat.

His heart stopped. He pulled back and looked down. "Excuse me?" He'd die a million deaths if she'd changed her mind about making love.

Pulling back had stopped her kisses. She moved her

soft hands to cup his cheeks. "I was too polite. What I meant to say was fuck me now."

He grinned. "Yes, ma'am."

"Condoms?"

He rolled off her long enough to open his bedside table and toss three on the bed.

"Have big plans, do you?" she asked with an arched brow.

"I'm ever hopeful."

He rolled the latex protection down his throbbing cock and resumed his top position. He looked down at her. "Okay? Or would you rather be on top?"

"Top, next time." She smiled and winked.

His heart leapt at her confirmation that there'd be more times together.

He caught her gaze as the head of his cock filled her entrance. Their gazes held as he pushed in inch by inch, going slowly to gauge her body's reaction.

When he was fully seated, her eyes closed with a soft exhale. "God, that feels so good," she said.

"It does," he agreed. It'd been years since he'd experienced such completeness as he felt at this exact moment. He began to move, pulling out before thrusting back inside with a rough drive of his hips. "I've never had this connection with anyone but you."

Her eyes filled with tears. "Nor have I." Her hips lifted off the bed to meet his hard thrusts, both of their breaths coming in pants and grunts.

Her hands fisted his sheets as her words shredded him. "Harder. Faster. There, Marc. Oh God, I've missed you, miss this. Harder." Her eyes flew open as her orgasm rolled through her, her sex squeezing his cock like a vise.

I still love you, he thought before he followed her over the cliff into his own release.

Neither was disappointed when Chloe spent the night with Annabelle at the Lamberts' place. They made love twice more that evening, finally falling asleep wrapped in each other's arms.

The following week was as exciting as it was exhausting. During the week, they tore out the rooms in the house. Each night, after Chloe had gone to bed, they tore at each other's bodies and souls. His room was more private, and she always joined him there. Their lovemaking had always been where they connected, where nothing was held back, no secrets left untold.

Now, as before, her touches and kisses left deep impressions on his heart. He loved her. He always had, and he'd accepted he always would. With time and maturity, he'd come to appreciate her intelligence, and instead of being threatened by it, he was proud of her.

By Thursday, they'd made it into the dining room with its yellowed, rose-patterned wallpaper and oncewhite wainscoting. He and Cash had considered just painting over the wallpaper, but Jenn and Chloe convinced him to let them steam it off, and that was their job for the day.

Cash had taken the day to meet with Dax, Cori, and their architect regarding the construction plans for the house they wanted to build. On Friday, they'd all be back with an engineer to assess the building site. While Marc was glad Dax and Cori would be building at the ranch, he was overjoyed that they had chosen an area close enough to him to be on the same parcel of land but far enough away that each house had a privacy buffer.

With Jenn and Chloe in the dining room working, he began cleaning up the bare kitchen. His mind was filtering through the latest cattle thefts when a cry echoed through the house. Dropping the load of debris he'd been carrying outside to the dumpster, he rushed toward the sound, worried that someone had gotten hurt. Instead, he found Jenn with her head shoved into a hole in the wall.

"What are you doing?" he said. "Are you okay?"

Jenn pulled her head out and looked at him with wide, excited eyes. "Chloe found this."

He frowned. "What is it?"

"It looks like a secret staircase," Chloe said, her voice shaking with exhilaration. "Pulling off this old wallpaper is hard work, so I took a break and leaned my weight on the wall. When the wall gave, my shoulders fell through."

"Let me see." Marc stuck his head through the opening, relieved no one was injured but shocked to find a secret rock staircase leading downward. "I had no idea this was here."

"I'll go get a flashlight and see where it goes," Chloe said and rushed off before he could tell her no.

"She's not going in there," Marc said.

"No, she's not, but I will," Jenn said.

He sighed. "You won't either. I don't want either of you going down there until we know if it's safe and what it is. I'll go."

"Really?" Jenn arched an eyebrow. "So it's okay if you do something risky, but not so much for me? Sexist, much?"

His back stiffened. "No, I'm not. I'm protective."

She laughed. "You are such a guy."

He winked. "Thank you, ma'am. You didn't complain about my manliness last night."

"Shh." She glanced around for Chloe.

"Jenn, honey, she's going to find out about us at some point."

"Yes, well," she said in a harsh whisper. "Now isn't the time."

"Found one," Chloe yelled as she charged back into the room. "Scoot over," she said to Marc. "I'm going in."

"Not hardly," he said sternly. "If anyone is going in there, it's me. Give me the light."

She huffed. "I'm smaller and lighter. It only makes sense for me to go down, right, Mom?"

Jenn shrugged. "I've been ordered away from the hole, so I guess it's up to you and Marc to fight it out."

"Marc, come on, man. You're a big old hulk of a man. I should go."

"And if there are snakes in there?" Marc asked.

She handed him the flashlight. "You should have led with that."

"I think, for safety, we should tie a rope around you," Jenn said. "Who knows if the wood supports are rotten, or the steps are slick, or if the steps abruptly stop. We should bring back appropriate gear tomorrow to check it out."

"I hate that you're probably right," he said. "Damn, I want to go in there."

"We all do," Jenn replied. "Once you check it out, then we can let Chloe go, okay, Chloe?"

"I'll never sleep tonight," she said. "What could it be?"

Marc chuckled. "You know, it's probably an old root cellar and nothing to get excited about."

Chloe's shoulders sagged. "I hadn't thought about that. I was thinking about slavery and the underground railroad."

"Just because it was called underground doesn't mean it was literally underground," Marc said.

"I know that," she said with a sneer only a teen could get right.

"Then, tomorrow, we explore. For now, let's call it a day and go home."

Home. He, Jenn, and Chloe going home. He liked how that sounded in his head.

After dinner and making sure Chloe wasn't around, Jenn kissed him. "I'm having so much fun."

"Fun?" He arched an eyebrow. "Just fun?"

She kissed the tip of his nose. "You know what I mean. Anyway, I'm going to my room and dying tonight. I'm exhausted."

"So, no sneaking into my room later? You're going to make me sleep all by myself in that big old bed?"

She shook her head. "I'm so beat all I could do is lay there."

"That's okay. I can do all the work."

She laughed. "See you in the morning."

He pulled a beer from the fridge and tossed the cap into the trash.

"Have you ever thought of going pro, Marc?" Chloe leaned against the door jamb watching him.

"In basketball or beer drinking?" he asked with a laugh.

"Did you ever think of doing anything other than being a sheriff?"

"Lots of things. I did construction a long time ago. I was in the Army for a few years. When I got out, I went into law enforcement. I found I liked helping people, and I had a knack for it, so I stayed. What are you thinking about doing after school? I don't think we've ever talked about that."

She pulled out a kitchen chair and sat. "I'm thinking astrophysics and maybe becoming an astronaut."

"Seriously?" He took a seat. "Wow. That's impressive."

She shrugged. "Thinking about it. Not sure."

"Lots of hard work, I'm thinking."

Nodding, she said, "It is, but I'm not nervous about the work. I'm..." Her voice trailed off.

"What are you nervous about, Chloe?"

"Mom. I don't want to leave mom alone. And I just found you. I don't want to leave you either."

He reached over and put his hand over hers. "Children are supposed to leave their parents. That's how life works."

"I understand that, but I only found out about you this year. It doesn't seem like I'll have enough time to spend with you if I leave for Harvard as planned."

"Your plan or Jenn's plan?"

Chloe's gaze dropped to the table. "Before we came back to Texas, I told her I wasn't going to Harvard. I think she was disappointed. I know she's always viewed Harvard as the pinnacle of universities. Of course, it has the programs I need to be an astrophysicist, but it's just so far away. Still, I think space is the future, and I want to be a part of it."

"That sounds very exciting. I hate to acknowledge this, but I have no idea what you need to study to do that."

"Astronomy and astrophysics, but it also takes a strong understanding of math and physics, and I do very well with both of those."

He frowned. "Is there a demand for that career?"

"One of the fastest growing careers."

"Interesting."

She yawned. "I'm headed to bed. Tomorrow is going to be so much fun." She stood. "I enjoyed our talk."

"Me, too."

After she left, he realized it was one of the first talks he'd had like this with his daughter, and for the first time, he really felt like a father. Did she see him as her dad or as Marc, her biological father? Would she ever call him Dad, or would he always be Marc? It wouldn't hurt his feelings if she called him Marc for the rest of his life, but calling him by his given name left an unseen, unspoken barrier between them.

He thought about Lon, his stepfather. Hadn't he done the exact same thing to Lon by refusing to call him Dad because of a stupid argument over a curfew? That dumb disagreement had been twenty-three years ago. At first, Marc had been angry and had punished Lon by refusing to call him Dad. Then, as time passed, the embarrassment at his ridiculous and childish actions kept him from going back to calling Lon Dad. Lon hadn't ever seemed to care that Marc refused to refer to him as his father, but maybe he'd hurt Lon without ever realizing the impact of his foolishness. Now that he was facing a similar issue with his own daughter, he could understand how Lon might be hurt but also understood why it was impossible for Lon to say anything, just as it was impossible for him to voice his thoughts to Chloe.

After tossing his empty beer bottle into the trash, he headed to bed, the subject of names on his mind. The next time he and his mother spoke, this would be on his list of topics. It might be time to rectify that situation.

Seventeen

ᢙᢙ

C offee had been brewed and breakfast cooked when he walked into the kitchen the next morning.

"It's about time," Chloe said. "Are you going to sleep all day?"

"It's five a.m. and still dark," Marc said as he poured himself a mug of coffee. "Where's your mom?"

"Still asleep." The disgust was loud and clear in Chloe's voice.

"Let her sleep. We have all day to explore."

"If the sun rises before she gets up, then I'll wake her."

He nodded. "I can agree with that."

"You can agree with what?" a yawning Jenn asked from the door.

He turned with a smile. "That Chloe can wake you up if the sun rises and you're still in bed."

Dressed in a dirty pair of jeans, a T-shirt that'd gotten torn sometime this past week, and her heavy-duty work boots, he still thought her beautiful. Jenn stretched her arms over her head, then leaned over, letting her arms dangle to the floor, her ass arched high into the air. If their daughter hadn't been standing right there, and if he hadn't sworn off door and wall sex, he'd have taken her against the wall, or on the table, or over the back of the sofa. He felt like a randy teen again.

They were the first ones to the property, which wasn't all that surprising since it was barely seven in the morning when he parked. The truck was vibrating with the excited energy from all of them. What was under his house? He reminded himself of what he'd told Chloe. It was probably some type of indoor access to a root cellar, but what if it wasn't?

Collecting the ropes and flashlights he'd loaded, they trooped into the house ready to explore its mysteries.

"This is so exciting," Chloe said.

"That it is," Jenn said. "What do you think is down there?"

Their daughter shrugged. "No clue, but I had trouble sleeping last night. Didn't you?"

Jenn smiled. "Are you kidding? I slept like the dead. You could've marched a university band through my bedroom, and I wouldn't have woken up. What about you, Marc? Sleep good?"

He gave her a side-eye. "Okay. I've slept better, but I survived."

She rolled her eyes with a snort.

"Seriously, I thought about this a lot last night. It doesn't make sense to climb through a hole in the wall as an indoor access. I want to spend some time looking for another way in," Marc told them.

While Jenn examined the wallpapered areas, he got on his knees to explore the wainscoting up closer.

"I'm finding nothing," Jenn said, "but you on your knees is a good look."

"Mom!" Chloe exclaimed.

Marc laughed. Their daughter had been looking around the house for other secret openings and had rejoined them without either of them noticing. He was starting to reply when he heard a click. "Did you hear that?"

Chloe hurried over. "I did."

He pushed on the wainscoting, and a section of the wall opened.

"Holy crap," Chloe said.

Jenn sighed. "Language."

"Sorry." Chloe tried to get closer, but Marc was already in the opening.

"There's a landing here that runs along the wall to that opening Chloe found." He stepped back into the room. "Time to explore."

"Not without a rope around you." Jenn fastened a safety rope around his waist while he slid on a flashlight fastened to a band that encircled his head.

He flicked on the light and tugged the rope. "Here I go." He stepped onto the creaky wooden landing. "If I don't return, remember the Alamo."

Jenn laughed. Chloe frowned.

The steps had been constructed of large rocks. They were damp and mossy, and he wondered where the moisture had come from. Plus, he wondered if the dampness would adversely affect his house. But as he stepped further down, he realized this had been here a long time, probably over a hundred years, so his concerns were most likely irrelevant.

When he stepped off the final stair, he turned to his left and stopped in stunned awe.

"Are you okay?" Jenn called down the stairs. He'd been talking to them as he made his way down, but then suddenly, he stopped speaking and the rope went slack. The quiet was more unnerving than the thought of snakes. She tried to convey a sense of maturity and strength around her daughter, but if anything happened to Marc, she'd never forgive herself. "Marc? Can you hear me?"

"Marc?" Chloe called. "You think he's okay?" she asked Jenn without looking backward.

"He's fine," came a deep voice from the living room.

Chloe screamed and hugged her mother, who wrapped her arms protectively around her daughter.

Marc walked in from the living room. "Sorry. I didn't mean to frighten you."

Chloe moved out of Jenn's embrace. "I wasn't scared, were you, Mom?"

"Nope, not me." Jenn lied with a big smile. "Where in the hell did you come from?" she asked Marc.

"Language," Chloe scolded in a voice that sounded remarkably similar to Jenn's.

"Outside," Marc said. "It's safe for you to go down. Take flashlights and be careful on the steps. They're a little slippery from moss."

Jenn gestured toward the small wall opening. "Lead the way."

"Go slow," he said and stepped inside the opening.

Chloe went next, with Jenn bringing up the rear. The steps were much as advertised...damp and slick. She kept her hand on the wall as she stepped down. When she finally stepped off the last set of rocks and found herself on solid ground, she breathed a sigh of relief. But then she turned the corner and gasped.

"Oh my!" she said in astonishment.

"Isn't this cool?" Chloe said.

"Are we in a cave?" Jenn asked, looking around at the underground room. It wasn't only the room that blew her away, but there were tables and chairs there. Against one wall was a long bar. "What is this?"

"I think maybe a hundred years ago this might've been a speakeasy. There's an old moonshine still around the corner. And listen."

Jenn tuned her ears and heard faint running water. "Water?"

"A spring," Marc said. "I think, maybe during prohibition, whoever owned this place made moonshine."

"That is too freaking cool," Chloe said. "Can I make this into my bedroom?"

"No!" Marc and Jenn said together.

"I'm glad you're both open to my ideas," Chloe said with an attitude.

"It looks too clean for no one to have been down here in a hundred years." Jenn dragged a finger across a table and held it up. "Some dirt, but not as much as I would expect."

He nodded. "I agree. I don't have answers for that."

"How'd you get out?" Jenn asked.

"Over here." Marc led them to another smaller room and then to a set of steps that led up. "This is the root cellar. I think that opening between the speakeasy and the root cellar was closed, but someone has opened it again and recently too."

"Yikes," Jenn said. "Not safe."

Marc lifted a board and placed it across the doors that opened out for the root cellar. "This should keep anyone from coming in for now."

"Where is everyone?" Cash's voice floated down from the dining room. "What the hell is this opening?"

"We're coming up," Marc shouted back.

"From where?" Cash shouted.

Once they'd shown Cash the underground room, they made their way back upstairs to the dining room. Cash had been surprised and amazed that, while he'd grown up in Whispering Springs, he'd never heard anything about a secret room. "My family...well, our family," he said to Marc, "has been in the area for over a hundred years. I can't wait to talk to Dad and see if he's ever heard anything about this."

"Before we spend time down there exploring, I want you to make sure it's safe," Jenn told Cash. "I want to know the ceiling isn't going to collapse and trap one of us down there."

Marc nodded. "Agreed."

"The engineer is meeting us today at Dax's place. I'll see if he's got time to stop by and take a look at it."

"That'd be great," Marc said.

"Y'all have made quite a dent in the work since I was here on Tuesday. I think Jenn was right about removing this wallpaper." Cash looked around the room. "I've been in the kitchen. Saving that big sink was a great idea. Next week, we'll get started on the cabinets."

For the rest of the day, Jenn and Chloe continued their work on the wallpaper while Marc finished hauling old lumber and trash to the dumpster outside.

Too tired at the end of the day to even think about cooking dinner, Jenn jumped on Marc's suggestion of picking up dinner from the Home Café.

They'd just sat down at the table when someone pounded loudly on the front door. Marc frowned.

"Jenn!" The shout came from the porch, followed by pounding on the door.

"Should I answer that?" Marc asked.

"I wouldn't," Chloe said calmly. She slathered butter and jelly on a biscuit. "It's just Mr. Dull and Boring."

"Chloe," Jenn scolded, but there wasn't much heat behind her words. She looked at Marc. "Kevin is a...friend."

"And he's awful," Chloe said as she chomped into her biscuit.

"Friend?" Marc's eyebrows arched. "All the way from Michigan? Well, we have to see what he needs."

He stood, but Jenn jumped to her feet. "I'll see what he needs. No reason to let your dinner get cold."

"Nonsense," Marc said draping his arm over her shoulders. "I'm nothing if not a good host."

Jenn's jaw tightened. *Dammit*, and she meant that for both Marc and Kevin.

Marc opened the door, his arm tight over Jenn's shoulders. "Can I help you?"

She elbowed him over. "Kevin, this is a surprise."

"Jenn, I need to talk to you." He eyed Marc. "Alone."

"What you need to say..." Marc stopped speaking when Jenn elbowed him again, but she put a little more muscle behind this jab.

"Okay." She looked at Marc with a plea for privacy in her eyes. "Give us a minute."

"I'll be inside with *our* daughter if you need me." He stepped back out of the door but didn't leave the room.

Jenn sighed and stepped onto the porch, making sure to close the door snuggly. "Now, Kevin, what do you need?"

His eyes flared. "Who is that man? And why is he calling Chloe his daughter?"

Jenn led him to a pair of chairs and indicated he should sit. He did.

"It doesn't matter who he is. Why are you here?"

"You took vacation." His voice was incredulous, as though announcing the discovery of live dinosaurs.

"Yeah? So?"

"You never take time off. Plus, I've given you enough time to reconsider my proposal. I had hoped you were saving your vacation days for our honeymoon."

She heard a crash from the living room.

"Kevin, we're not getting married. Not now, not ever."

"Because of him?" he sneered. "Are you fucking him?" He held up a hand. "It doesn't matter. I've come to take you and Chloe home where you belong. Then we can discuss our future. I've given you time to come to your senses, but it looks like I'll have to be more forceful in making you understand."

She blew out a long breath. "I'm going to put this into words you'll understand. I'm not going home, not now anyway. I'm not marrying you. I'm not marrying anyone. We have no future. And if you get forceful, that man inside the house, who I suspect is looking out the window, will probably take your head off."

"Honey, think about this. We're good together. You deserve a smart, professional man in your life, not some redneck, Texas cowboy who can't give you the life you deserve."

The front door slammed open, and Marc stepped out with a glare. "She told you no. You need to leave...now!"

With his hands fisted at his sides, Kevin glared back at Marc. While she didn't want a fight and didn't relish the idea of anyone getting hurt, she might have felt a secret thrill at two men glaring at each other over her. She'd take that secret to her grave.

"You better go, Kevin." She moved toward him.

He nodded once. "I'm returning to Michigan tomorrow. I think you and Chloe should come home to where you belong. Give it a hard thought tonight. I'm staying at the Riverside Inn."

"I hate you came all this way, but I thought I made myself clear. While I'll always think of you as a friend, that's all. You need to move on."

"And the first step is off my porch," Marc said with a growl.

"Don't threaten me, cowboy. I'll have you arrested like that." He snapped his fingers.

Jenn hid her smile and put her hand on Marc's chest to stop him from throwing Kevin into the yard. "Have a safe trip home, Kevin."

"You're making a mistake," he said.

"Thank you for your concern, but I can only hold the cowboy back so long."

She would swear Marc growled behind her.

Kevin slipped past and down the stairs. "Call me if you change your mind."

"I won't."

They remained on the porch until his car drove away. Only then did they return to the kitchen.

Chloe jumped to her feet when they returned. "I'm going to my room. Reading a fabulous book and, um, putting on my headphones with loud music. Won't hear a thing. Not a thing." She took a couple of steps and came back to grab her plate, drink, and fork, then left again. "Can't hear a thing," she shouted over her shoulder. The sound of her bedroom door slamming echoed through the quiet house.

"Well," Jenn said. "I...um..."

"You told me you weren't seeing anyone."

She winced. "I don't think I said that, but it doesn't matter. Things with Kevin were never serious."

He crossed his arms, which made all the muscles in his forearms and biceps pop. Her mouth watered at the sight.

"Sounded serious to me."

"He was more serious than I was. I broke it with him before I left Michigan."

"He asked you to marry him." It wasn't a question.

"Yes, he did, but I said no." She laid her hands over his folded arms. "I wouldn't be sleeping with you if I were in love with another man."

Marc blew out a long breath. "I know that. I was just...I don't know. I didn't like him showing up here."

She smiled. "I think you were jealous."

"Fuck, yes, I was jealous. He's younger and more attractive. Probably has more money than I do too. I can't compete with that."

Sliding her hands up his chest and around his neck, she said, "Younger, yes. More attractive? Only in his dreams. You have something he doesn't?"

"What's that?"

"Me."

"Yeah?" A smile began to slowly curl the corners of his mouth.

"Yeah."

He tilted his head toward the bedrooms. "I love noise-cancelling headphones."

Her body heated from her head to her toes. A smile crept onto her lips. "Even with those, we'll have to be quiet."

"I'm not the one who screams my name when she comes."

"You'll just have to find a way to keep my mouth occupied."

He pumped his eyebrows. "I do have a few ideas."

He took her hand, and they hurried to his bedroom, the furthest room from Chloe's. As soon as the door closed, he had her against the wood, his mouth on hers in a savage kiss that left her breathless. His hands roamed up and down her sides, finally sliding under her T-shirt. He pushed the shirt up, breaking the kiss only long enough to get the material over her head, and then fused his mouth to hers again.

A moan built inside her, along with a tightening spring of tension.

Flicking the latch on the front of her bra, the two cups sprung to the side, giving him unimpeded access.

"I fucking love your tits," he said against her lips before kissing his way over her chin and down her neck until he could latch onto one of her nipples.

Her nails scraped through his hair as she held his head firmly to her. "Good," she said with a gasp, "because my tits love your mouth."

Her words seemed to drive him to suck harder while rolling and pinching the other nipple.

He glided his hands over her ribcage and down to the waistband of her shorts. He inserted a finger under the elastic band, rimming her waist with the pad of his finger. Then, his hand was there, pushing her shorts down and over her hips. As the waistband swept past the elastic of her panties, he caught them and jerked those down too. His body followed the descent of her clothing to the floor until he was on his knees in front of her. He pressed a kiss on her abdomen, then licked, kissed, and bit his way down to her opening.

Knowing what he liked, she widened her stance,

wanting his mouth and tongue to soothe the ache between her thighs.

He ran his tongue along the seam of her sex until he could flick her clit. He circled her throbbing nub before licking her front to back.

The tension spring inside her coiled tight. Her heart raced as her breathing became erratic. Her toes curled as the sensations overwhelmed her. She slammed her fist between her lips as a million fireworks shot off in her belly. She moaned and sagged against the door.

He rose with an arrogant expression on his face and held out his hand. "Come to bed with me."

Taking his hand, she let him lead her from the door to his massive king-sized bed. She climbed onto the mattress and then watched as he removed the rest of his clothing. He wasn't the boy she'd known, not by a long shot. He was a man, a strong man with well-formed muscles and a confidence she found sexier than hell.

Of course, she loved him. She'd always loved him. Loving him had never been the problem. Her fear of losing him had, but hadn't her actions caused that anyway?

Their gazes met and held as he grasped his hard, long cock and stroked himself. She licked her lips, desperate for another taste of him. She began to move toward him, but he stopped her.

"Honey, if your luscious mouth gets even close to my dick, I'm going to explode."

A smug smile came to her lips. She licked them again. "You mean these lips?" She made an exaggerated sweep with her tongue over her already wet lips.

"Fuck, Jenny. You'll always be the sexiest woman I'll ever know."

She held out her arms. "Don't make me wait."

He grabbed a condom from his bedside and ripped open the foil. After rolling it down his straining cock, he joined her on the bed and then joined them as one.

Later, as they lay in the afterglow, she rolled onto her side and looked at him. "I have an idea."

He gave her a leer and arched his brow. "Give me a little more time and we'll do your idea. I'm not sixteen anymore."

She chuckled and draped an arm across him, loving the feel of his crinkly chest hair on the skin of her forearm. "Well, that too, but let's introduce my Kevin to your Angel. They seem perfect for each other."

He laughed, rolled on top of her, and kissed her. "Great idea. They can keep each other company while keeping out of our lives."

Eighteen

As Kevin Bland had promised, he showed up the next morning ready to collect Jenn and Chloe.

When the rental car pulled into the drive, Jenn lifted her coffee and looked out the window. She sighed and set her mug on the table.

"That man is either stupid, hard-of-hearing, or has an ego the size of Texas," Marc said with a shake of his head.

"Not stupid," Jenn answered. "And as far as I know, not hard of hearing, but his ego can compete with a Texan's ego."

Chloe walked in and looked out the window. "I'll go tell him to fuck off."

"Chloe!" Jenn said, but in reality, she totally wanted to do the same.

Marc stood, his gut ready for a fight. He could take that guy...probably. "I'll handle it."

Jenn rose. "No. This is my problem to handle." She looked at Marc. "Which reminds me, what did you ever do about *your* problem?"

"She means that Angel woman," Chloe said from behind him.

"Thanks, but he knows exactly what I'm talking about," Jenn said. She started toward the front door, then looked back at Marc. "Stay here. I've got this. Chloe?"

Chloe saluted. "I've got this, Mom."

Marc looked at his daughter and smiled. "You do, do you? And what are you going to do if I run out the door and beat the crap out of the guy?"

With a mischievous grin and a shrug, Chloe asked, "Cheer from the porch?"

He rejoined Chloe at the table and watched Jenn face her ex. He couldn't hear their conversation, but from both their stances, it was apparent the words were harsh. Kevin reached out and took Jenn's shoulders. Marc's back stiffened.

As he started to stand, Chloe put her hand on his shoulder and pushed down. "She's got this," Chloe said. "Trust me."

About that time, Jenn swung her arm and slapped him firm enough his head jerked to the side. The shock on Kevin's face made Marc's heart sing. Kevin shook his fist, got into the car, and squealed out of the driveway, leaving a long black mark.

"That's going to be fun to remove," Chloe said as she took a bite of jelly-covered toast.

Marc rubbed his cheek. "Ouch. That must have smarted."

Jenn walked in and brushed her hands together. "I think that does it. Are you two going to dawdle all day? We've got a house to work on."

The renovation of his house continued. Chloe's fascination with prohibition had her researching the property's history as far back as she could on the internet. As he'd promised, Cash talked with his parents about the property's history, which was a little murky.

Being with Jenn again, talking and laughing all day while spending each night together, made him happier than he'd been in a long time. He'd believed himself content with his life, and getting the ranch was his ultimate fantasy. However, he had begun to dread the day Jenn and Chloe would leave. He had little doubt she would go home. She'd never promised him more than here and now, but that wasn't what he wanted. He wanted it all...the ranch, the woman, and their child. How he could achieve all that played majorly in his mind.

Chloe's birthday was coming up on Saturday. Cori had offered her parents' house and pool for a party, but before Jenn accepted, Marc had gotten a call from Lane Montgomery, wanting to host the party at their house with all the Montgomerys and anyone else Chloe wanted to invite. After discussing it with Jenn and Chloe, he took Lane up on his offer to host the party on Sunday afternoon, July the first.

Even though the date for the Montgomery party was after Chloe's birthday, Jenn had told him that she still wanted to surprise Chloe with her grandparents and her Bronco on her special day. The truck had arrived early in the week. Cori and Dax had taken the SUV to Cori's house to hide, promising to drive it over on Saturday for dinner and cake.

Friday evening, dirty, exhausted, and starving, Jenn,

Chloe, and he sat at the table eating pizza when someone knocked at the door.

"I swear if that's another old boyfriend..." Marc started, but before he finished, the door opened.

"Where's everyone?" Cora Cooper called.

Marc shoved his chair back and stood. "Mom! Lon! We're in the kitchen."

His parents hurried in.

"I didn't see you drive up," Marc said, glancing outside, the dropping sun still providing more than adequate light to see his yard and drive.

"We wanted to surprise you." Cora hugged him and kissed his cheek. "My prize pupil." She hugged Chloe. "You cannot know how much I've loved having you in my class." She chuckled. "You totally intimidated my graduate students. And Jenn. You look wonderful."

Jenn looked down at her sweaty shirt. "You're sweet but blind, Cora."

His mother laughed. "Love will do that."

"What are you doing here?" Marc asked. "Not that I'm not thrilled to see you, but I wasn't expecting you until next week."

"The first birthday with my granddaughter? You better believe I'm not missing that."

Marc nodded. "Lane called you."

"He did." She popped him on the shoulder. "As you should have." She looked at Jenn and wagged a finger. "Or you."

"I'm glad you're here," Jenn said.

"Y'all want some pizza?" Marc asked.

"No, we're not staying. Lane and Jackie are expecting us at their house in a little bit. I just needed to hug my granddaughter." Standing behind Chloe, she wrapped her arms around Chloe's shoulders and hugged her tightly until the teen squeaked. "Sorry," Cora said and sniffed. "I didn't think I would ever have grandchildren." She hugged Chloe again.

"Mom," Marc said. "Let her breathe."

Lon chuckled. "I've had to talk her out of flying down here every day since you told us about Chloe." He walked over to where his wife stood. "We're so happy, Chloe. And, the good news is, we are the type of grandparents with too much money who want to spoil our grandchild."

"Oh great," Jenn snarked with a roll of her eyes. "Just what Chloe needs...more spoiling. My parents are bad enough."

"Yay," Chloe said. "I love having a new set of grandparents to train."

Cora and Lon laughed.

"We're headed on to Lane's," Cora said. "We just got into town and had to stop by and hug Chloe."

"And not your own son?" Marc asked with fake hurt feelings as he rubbed his non-crying eyes.

Jenn snickered, as did Chloe.

"Tomorrow's the big day, huh?" Cora said with a smile.

Chloe's eyes lit up. "I'll be sixteen. When we get back to Michigan, I can drive without an adult."

Jenn and Marc exchanged quick glances.

"I don't know what teens like these days, so why

don't Lon and I pick you up tomorrow, and we'll go shopping in Dallas? Anything you want."

"Anything?" Chloe asked with wide eyes.

"Within reason," Jenn said. "Thank you both. That's a very nice offer."

"Okay, then. We're off. We'll see you about nine, Chloe. Breakfast and shopping?"

His daughter grinned, and he could almost see dollar signs floating out of her ears. "Yep."

After his parents left, Chloe went to her room, explaining, "I need to do some research on what stores are there."

"Anything you could possibly want," Marc told her.

"This is going to be so much fun." She put her dirty dishes in the dishwasher and danced from the room. He wasn't sure her feet touched the floor.

"This is awfully nice of your parents."

He started to correct her, to remind her that Lon was not his father, but he stopped. Meeting Chloe and coming to love her like he did was making him reevaluate a lot of things.

"Trust me, Mom will have more fun than Chloe. I feel for Lon, though. It's going to be a long day."

"I need a shower," Jenn announced as she stood.

He waggled his eyebrows. "You know you're welcome to use mine."

"I'm thinking my back got very, very dirty today."

He leapt up. "Let me see what I can do about that."

. . .

When Marc woke, Jenn was gone from his bed. It wasn't the first time. She felt strongly that their sleeping in the same bed would give Chloe the wrong impression. He should have asked her exactly what she meant by the wrong impression, but he wasn't sure he would have liked her answer. Did she mean the wrong impression in that they were having sex without being married? The wrong impression in that she and he were together as a couple again? Or the wrong impression that they would be staying in Texas permanently?

She wasn't in the kitchen when he walked in. The coffee pot was cold and empty. Last night's dinner dishes still littered the table. Outside, the sun was just beginning to break on the horizon.

While the coffee brewed, he loaded the dishwasher and started it. Once he had coffee in hand, he went onto the back deck to see the morning start. On these hot Texas days, the only time the temperature was tolerable to be outside was early morning, and he thrived on being outside.

He hadn't been there long when he heard the French doors open. Expecting Jenn, he was surprised to see Chloe joining him.

"Good morning," he said. "Sleep good?"

She nodded. "Great."

When she stood there, he said, "Have a seat. Got something on your mind?"

She nodded again and sat. "Are you in love with Mom?"

His heart skittered to a bumpy stop before racing off. "I care very much about your mom."

"Yes, but are you in love with her?" The teen leaned toward him. "I need to know."

"Can I ask why you need to know?"

She took a sip of coffee and leaned back in her chair. "Mom hasn't been this happy in years. Even when David was alive, she was okay. She worked all the time and was gone a lot. But down here, she's just happy and easier to be around."

"She worked all the time?"

"God, yes. She'd be gone for surgery before I woke up. Some nights, she'd come in to tell me goodnight long after I went to bed. She and David...." She shrugged. "I don't know how to explain it, but she's different when she's around you."

"Did Jenn and David fight?" He shouldn't be prying. He knew that, but his curiosity about her life between their divorce and now was growing like a cancer inside. Questions to Jenn about David or about their life were always answered by her, but in ways that left him with more questions.

"No. They never fought. They were...like..." She paused and then said, "They were so polite to each other. They never had raised voices or any disagreements, or at least I can't remember any."

"Maybe you don't remember," he suggested. "Time will do that to memories. Sometimes, we only want to remember the good times, not the bad."

"It's not that. Her face was so serious all the time. I heard her snort the other day, and..." She looked at him with wide eyes, "I've never heard her snort in my life." She turned her gaze over the yard. "And all her kidding and laughter. That's odd too."

"Odd?"

"You know, new." She turned her chair to face him. "That's why I'm worried. What if she's in love with you, and you do something that hurts her again?"

He dropped his feet to the deck and took her hands. "I would never hurt your mom, not again. We were both hurt by each other a long time ago, but we're older and wiser."

"Older, for sure," she said with an evil grin.

He laughed. "True, but don't worry about your mom. I promise not to make her cry—except for tears of happiness."

"Thank you."

"Now, do you have your stores lined out for today?"

"Yes. I got a text from your mom last night. Your Aunt Jackie and Aunt Nadine are going with us, and we're leaving Lon at home."

Marc laughed. "I'm sure he's not too broken-hearted."

"This is going to be so much fun."

"What's going to be fun?" Jenn asked as she walked out.

"She's going with my mom and her sisters-in-law today. Apparently, my aunts decided to tag along for a girls' day out."

Chloe frowned. "What should I call them? Should I call your mom Cora? Dr. Cooper? Do I call them Mrs. Montgomery, or what? I mean, two Mrs. Montgomerys will be confusing."

"My suggestion?" Jenn said. "Ask them what they want to be called. I've found people prefer that."

"I agree, but I know my mom will not want to be called Dr. Cooper or anything like that."

A grin crept onto Chloe's face. "Grandma Cooper?"

Marc laughed. "I'd love to be there when you use that term. But Jenn's right. Ask her what she wants you to call her. She might want Cora. On the other hand, she's wanted a grandchild for so long she's probably practiced some grandmother names. She might have one she wants you to use."

"She probably expected to start with a baby." Chloe winced. "I bet she would've loved to cuddle a baby instead of an almost grown-up."

"First, you're a long way from grown up," Jenn said as she sat in a chair near her daughter. "And second, you were a horrible baby, so she got the best end of this deal."

"Mom!" Chloe said indignantly.

Jenn shrugged as she took a sip of coffee. She looked at Marc. "She was colicky for the first three months of life. Nothing made her happy and..." she leaned over to squeeze her daughter's cheeks, "and not much has changed."

Marc laughed as Chloe rolled her eyes.

"They're coming earlier than Cora said last night, so I need to go get ready." She stood and pointed to her mother and then to Marc. "You two stay out of trouble today."

Jenn slapped her hand to her chest in mock horrification. "Us? We would never..."

Marc nodded. "Total innocents here."

Chloe left laughing.

Marc sighed and smiled. "Damn, Jenn. She's incredible. You've done a great job with her."

"I wish I could say it was all me, but so much of it was David. He was so good with her."

"Maybe he was important in those early days, but now? You two have a great relationship, and if you hadn't been an important part of her life before he died, I doubt you would have this close relationship now."

"Maybe. I'm going to head in and catch the Saturday morning shows."

He stood. "Sounds like a plan."

They were in the living room when a large, silver SUV pulled into the drive.

"Chloe, they're here," Jenn called.

"Coming." Chloe raced into the living room. "This look okay?"

Jenn frowned and muted the television sound. "What are you wearing?"

"A skirt."

"I know it's a skirt, but... Is that my skirt?"

"Well, yeah. You wore my jeans the last time we were here."

"I don't mind you wearing it, but it's not usually your style."

"Well, Grandma Cora said—"

"Grandma Cora?" Marc asked.

"Yeah, that's what she said she wanted to be called. Anyway, Grandma Cora said that Aunt Jackie—"

"Aunt Jackie?" Marc arched a brow.

"Yes," Chloe said with exasperation. "Aunt Jackie and

Aunt Nadine. I did what you suggested and asked them what they wanted to be called when Grandma Cora texted me to say they were on the way. Anyway, Aunt Jackie said she needed a new outfit for Dax and Cori's party this week, so we'll be trying on clothes and a skirt is easier to take on and off."

A car horn tooted.

"That's them. I've gotta go. See you later."

Chloe flew out the door, slamming it behind her.

The sudden quiet was startling. Jenn looked at Marc. "I think we've got a few hours with no one here but us. Whatever will we do with our time?"

He stood and pulled her to her feet. "I have a few ideas."

"I bet you do."

It was close to one when the baby blue Bronco pulled into the drive. Jenn looked out the window and laughed.

"What's so funny?" Marc slipped his arms around her waist.

"Check out Chloe's car."

Cori had pulled in behind the blue SUV. Helium-filled balloons danced in the light breeze from each door handle and the rear hatch handle. A large white bow sat on the SUV's top. A banner with HAPPY 16TH BIRTHDAY CHLOE ran across the windshield.

"She is going to go crazy when she sees this," Jenn said. She leaned back into his embrace.

Nothing had ever felt so right than having her in his arms. "She'll be surprised?"

She snorted, and he thought about what Chloe had told him that morning. Jenn did laugh a lot, and she smiled and flirted with him. Maybe she was happy here. Maybe there was a chance for a long-term future for them. He barely dared to hope.

"Do I need to go get her cake?"

Jenn nodded. "Please. Porchia said to leave the cake design to her, so I have no idea what it'll look like, but I've learned it doesn't matter. Anything she makes is fabulous."

"I'm going to take Dax with me. I need to chat with him."

"Send Cori in to keep me company."

"Will do." He turned her in his arms until he could kiss her. Even now, the taste of her mouth sent lust coursing through his veins. "Mmm," he moaned. "You taste good."

She pushed him back with a laugh. "That's coffee on my breath."

"Like I said, tastes so good."

"Go on. I need to get things together for dinner."

"What time will your parents be here?"

"I'm not sure. They said not to worry about them. They'd rent a car."

"Okay," He kissed her again and held her tight. "This feels good. Are you sure we have to have guests for dinner?"

With a snort and a chuckle, she stepped out of his reach. "Go get the cake."

He and Dax loaded into his departmental SUV and headed to Porchia's bakery.

"I feel bad," he confessed to Dax.

"About what?"

"I've been so consumed with the house renovation I totally forgot to throw you a bachelor party."

"Well, how can you throw a bachelor party when no wedding is on the schedule?"

"True."

"Plus, I didn't want one. A bunch of drunk guys in a bar? I've done that scene and have no interest in doing it again. No, Cori and I talked about those parties and neither of us had any interest. That's one of the advantages of our little surprise this week. No bachelor or bachelorette parties. No wedding showers. No fuss. Just us starting our life together."

"You have the license?"

"Yep. You do your online preacher registration?"

Marc grinned. "You may refer to me as Brother Love and Light."

Dax chuckled. "No shit?"

"Nope. They wanted me to name myself, so I did." He glanced over. "I'm glad Cori's mom was able to get the country club for the wedding. It'll be nicer and cooler than our ranch."

"Well, Tuesday night isn't a big draw for ballroom rentals. Plus, throw in July the third, and it was wide open."

"How many people are coming?"

Dax shrugged. "I have no idea. I invited you, Sami, and Mom and Dad. That was the extent of my list. Cori invited a bunch of her friends, and then we told her mom to invite whomever she wanted. Since the Lamberts are paying for the party, Cori and I decided to turn her mom loose with the invitation list and food. Neither of us cares what she serves."

"Is Porchia doing a cake for y'all?"

Dax chuckled. "Cori's mom ordered an engagement cake. Cori and I met with Porchia and let her in on the big surprise. She promised to keep it under her hat. So, there will be a cake, just not what was ordered. Cori said she trusts Porchia, so..." He shrugged. "I honestly don't care."

"I hear ya."

At the bakery, Porchia was working behind the counter when they entered.

"Good morning, gentlemen," she called. "I've got your cake ready, Marc."

"Great. I'll pay while you box it up."

"I want you to see it before it goes in the box."

As she turned toward the refrigerated cake case behind her, Marc saw what she was reaching for and burst out laughing. She pulled out a 3-D rendition of Chloe's baby blue Bronco. She hadn't just drawn the SUV on top of a cake or put a plastic car on top. The entire cake was the car.

"That's incredible," he said.

She smiled brightly. "I had never done anything like this before and wanted to give it a shot." She held up the cake and turned it so he and Dax could see all sides. "I'm going to use it in my advertising if you don't mind."

"Have at it. Chloe is going to lose her mind when she sees it. I hope she'll cut it."

Porchia laughed. "Trust me. It's cake, and it'll be good. Take lots of pictures tonight."

She boxed up the cake-car and looked at Dax. "Any questions from you?"

"We ready to go?"

She nodded. "Yes. Luckily for you, I'm friends with the catering manager at the club, so arrangements have been made."

Marc picked up the box. "See you tomorrow?"

"And Tuesday," she replied.

Marc had sent a text to his mom asking her to alert them before bringing home Chloe. Jenn wanted to get pictures of their daughter's face when she saw her Bronco. At a little before four, the text came that they were around the corner. The four adults headed to the front yard and waited.

"I hate that my parents are going to miss this," Jenn said to Marc.

"Planes are late all the time. I wouldn't be worried about them."

The silver SUV pulled into the drive, and a rear door flew open.

"Ohmigod, ohmigod," Chloe shouted. "My car. You got me my car." She threw her arms around Jenn, then Marc, and then across the hood of the Bronco. "I'm so glad to see you," she crooned to the SUV.

Jenn was grinning brightly as she snapped pictures.

"Chloe," Cora called from the SUV. "Didn't you forget something?"

Chloe's eyes popped wide. "Mimi and Poppa."

"Do what?" Jenn said. She'd been expecting her

parents to arrive at any moment, but how did Chloe know about them?

From the open rear door, Adele Winslow stepped onto the drive.

"Surprise," Adele said.

"Mom!" Jenn hurried over and hugged her mother.

"We wanted to surprise you," her mom said. "When Cora called and told me about taking our girl shopping, well, I just had to be there. So, your father and I flew in early this morning. He took the rental car to spend the day with Lon. They'll be along shortly, I'm sure."

"Hello, Adele," Marc said. "Good to see you."

"You, too, Marc. Dax, I hear congratulations are in order."

Dax put his arm around Cori. "This is Cori Lambert, my fiancée."

"Nice to meet you, Cori."

"I hope you'll be around long enough to attend the engagement party on Tuesday."

"We plan to." She looked at Dax. "Your mom invited us. I hope you don't mind."

"Not at all. We're happy to have you."

Marc helped his mom unload more shopping bags than he wanted to count. Lon and Roger arrived shortly after, and the evening party got started.

Chloe moved to his den and gave her room to her Mimi and Poppa. While Marc was happy to host his ex-in-laws, their presence put an end to sleeping with Jenn. His bed, always the most comfortable piece of furniture in his house, suddenly became too large and too cold. He missed Jenn next to him.

Sunday's pool party was a boisterous affair with children ranging in age from a few years up to Noah Graham at eighteen. Jackie had hired Noah as the lifeguard, leaving the adults free to sit a distance from the noise, all the children still within sight but with some of the responsibility off their shoulders.

Since Dax and Cori's party was on Tuesday, Marc had decided to give the house renovation a break. On Monday, he went into work. He'd kept in touch with his deputy sheriffs to ensure nothing major arose that he needed to deal with, and nothing had. But it didn't hurt to drop by and check the mail he was sure had accumulated on his desk.

The mail hadn't fallen off the desktop to the floor—yet—but it was leaning precariously. He sat, lifted the first envelope, and slit it open.

"Sheriff?"

Marc looked up at Tiffany Yeats standing at his door. "Hi, Tiffany. What's up?"

Her eyes shifted nervously around. She looked over her shoulder and then back to him. "Can I talk to you?"

"Sure. Come in."

She shut the door, and he heard the lock click into place. Warning alarms blared in his head. He started making mental plans for an appropriate reaction when she made a pass at him.

"Thanks." She pulled around the chair from in front of his desk until she was sitting beside him.

"Um, Tiffany? What's happening here?"

"I need to talk to you," she whispered. "And I don't want anyone to hear."

Her voice was so low and quiet he could barely hear her.

"Okay, shoot," he said, not having a clue what was going on right now.

"You know I got into a lot of trouble growing up."

He nodded. "I do, and I'm proud of how you've turned your life around."

"I like working here."

"Good to hear. You've done a great job." He worked to keep a confused frown off his face.

"My Grandpa Yeats got me out of a lot of trouble back then."

"I know, Tiffany. To tell you the truth, it was Judge Yeats who asked me to hire you."

"That's what I want to talk to you about."

This time, his frown formed before he could stop it. "Why don't you just tell me what you're trying to say."

She sighed, and tears glistened in her eyes. Dammit. He hated female tears.

She sniffed. "I'm sorry. I just...I don't want to do this anymore."

"Work for me? Work in this department? I don't understand. You seem so happy here."

"I am happy here. That's the problem." She sniffed again, then pulled a tissue from her pocket and blew her nose. "My grandpa put me here to spy, and I hate it. You're a good man, Marc. A good sheriff. Everyone who works here knows that."

It was as if someone had hit him with a taser. He jerked back. "Spy on me?"

"Well, you and the department."

"Why? What did he want you to find out?"

"He said the Montgomerys put you into this position to protect them and that you weren't qualified for the job. He has it in his mind that if you do a bad job, he can get you replaced."

"Is there someone in particular he wants in here?"

She nodded. "My uncle."

"Ah."

Her uncle was Jasper Yeats, a local whom Marc had beaten in the election.

"And now, Grandpa Yeats is mad at me because I told him I didn't want to do this anymore."

"What exactly have you been doing?"

"He wants all the information on the cattle rustling."

A light bulb flashed on in Marc's brain. "He thinks if the cattle thefts continue, he'll be able to convince the town I can't do the job?"

"Worse." She leaned so close Marc could smell her vanilla-scented shampoo. "You remember Dancy Little?"

"Sort of. Wasn't he the guy you got busted with back when you were a teen?"

She nodded. "Well, Dancy and his brother, Danny, got into trouble over some stolen cars. Grandpa Yeats was their judge. They're working for Grandpa now."

"In what way?"

"They're the ones stealing cows. Well, them and their friend Frank Moser. He's the one who got hurt at the D&R."

"Are you telling me that your grandfather, Judge Yeats, is behind all these cattle thefts?"

She nodded. "There's a fourth guy working with

them, but I don't know him. I just know he lives on Grandpa's ranch and takes care of the place."

"Are the cattle at that ranch?"

She shrugged. "I don't know. I think so, but I really don't know. Are you going to fire me?"

"No, but I need to know what you've told him."

"Nothing, and that's why he's so mad. I told him you were keeping all the reports locked up, so I couldn't find out anything about the investigation. He didn't like that. And then when you bought the ranch he wanted, well, he got crazy mad." She looked at him with wide eyes. "Dancy told me that he, Danny, and Frank had been meeting with Grandpa Yeats in some secret, underground room on that ranch you bought. Said nobody remembered that old room, and it was perfect since they'd never be seen with Grandpa in public, and nobody would ever think to connect them."

Marc nodded. He'd suspected the judge had wanted his ranch. He hadn't, however, suspected that Judge Yeats was involved with the cattle rustling. "Do you have anything else you need to tell me?"

Her fingers twisted nervously in her lap. "They're going to steal some more cattle. I heard Grandpa talking on the phone."

Marc's jaw tightened. "Where and when? Do you know?"

"Wednesday night. During the July Fourth fireworks. Most of our department will be on traffic duty that night, so we'll be a little light here. Same with Chief Gruber's department."

"Where?"

"They're hitting the Halo M."

"Travis Montgomery's place?"

She nodded. "That's what I heard. I couldn't ask questions because I didn't want him to know I heard anything. Don't fire me, Sheriff. I really like this job."

"Thanks for the information, Tiffany, and I don't intend to fire you. Go back to work, and don't say anything about this to anyone else. Promise?"

"Yes, sir."

He sat there stewing over what Tiffany Yeats had just told him. It was time to bring the cattle rustling to an end and give Judge Yeats a taste of real justice.

He picked up the phone and placed a call to Harvey Cole. The Texas Ranger would be mighty interested in what Tiffany had had to say.

Nineteen

❧

Marc was adjusting his red bowtie when there was a knock at his bedroom door. "Come in."

"Are you decent?" Jenn asked.

"I'm dressed, but around you, I'm never decent." He gave her his best leer and licked his lips.

She laughed. "Wow." She walked into his room. "You look fancy."

He looked down at his khaki pants, long-sleeved, white oxford shirt—rolled up on his forearms—and red suspenders with matching bowtie. He held out his arms. "You want this. You can admit it."

She snorted. "Oh yeah, baby." With a grin, she walked over to straighten his tie. "I've missed you," she whispered.

"Yeah, that's what letting your parents stay in Chloe's room does for our sex life."

She smiled, but before she could respond, Chloe asked from the door. "What do you think about this outfit?"

Jenn turned. Marc studied their daughter. Her sleeveless dress was black with a white polka dot design that cut in at her waist and flared out into a full skirt on the bottom. She wore a pair of white sandals with small heels.

"Oh honey," Jenn cooed. "You look so grown up."

Chloe spun around with her arms out. "Aunt Jackie said this made me look mature. Do you think so?"

"I think your Aunt Jackie has excellent taste in clothes. Do I want to know what it cost?" Jenn asked.

"Nope. Grandma Cora said if you asked, I was to say either none of your business or ten dollars." Chloe grinned. "None of your business. I like that."

Her mother gave her a mock glare. "I can still send your Bronco back to Michigan."

"You wouldn't," Chloe gasped.

"No, I wouldn't. When are you leaving?"

Chloe had asked to drive her own Bronco to the party since arriving with her mother looked so juvenile.

"When you do, I guess. I'm picking up Annabelle on the way. Noah is meeting us there."

"I'm glad you've made some friends," Jenn said.

Chloe smiled. "Me too."

"I think we need to stop yakking and get moving," Marc said as he put his hand on Jenn's lower back. "Have you seen your grandparents?" he asked Chloe.

"They've been ready forever. Poppa is watching the news, and Mimi is reading a book."

"Okay, then. Let's round up the troops and get moving."

The parking lot of the Whispering Springs Country

Club was filling quickly, and he was lucky to find a parking spot at the end of a row.

"Looks like Cori's mom outdid herself." Jenn gestured to all the parked cars.

"You've met Clover Jean. Would you turn down an invitation to a party she was hosting?"

Jenn chuckled. "Nope. You know it's going to be over the top."

"Of course, it is. That's Clover Jean in a nutshell. Let's go."

"You have what you're going to say later?"

Marc nodded. "I have it."

"Then let's go get this party started."

Jenn was wrong. The party had already started when they got there. A uniformed server handed them glasses of champagne as they entered the elaborate ballroom. Fresh floral arrangements were everywhere he looked. On the tables. In an arch over the entry door. Hung from swags in the windows.

"Just think what she would have done with time and insider information about today," Marc whispered.

She clinked her champagne flute against his. "I completely understand Cori's reasoning now."

"You haven't met Cori's older sister, have you?"

Jenn shook her head.

"Come on. I'll introduce you."

Marc put his hand on the small of her back—something he loved to do—and steered her toward Elsie Belle Lambert Billings. As usual, Elsie Belle held court as people flocked around her. At close to their age, Elsie Belle continued to maintain her stunningly beautiful appearance. Trim figure. Flawless makeup and hair. He wondered what Jenn would think of the town's Miss Texas.

"Elsie Belle, I'd like you to meet Dr. Jennifer Tate. Jenn, this is Cori's sister, Elsie Belle Lambert Billings."

"Marc," Elsie Belle said. "How good to see you." She bussed a kiss on his cheek. She then held out both hands to Jenn, who took them. "Dr. Tate, I am so thrilled to meet you. Your daughter is a delight and, I might add, a good influence on our younger sister Annabelle."

"Jenn, please, and thank you for your nice comments about Chloe. I am so thankful Cori took her under her wing and introduced her to Annabelle."

"We are too. The entire family thinks she's delightful."

Jenn laughed. "I wouldn't go that far, but thank you."

"Where's your husband?" Marc asked. "I haven't seen him."

Elsie Belle waved a hand. "He's in Madrid on a business trip. Oscar is always traveling and making business deals." She directed her comments to Jenn. "I miss him when he's gone, but I've grown accustomed to his travels."

"I'm sorry I won't get to meet him."

"Me too."

"Clover Jean went all out," Marc said.

"Mom's thrilled. To tell you the truth, I think she was worried Cori would never marry, so Mom thinks your brother is the greatest."

Marc chuckled. "We feel the same about her." He looked around. "Have you seen the feted couple?"

"They're around somewhere. Cori was leading poor Dax from person to person, introducing him. Oh, wait. I see them over by the bar."

"If you'll excuse us," he said, "I think we should go say our hellos."

The party had started at seven. It was now a little past seven-thirty, and he wondered when the happy couple planned to pull the trigger on the surprise. As Elsie Belle had pointed out, Dax and Cori stood by the bar studying the crowd.

"You're here," Dax said, relief evident in his voice.

"Is everything okay?" Marc asked.

"He's nervous," Cori said and put her arm through his.

"I'm not changing my mind," Dax said. "I'm just wondering if we slipped away for ten minutes or so whether anyone would notice."

"Probably," Marc said, "but so what? It's not like they'll come looking for you. They'll probably think the engaged couple is off somewhere sharing a few kisses." Marc pumped his eyebrows for effect.

"You're probably right," Dax agreed. "Okay, give us about ten minutes, and then we'll be back."

"Cori, can I do anything to help you?" Jenn asked.

"Yes. Please. Come with me and help get me into my dress without messing up my hair or my makeup. Elsie Belle took hours to do those."

Jenn smiled. "And you look beautiful. Let's go."

As soon as the ladies disappeared, Dax said, "I'm gone. See you in a little bit."

Marc exchanged his empty champagne glass for a bourbon on the rocks and wandered away from the bar. Shade Gruber greeted him with a nod, and Marc moved that way.

"You set for tomorrow?" Police Chief Gruber asked.

"I am. What about on your end?"

"Ready. Spoke with Cole today. He's already in town with men but keeping a low profile. Well, well, well. Look who just walked in."

Marc turned far enough to see Judge Darrel Yeats enter the room accompanied by his son, Jasper Yeats.

"You know his son Jasper?" Marc asked.

"Only by reputation, and let's say, I've not been impressed by what I heard."

An arm wrapped around his waist from the side. "I'm back," Jenn said. "Hello, Chief Gruber."

"Shade, please. Nice to see you again, Jenn. I'm sorry Vivi couldn't be here tonight. I know she would've enjoyed meeting you."

Abruptly, the background music stopped, leaving only the sounds of talking and laughing in the room, and then those stopped too as people began to glance around with questioning expressions.

"What's going on?" Clover Jean demanded of the closest server, who replied with a shrug.

"Can I have your attention, please?" Dax's voice came over the speakers.

"Can *we* have your attention?" Cori corrected.

"You're right, honey," Dax said into the microphone.

"Can Cori and I have your attention? Look toward the rear of the room, please."

The crowd turned en masse toward the closed doors. The Wedding March began playing over the speakers. The doors opened, and the honored couple stepped through. Cori was dressed in a long, white, form-fitting dress with a short train. His brother wore a formal black tux with tails. Cori's arm was linked through Dax's, and she carried a large white, cascading floral arrangement.

"I think that's my cue," Marc said and headed toward the front of the room.

Clover Jean began to cry. Her husband put his arm around her.

Cori lifted a mic to her mouth. "Everyone we love and want to share our special day with is here today. We thought there's no reason to drag you out again later this summer, so..."

"Welcome to our wedding," they said in unison.

The crowd applauded and then moved toward the sides of the room, forming an aisle for them to walk down. As they neared to where Marc waited, he smiled. His heart was overflowing with happiness for his brother, who deserved every second of joy for the rest of his life.

At the front of the room, Cori asked her sisters to join her. Dax asked his dad to stand with him.

Cori handed the portable mic to Marc.

"Well, as you have figured out, this is no longer an engagement party," Marc began. "Welcome to Dax and Cori's wedding." He pulled a folded piece of paper from his front pocket. "Are you two ready?"

They both nodded, and Marc started speaking.

. . .

"Wow," Jenn's mother said as she dropped onto his living room sofa at the end of the evening. "I'm so glad your mother invited us to the party tonight. Your brother and his new wife sure surprised everyone."

"Really?" Marc asked, sitting beside her. "You didn't have an inkling?"

"Nope. Not a one, but well done." Adele caressed his cheek with her hand. "Well done, Dr. Love and Light."

Marc laughed.

"I can't believe you guys didn't tell me," Chloe complained.

"No way," Jenn said as she took a seat. "You would've burst trying to keep that news."

"I would have kept it."

"From your new BFF, Annabelle?" Jenn asked with an arched brow.

Chloe chewed on her lip. "Yeah, probably better. Besides, what a cool surprise."

"Well, Roger and I are exhausted, right, dear?" Adele said.

Roger, who'd remained standing, nodded. "I'm headed to bed. I'm old and tired, and I spent way too long on the dancefloor."

"Give me a hand," Adele said, extending her arm upward. Her husband pulled her to standing. "I'm going to sleep like a baby. Don't wake us in the morning. When you see us, you see us."

"I'm going too," Chloe announced. "I'm putting on

my noise-cancelling headphones so I won't hear a thing." She looked at her mother. "So, you kids keep it down."

Jenn and Marc chuckled as the three left the room. Marc patted the sofa cushion, and Jenn moved over next to him.

"I hate you have to work tomorrow night," she said.

He draped an arm around her shoulders. "Me, too, but with it being the fourth, the department will be spread all over the county dealing with illegal fireworks and drunks."

She snuggled next to him. "Any idea when you'll be home?"

"No clue, but I like the sound of home on your lips." He kissed her, and a ball of lust lit in his gut.

"I can't believe we've been here over three weeks."

"Missing work?"

She shook her head. "Not as much as I thought I would." She stretched her arms over her head. "I can't remember when I've been so relaxed. I hate the thought of heading home soon," she said with a sigh.

His heart fractured. "You're leaving?"

"Eventually. We have to." She smiled. "But not tonight." She kissed him. "Let's go be very quiet. There's something about weddings that makes me horny."

"I'll make a note to get more wedding invitations in the future." She was laughing when he pulled her up to stand, and they headed to his room like a couple of high school teenagers breaking the rules.

. . .

Jenn woke up in her bed. She'd left Marc's room somewhere around four, crossing her fingers she wouldn't run into anyone needing to use the hall bath at that time. Luckily, the coast had been clear. She'd dropped into a deep sleep the second her head hit the pillow. Now, she stretched and looked at the bright sunlight outside. She should probably get up, but this bed felt so good. She snuggled into the sheets again. Maybe just for a couple of minutes more...

The next time she woke, her phone's clock said she'd slept until noon. She couldn't remember sleeping until noon since she'd found out she was pregnant; back then, she'd wanted to sleep all the time. The house was remarkably quiet. And worse, she didn't smell any coffee.

She dressed and headed down to see where everyone else was. To her surprise, she found her mother sitting and talking with Cora.

"Good morning, ladies."

"Don't you mean good afternoon?" her mother said with a laugh.

Jenn grinned. "What can I say? I was exhausted." She stretched and yawned. "But man, I slept great. Hey, Cora. I didn't know you were here. Nice wedding yesterday, wasn't it?"

Cora's eyes turned dreamy. "Dax was so handsome, wasn't he? And Cori looked beautiful. Those two sneakers. I can't believe they pulled a surprise wedding on us."

Jenn chuckled. "They were determined, but be glad it was inside with air conditioning. Their first plan had been for outside at Singer Ranch."

"Oh Lord," Adele said. "I'd have melted."

"Me too," Jenn agreed. "In the end, they didn't care where it took place, only that it did. Still, Clover Jean did an incredible job with the decorations and food for a mother of the bride who didn't know she was the mother of the bride."

The three women laughed.

"Where's Chloe?"

Cora's eyes sparkled at the mention of her granddaughter. "Her friend Annabelle called and offered to show Chloe all the *quote* cool places *unquote* to hang out in Whispering Springs. Chloe grabbed her swimming suit and a change of clothes and then headed out about ten. Marc was still here, and he said it was fine, so we let her go. Did we do the wrong thing?"

"No, not at all. Annabelle is a great kid. I'm sure they'll have fun running around." She looked toward the kitchen.

"Marc's already left," Cora said. "Something about meeting with Chief Gruber about tonight's patrols...?"

"Right," she said with a yawn. "Did both of you have breakfast, or I guess it's lunch now."

"Don't worry about us, dear. We're used to taking care of ourselves," her mother said. "But we can keep you company while you fix yourself something."

"That'd be nice." Jenn said. "The three of us haven't sat down together in a long time."

"Need help getting up off the sofa, old woman?" Adele asked Cora, who laughed.

"Hush. You're the same age I am."

Jenn was smiling at the two old friends' relationship. That was one thing missing from her life. She'd left her old friends when she'd gone to college and had long since lost contact with them. Since being here in Whispering Springs, all the Montgomery women had reached out to her. She'd laughed more with them during Chloe's birthday party at the Montgomery house than she had in forever. At work, she had some people she ate lunch with, or maybe had drinks with after hours, but she couldn't really call them friends; they were more acquaintances than friends.

The two old friends were still playfully exchanging insults as they followed Jenn into the kitchen.

"I'm getting some iced tea," Adele said. "You want a glass, Cora?"

"God, yes. I miss good iced tea."

"Yeah, it's not much of a Maine thing," Jenn's mother said as she poured them two glasses.

Cora chuckled. "Not a restaurant in that state can make a decent glass of cold tea. Texas may have its problems, but good iced tea isn't one of them. Stay here long enough, and I guarantee you'll get hooked."

Jenn pulled the leftover egg and sausage casserole from yesterday and cut a square. While it was heating in the microwave, she brewed herself a cup of coffee. When the square of casserole was hot, she joined the two women at the table. Condensation rolled down their iced tea glasses, leaving wet circles on the tabletop.

"Where's Dad?" she asked.

"Oh, he and Lon are out running around somewhere," her mother said.

"I know where they are," Cora said. "Lon discovered

there's a Fisherman's Pro Shop in Dallas, so I have very little doubt that's where they're headed."

The two men were both diehard fishermen back home in Maine.

Adele sighed with a smile and a shake of her head. "No wonder Roger didn't tell me where they were going. I dread what they'll bring back and try to get on the plane to Maine."

Jenn nodded and ate. Sometimes, she'd swear reheated leftover food was tastier than when it was fresh from the oven, like right now.

"When are you headed home?" her mother asked.

Jenn shrugged. "Don't know for sure. Probably a little later this month."

"How has it been, working from here?"

"It wasn't too bad initially, but then we started tearing up Marc's house, and I didn't get a heck of a lot done after that. At night, I was too exhausted, but the distance part worked okay. I need to go back to the office for a few days and play catch up."

"You're leaving?" Cora asked with a frown. "What about Chloe?"

"What about Chloe?" Jenn's brow furrowed in confusion.

"She mentioned attending school here in Texas to get an astrophysics degree."

Jenn shook her head. "Harvard has one of the top programs in the United States, and she's already gotten an early admission, so I don't think that'll be happening."

"Hmm," Cora replied.

Jenn and Adele turned toward Cora.

"Harvard is an excellent school, Cora. Are you thinking she shouldn't go there?" Adele asked.

"It's just...well...I mean, Marc's just meeting his daughter, and I thought...well, continuing her education here would give them time to catch up on their relationship."

Jenn sat back in her chair and frowned. "You seem to be implying that I've kept Marc away from his daughter. Or that by sending her to Harvard, I'm still trying to keep them apart." Jenn set her fork on the side of her plate. "Nothing could be further from the truth. I didn't know Marc was her biological father until recently. And as far as catching up on their relationship, I stayed here in his house for that exact reason...so they can be together."

Cora leaned back in her chair. "Is that so?"

"Okay, you two," Adele said. "Take it down a notch. We all want what's best for Chloe."

"You're right," Cora said. "I'd kind of hoped she'd end up here in Texas so Marc would be able to see her more. Having her in class this summer has been eye-opening. Even if she wasn't my granddaughter, I'd have to say she's one of the brightest students I've taught." She sighed. "And yes, I know Harvard is an excellent school, and I do want her to get an education worthy of that brain of hers, but I'm feeling all protective of Marc." She smiled wistfully. "He was my first baby, and I guess he always will be."

Adele took her friend's hand. "I know exactly what you mean." She nodded toward Jenn. "That's my baby, and I'd fight to the death for her too."

Jenn grinned. "You two old women fighting? Now, that's something I'd pay to see."

"Hush," her mother said with no heat in her admonishment.

Cora chuckled, then asked, "Are you really planning on going back to Michigan?"

"Well, yeah," Jenn said. "I'm only here for Chloe. I wanted her to spend some time with Marc."

"Only here for Chloe?" her mother said. "Is that so?"

"Yes, that's so," Jenn answered.

Adele and Cora exchanged looks.

"What?" Jenn asked.

"Honey," her mother started, laying her hand on Jenn's arm, "you and Marc...well...you seem to have gotten close." Her mom emphasized the word close.

With wide eyes, Jenn asked, "What do you mean by that?"

"I can tell you," Cora said. "When Marc looks at you, his eyes say it all. Same with you."

"Reminds me of when you were dating," Adele said, nodding. "Both of you would wear these goofy expressions." She shrugged. "You had them on yesterday."

"That's it," Cora said. "Those lovey-dovey looks when you thought no one was looking."

Jenn shook her head. "You're both crazy. You're seeing something that isn't there. Marc and I are friends. We share a daughter. That's it."

Adele shook her head. "I'm not saying you and Marc should get back together."

"Nor am I," Cora added. "When you and Marc split, it almost killed him."

"And you," Adele said. "David came along—and don't get me wrong, we loved David—but you jumped into that relationship very fast. Your father and I worried you had married him on the rebound, but then you and he stayed married, and life moved on. However, you never looked at him like you look at Marc. And there were no more children, which concerned us too."

"You and Dad worry too much," Jenn said. "I was fine back then, and I'm fine now."

"Marc wasn't," Cora said. "He wasn't fine. When you left him, he didn't care if he lived or died. Lon and I were scared he would die in the military because he didn't care about living."

"But look at him," Jenn insisted, "he's doing great."

"You keep telling yourself that you're fine and he's fine, but are you?" Adele asked.

Cora reached for Jenn's hand. "Marc wasn't the easiest person to live with back then. Lon and I know that. Marc watched you bettering yourself in college. He imagined you having this exciting campus experience and then coming home to a man who felt he had no real future. Lon and I didn't want him to join the military, but he told us he had to do something to make life better for his family. I suggested college, but he didn't believe he was smart enough."

"Well, that's crap," Jenn said. "I don't know why he doesn't think he's smart. He's said something like that to me. Look at what we made. Chloe is a brain, and she didn't get that all from me."

Cora nodded. "I agree, but his grades were bleh in

high school, and in his mind, those grades reinforced all those feelings of insecurity he had."

Jenn scoffed. "He played around in high school. Sports were more important than studying."

"I know that. You know that. But what he remembers is that you were valedictorian of your class, and then you were doing well in college."

"Cora and I have discussed this," Adele said.

"I'm sure you have," Jenn said with derision.

"And," her mother continued speaking over Jenn, "I agree with Cora. I wish we'd seen what was happening back then, tried to step in—"

"You mean interfere," Jenn said.

"Sure, you can use interfere, but that's not how we saw it," Adele said. "We loved you both and watching you throw away what you had was—"

"Painful," Cora finished.

"I couldn't be a military wife," Jenn said. "I told Marc that, more than once, actually. I didn't want to move around. I didn't want to wait for two soldiers to show up at my door and tell me my husband was dead. It'd be like living on pins and needles every day." She shook her head. "He knew how I felt, and he joined up anyway." She pressed her hand to her heart. "The day he told me... well...I still have nightmares about it. He knew, and he did it anyway." She looked at the two mothers. "Can't you see? If I felt so strongly about something, and he did it anyway, what kind of life would we have? I felt he ignored my wishes. Disregarded my opinions and feelings." She shook her head. "I just couldn't stay married to him, ready to be a military widow at twenty-two. I just couldn't watch him die, so I ran. Maybe not my best reaction, but the only one I felt I had."

The three women sat and digested the things that'd been said.

"I have to tell you, Jenn, I was mad at you for a lot of years," Cora said. "You hurt my son, and that brought out all my maternal rage."

Jenn frowned. "I saw you whenever I visited my parents. I had no idea you were harboring these feelings. Why haven't you said something before now?"

"Because your mother told me you'd married, had a husband with a baby on the way, and were working your way through medical school, so I thought, 'Let it go, Cora. She's moved on, and Marc will too.'" She took Jenn's hand. "I honestly don't believe he ever got over you."

Jenn gave a sad smile. "I don't think I would've understood your hurt for me and for Marc, without having had Chloe. I'm so sorry we caused you both so much pain for so long." She sighed. "Your impressions of our marriage are right and wrong. We were so young and immature. We made a lot of mistakes, which you should understand since you made a lot of mistakes with your family when you were our age."

"You're right," Cora nodded sadly. "And my own stubbornness made me lose so much time with my brothers."

"Well, Marc and I were young. I thought marriage should be easy, like going steady. If a couple had to work at it, then something was wrong." Jenn shook her head. "Sometimes, I wish I could go back and do things differently, but then I realize if I did that, everything would change. Chloe might not be here, and I would give up anything for her." She reached over and took Cora's hand. "I like where I am in life, and I think Marc is happy where he is. We might not be sitting here today if we'd stayed on the same path."

"Explain something to me," Cora said.

"Okay. What?"

"All three of my children served in the military. I wasn't thrilled with their choices, but I supported them. Why couldn't you support Marc?"

Jenn's gaze flicked to her mother and then back to Cora. She was sure she'd told them both why she wouldn't stay, but sometimes, you had to hear something difficult more than once to make it sink in.

She twisted the coffee mug in front of her. "Marc and I have discussed this, and I think he understands my position now." She looked into Cora's eyes. "I loved Marc with every cell in my body. He was everything to me. But I couldn't watch him die, and every time I thought about him being overseas or in harm's way, I couldn't function. My brain would literally shut down. I was deep into medical school. I needed every advantage if I wanted to finish. His death would have killed me. I believed putting distance between us would help me survive if something bad happened."

"But don't you see? What you and he did was as much a death as if one of you had actually died."

Adele put her hand over Cora's and squeezed. "You and I were once that age, and we made decisions that couldn't be undone," Adele said. "With age comes life experiences and wisdom. It's easy for us to say what we would've done had we been in her shoes, but we can't. We've talked about this. We had to let them make their own life decisions, even if we disagreed with them."

Jenn sighed. "I was terrified of him dying and in my magical thinking, I thought if I left, then he wouldn't die. I know it doesn't make sense, but back then, it did."

Cora studied Jenn's face. "Are you still in love with him?"

"Cora, don't push," Adele said.

Jenn searched her heart for the answer, but she didn't have to look long. Of course, she loved Marc. Always had, and always would. "I love Marc," she said. "I don't know if we will ever be a couple again, but I love him enough to share the most precious thing I have with him."

"So, you plan to go back to Michigan." It wasn't a question.

"My job is there. My life is there. But with Chloe, he'll always be a part of our lives."

"But if he asked you to stay?" His mother continued to press the issue.

He had, sort of, told her he wanted a relationship, but *where* hadn't been in the discussion. Would he move to Michigan to be with her? He was asking her to make all the sacrifices. What was he willing to forfeit to be with her? That was something he and she had to discuss. That was not a subject for his mother or hers.

She smiled. "I guess we'll cross that bridge when we get to it." She rubbed her hands together and said, "Now, I know you two didn't stay here to talk about a divorce from sixteen years ago. What's on the agenda?"

Both mothers got the hint, and the conversation changed to shopping and fireworks. The plan was to shop the Fourth of July sales in Dallas, then meet her dad and Lon at Riverside Inn for dinner on the rooftop bar, followed by fireworks over the river. The shopping would be fun, but she wished Marc could be with them for dinner. She hoped he and his deputies didn't have to deal with too many drunk drivers.

They returned from their Dallas shopping trip at close to seven-thirty. Since the sun liked to stay up late in the summer, fireworks weren't scheduled to start until after nine that evening. The rooftop was a popular place on this date, but luckily, reservations had secured them a table for five. Chloe had sent a message that she and Annabelle were with a group of Annabelle's friends at the river for the show.

"I wish Marc could've made it," Cora said.

"I do too," Jenn agreed. "But you know the job is important to him."

"It is, but there are other things just as important."

Jenn sipped her wine and didn't respond. He'd been on his best behavior over the time she and Chloe had been there, but did he put the job before everything else? Maybe he wasn't over her, as Cora had said, and that's why he'd never remarried. Or maybe other women weren't willing to come in second to the job.

Dessert had been served when the first burst of sparkles lit up in the sky.

"It's started," Adele said and turned her chair. "I love fireworks," she said to the table at large.

Jenn grinned. Her mother had never found a fireworks display she hadn't loved.

A local radio station had coordinated music to go with the show. As things boomed and burst around them, the sounds of music and "Ohhs" and "Ahhs" filled the rooftop. And yes, some of those ohhs and ahhs came from Jenn. She was her mother's daughter after all.

"Dr. Tate?"

Jenn moved her gaze from the sky to the uniformed deputy standing beside her and smiled. "I'm Dr. Tate."

"I've been asked to come get you. Sheriff Singer has been shot and taken to Whispering Springs Hospital. He's asking for you."

Twenty

The ride to the hospital in the departmental cruiser with siren and lights seemed to take forever. Jenn could barely draw a breath. Her heart raced as fast as the deputy drove the car. Behind them, the two sets of parents were in Jenn's SUV on the cruiser's bumper. Her car's emergency flashers hit her eyes in the side mirror.

Sonofabitch. Sonofabitch. He can't die. He can't die. The mantra refrain echoed in her head.

Andy of Mayberry, her ass. Speeding tickets and loose cattle didn't fire guns at cops. This was her nightmare come to reality, except it was a departmental deputy coming for her instead of soldiers.

This was her fault. He'd been safe until she'd come back into his life, just like she'd believed all those years ago. She didn't care that it made no sense. This was her fault.

The deputy whipped into the emergency drive, and Jenn was out of the vehicle before he came to a complete stop. A scrub-clad Dr. Lydia Montgomery stood in the ambulance bay. She called Jenn's name as soon as Jenn had the door open.

She raced over. "Where is he? What happened? Is he...."

"He's not dead," Lydia said. "He's getting prepped for surgery."

"Who's doing the surgery? Do you have a trauma doctor in this town? What about airlifting him to Dallas?"

Lydia reached out for Jenn's hand. "Caroline has tons of emergency medicine experience. She's with him, and—"

"Where's our son?" Cora cried as she and Lon hurried over.

"As I was just explaining, he's being prepped for surgery. He wants to see Jenn before he'll agree to the anesthesia. Come on. I'll take you to him." She gestured to a scrub-clad woman. "Nancy will take you to the surgery waiting room," she told Cora and Lon. "Caroline will find you there after it's over."

"I demand to see our son," Lon said.

"I understand," Lydia said, her voice calm. "But you can't. Not now. Afterward, you can. Now, go with Nancy."

Adele put her arm around Cora, and the two women wept as they trailed Nancy inside and to the elevators for the fourth floor. Lon and Roger followed closely behind.

"Now, they're gone," Jenn said. "How bad is it?"

Lydia led her toward the ambulance entry. "Three bullets. He's lucky. As far as we can tell, none of them hit vital arteries."

Jenn scoffed. "Lucky?" She growled under her breath.

They rushed to the operating room preoperative area. Dressed in clean, red scrubs, her hair covered with a surgical cap, Caroline was completing notes at the nurses' station. She looked up when the door opened to admit them.

"Oh good, you're here." She stood. "He's a stubborn sonofabitch who refuses any anesthesia until he can talk to you. Can you make it quick? I have to get him into surgery."

Jenn's lips tightened. "Yes, it'll be quick because I'm going to kill him."

Caroline shrugged. "Okay, but make it fast."

Jenn charged toward the bed that held Marc. The sheets were white. He was whiter. The area around his mouth was tight with what she suspected was pain. His wide shoulders filled the narrow bed. His eyes opened as she neared.

"You came." His voice was thin and reedy.

"You ass. Of course, I came." She sniffed. "You lied. You said you were Andy of Mayberry. He never got shot."

He grimaced, and she knew she needed to make this quick.

"I have to tell you something in case I don't make it."

"You're going to make it," she said and prayed like hell she was right.

"I love you, Jenn. I always have, and I always will. I need you with me."

"What? Where?"

"In my surgery. I want you there. I need..." He

coughed and gasped. "I need you there. You won't let me die."

From behind her, Caroline said, "She's not on staff. She can't do surgery."

"I just need her in the room with me," Marc said. His voice had grown weaker.

"Give me scrubs," Jenn said.

He smiled and relaxed into the sheets.

"Get Anesthesia. We're going now," Caroline said.

In the operating room, Caroline's surgical skills left no doubt of her talent and expertise. From Jenn's perspective, the entire OR staff was impressive. They were efficient and ready with instruments before Caroline asked.

As Lydia had told her, he had three wounds. One through the right shoulder, which was a lot of muscle destruction but would heal. A second bullet had grazed the side of his head, removing some of those gray hairs she loved so much. But the wound wasn't deep and was easily cared for. The final bullet had pierced his side. A through and through that nicked his liver and bowel. Other than the head graze, the other two were serious injuries. Life-threatening, yes, but as she watched Caroline work, she felt she could move those to painful, but the patient would live.

"He's a tough man, your guy," Caroline said.

"He's not..." Jenn stopped speaking then said, "Do you know what happened?"

"Some. There was a stakeout today. You know about the cattle rustling that's been going on?"

"Yes."

"Marc got a tip that there was going to be a hit tonight, at our ranch, of all places. His department, along with the police SWAT team and the Texas Rangers' Rustling division hid in wait for the thieves. They were expecting three, maybe four guys, but there were eight."

"Eight! How was Marc the only one hurt?"

"He wasn't. A couple of Rangers were airlifted to Dallas. I think one Ranger was killed. No one else from the sheriff's department was hurt, nor the police SWAT team, or at least that's what I heard."

"Marc should've gone to a Level I trauma center too. Not that you aren't capable," she added. "It's obvious you know what you're doing."

Caroline's eyes met hers. "He refused to go. He'd insisted you had to be with him."

"Idiot. Stubborn fool."

Caroline chuckled as she pulled a suture through his skin. "He is that, but if I'd thought for one second I couldn't handle this, I would've sent him regardless of what he wanted. We're lucky his injuries didn't require a shoulder or hip replacement. That would have required sending him to Dallas. One of the Rangers was shot in the knee. so..."

Jenn winced under her mask. "That's going to be a heck of a repair surgery."

"Exactly. Like I told you, Marc was unbelievably lucky. He was hit with .22 caliber bullets, so the damage isn't as extensive as I'd feared. I'll be worried more about infection than anything. Well, that's not true. This shoulder is going to need rehabbing, and that's going to be a bitch."

By the time Marc was rolled into recovery, five hours had passed. The circulating nurse had kept the families up-to-date. After her second trip to the waiting room to inform the families of Marc's status, she'd reported back that the room was full of cops from every department. Jenn knew that was how it was with close departments. When one of them was injured, then they were all injured. She didn't know what had happened to the thieves, but that could wait. Her attention was focused on Marc.

Cora and Lon were allowed into the recovery room to see him. Their faces were red and swollen from extended crying. Cora hugged Jenn as Lon walked to the other side of the bed and took Marc's hand.

"How's he doing?" Cora asked.

Jenn nodded. "Good. Holding his own. Lost a lot of blood, but he's had a couple of units. Dr. Montgomery got all the debris out. She saved the bullet from his shoulder in case it's needed for evidence. Did you get the story of what happened?"

"I don't understand who all the people are, but one of the deputies said a judge was involved, along with a gang of criminals who'd been tried in his court. Two of the thieves died, and I say good riddance. I know I shouldn't be like that, but..."

"No one would blame you," Jenn said.

"I think I heard a couple of others were shot and taken to Dallas, and everyone else is in jail." Cora shook her head. "I never thought..." Her eyes filled with tears. "He could've died."

Jenn wrapped her ex-mother-in-law in her arms. "But

274

he didn't, and he won't, or at least he won't from this. He's got a rough recovery ahead of him, so it's not over. You'll have years to nag him."

Cora smiled through her tears. "So will you, dear."

Jenn heard her words, but she had no response.

Marc was moved to a private room around six in the morning. She'd sent both sets of parents home around five to get some rest, but getting Chloe to leave had been impossible.

Chloe had shown up at the hospital while Marc had been in surgery. The word had gotten to her from Annabelle, who'd gotten a text from Cori. Adele had told Jenn that Chloe had been almost inconsolable when she'd arrived at the hospital. It was only after she'd been permitted to briefly see Marc that the teen had calmed down. Jenn had tried to send her home with her grandparents, but her daughter had refused to leave. So, when it came time to roll his bed from recovery to his room, Chloe had been there, taking every step with her.

The room had a sofa and a recliner. Jenn got Chloe settled on the sofa with a pillow and blanket and convinced her to try to get some rest. For a long time, her attention shifted from her daughter to Marc and back to Chloe. Jenn's heart ached for both of them. Luckily, Chloe wouldn't lose the father she'd come to love, at least not this time, but what about the future? Why did Marc have to pick careers that risked his life?

She didn't know when she dropped off to sleep or how long she was out, but the aroma of coffee jolted her awake. Chloe was standing beside Marc's bed watching him sleep, her fingers wrapped around a tall to-go mug.

"Hey," Jenn whispered.

"Hey," Chloe replied. "I got you a cup of coffee." She gestured to a second paper cup on the bedside stand.

"Thanks. Where did this come from?"

"The day deputy brought them."

Jenn frowned. "Day deputy?"

"Yeah, there's a cop standing outside the door."

"Why? Like for protection?"

Chloe shrugged. "I don't know. Mom?"

"Yeah, hon."

"Is Marc going to die?"

Jenn joined her daughter at the bedside. "Not today, he's not." She put her arm around her daughter's shoulders. "I'm sorry, Chloe. I know how scary this all must be."

The teen nodded. "I freaked out when I heard last night. I mean, I just met him and thought, 'I just got him. I can't lose a second dad.'"

Jenn hugged her daughter. "You're not going to lose him. He's going to be in your life for a long, long time."

"I can't leave him. I have to stay here in Texas. You know that, right?"

"We can stay for a while longer," Jenn said.

"No, you're not getting what I'm saying. I'm saying I'm not going back to Michigan, and I'm not going away to Harvard. I know passing up Harvard is a big deal, but it's just a school. I don't want to go that far away."

Jenn smiled. "Chloe, you're sixteen. That's a decision you don't have to make tonight. You've got time. Seeing your..." Jenn hesitated, then said the words she'd yet to use, "your father hurt like this, well, it'll take some time to process it. But he's going to live. He'll recover, and you'll have the rest of your life to be with him."

Marc's groan drew both their attentions back to the patient. His eyes opened to slits. "Jenny?"

"I'm here, Marc." She took his hand.

"You stayed."

"Of course, I stayed." She squeezed his hand. "Get some rest. Chloe and I are here if you need anything."

His eyelids lowered, and he was out again."

"See?" she said to Chloe. "He's going to be fine."

The door opened slowly, and Cora's head popped in. "Can we come in?"

Jenn nodded. "Chloe and I will step out and let you have some time with him."

"I'm not leaving," Chloe said stubbornly.

"I'm going to take a walk, stretch my legs," Jenn said. "I could use the company."

Her daughter's jaw set. "Nope."

"Okay, then." Jenn picked up the coffee and met Cora and Lon in the hall. "He's doing well. Vital signs are good. No bleeding. The main thing now is that he needs his rest."

"What you're saying is we can't stay long," Lon said.

"That's what I'm saying. I'm not his doctor, but if I were, that's what I would tell you."

Once Marc's parents went in, Jenn looked at the deputy sitting outside the room. "Why are you here? Is he still in danger?"

The young deputy stood and shook his head. "No. We're sure we have everyone involved in last night's shooting. But the department wanted to show our respect by keeping someone here with him until he goes home. Sheriff Singer is the best sheriff we've ever had. Everyone thinks he's great. What he did last night, well, he didn't have to go himself. He could have stayed in the office and gotten reports, but he always tells us that he'd never ask us to do anything that he himself wouldn't do. He's a great boss, Dr. Tate."

"Thank you. I'll be back if anyone needs me." She needed some air and some time to process the last twelve hours. Of course, she was relieved and happy Marc was going to live. On the other hand, the deputy had confirmed her fears that Marc *had* put himself in harm's way when he didn't have to. How was this any different than what she'd walked away from all those years ago? He'd asked her to give them a chance, but he'd lied about the dangers of his job. He knew she didn't want to live in fear that he would die on the job. Hadn't she explained that clearly to him?

She thought about David. She'd buried one husband. Losing David had been horribly sad, but Marc's death would destroy her. Even the thought of his death had her gasping for air.

She couldn't do this. It would take time, but in five or ten years, she'd stop thinking about Marc the first thing in the morning. She'd stop looking at the stars and wonder if he was looking at them at the same time. He'd stop being the last thing she thought about when she went to bed. It would be rough. She knew that. She'd been through it before, but this time, she was older and wiser.

But this time, she knew they shared a daughter. Did that change everything?

By the time she returned to Marc's room, she'd made no long-term decision, but she had decided to go back to his house to shower and change into fresh clothes.

Cora was sitting in the recliner, which had been pulled up to the bed. She held Marc's hand and stared at his face.

Lon was on the couch, a concerned look on his face.

Chloe hadn't moved. She remained beside Marc, holding his other hand.

"Chloe, I think we should take a break," Jenn said.

"But—"

"You need some food," Jenn said. "Maybe a shower and some fresh clothes too. His recovery isn't a sprint. It's a marathon. He'll be here when you come back."

Chloe looked at Marc and then at Jenn. "Do you think he would mind if I called him Dad instead of Marc?"

A warm glow grew in Jenn's belly. "I think he would love it."

"Oh!" Chloe said. "He just squeezed my hand."

"Marc?' Jenn stepped up to the bed. "Squeeze Chloe's hand if you can hear me."

She saw the tendons in his hand move as he squeezed. She smiled. "I knew you were in there somewhere. Your mom and Lon are here. Chloe and I are going home for just a little while to eat and change clothes."

"Stay." His voice was raspy and quiet.

"We'll be back," she assured him. "Your mom is here."

Lon had driven her SUV to the hospital while Cora had followed in their rental car, so Jenn had a way to leave. The only way she could get Chloe to go also was to promise her that she could drive her Bronco back to the hospital if she got ready to leave Marc's house before Jenn did.

By Thursday, Marc was awake...in pain but awake. Cora refused to consider going home to Maine until Marc discharged from the hospital. His doctors kept him until Friday, then discharged him home. Jenn drove him back to his house since her SUV was large enough he could be as comfortable as one could be while recovering from bullet wounds and surgery.

She pulled into his drive and parked. "Hold on, and let me help you."

"I've got it." Then he winced when he moved his right arm. "I'll wait."

"That's what I thought."

His legs weren't injured, but the shot in his side made walking painful. He settled on the sofa against Jenn's wishes. His mother fluttered around, fluffing his pillow and covering him with a blanket...in July... in Texas. Probably overkill, Jenn thought to herself.

Cora declared she was staying to help. Chloe announced she was going nowhere either. Jenn, however, felt superfluous after a couple of days. She was working from Marc's office, but she needed to actually return to her headquarters office. A month away was leaving her twitchy.

On Monday, the house was quiet. Cora was napping and Chloe had been persuaded to go to lunch with her new friends. It was time to have her talk with Marc.

He was stretched out on the sofa watching the news. She pulled up a chair.

"We need to talk."

He clicked off the television. "Okay."

"I'm going home." Maybe she shouldn't have blurted it out so bluntly, but she decided to rip off the bandage, so to speak. "I need to go home," she corrected. "I'd thought I'd be able to work from here and fly back a couple of times a month, but I haven't been to my office in over four weeks. Things are piling up."

His eyes shuttered. "When will you be back?"

"That's the thing, Marc. I'll only be coming for a day here or there. Chloe wants to stay and help you, and I've agreed to let her stay put here until school starts in August. By then, you should be getting back on your feet. You'll have physical therapy on your shoulder, but you won't need her as much."

"But I'm not back on my feet," he said. "I need you here to help me."

His words were sharp daggers in her already guilt-ridden body. "Cora is going to stay. I can't let Chloe spend the summer sleeping on the sofa in your office. Either Cora can move to the room I've been using, or Chloe can, but my leaving frees up that bed. Between the two of them, you have more than adequate help."

His mouth tightened. "You're leaving me again."

"When I came, I told you it was temporary."

"I asked you to stay."

"No, you asked me to think about us as a couple again, and I have." She laid her hand on his arm. "You lied to me, Marc. You told me your job wasn't dangerous, and yet, here we sit with you recovering from bullet wounds."

"This isn't usual, Jenn. Wednesday night was the first time I've fired my weapon outside of a gun range since I got out of the military, and even then, I didn't shoot at people. Honey, you've got to believe me. This will never happen again."

Her eyes welled with tears. "I'm sorry. I can't take that chance."

"So, if you live in Michigan and I live in Texas, I'll never get physically injured again? Is that what you're saying?"

"Marc..."

"That's bullshit, Jenn, and you know it."

"I have to protect my heart."

"And what about our daughter? You're not worried about protecting her heart?"

Jenn stood and paced across the room. "That's not fair, Marc."

"If playing unfair will keep you here, I'll do whatever it takes." He adjusted his position and groaned lightly.

She walked back over. "Do you need some of your pain meds?"

He shook his head. "I need you, Jenn. I love you. Don't you know that?"

"I know you do. I love you too."

"Then I don't understand. Why can't you stay with me?"

With a sad sigh, she sat. "Two reasons. First, when your deputy showed up at dinner to tell me you'd been shot, it was my every nightmare. And second, I've buried one husband. I can't do it again."

He held out his hand, and she took it. "There are no guarantees in life, honey. I can't promise I'll outlive you, but I'll do my damnedest. My job isn't really all that dangerous. Heck, you driving back to Michigan is riskier. Check the stats, and you'll see I'm right."

"But my job..."

"Fuck your job," he said. "I don't care if you never work. I'll never be rich, but we'll get by."

She stood and shook her head. "I can't. I'm sorry."

Jenn drove home to Michigan alone. Chloe stayed, as she'd wanted. She'd started calling Marc "Dad," and Jenn didn't remember ever seeing him smile as broadly as he did the first time he heard that word from Chloe.

Work was chaotic from the moment she arrived back in Michigan. Playing catch-up took the rest of July. She called and stayed in touch with Chloe. Sometimes she spoke with Marc, but those conversations always left her crying. He stopped asking her to come back to Texas. and he never told her that he loved her again. They talked like divorced parents, their common denominator being their child.

Cora stayed until mid-August. Marc was up and doing physical therapy. He could drive again and was planning on returning to desk duty soon. Jenn was happy to hear he was doing well and planning on resuming his life.

Unfortunately, she hadn't recovered from her time in

Texas and with Marc yet. Her dreams were filled with memories of July the Fourth. She had more nightmares than sleep these days.

Stroker needed her to fly to Amsterdam to check on the progress of the new manufacturing facility. At one time, she'd looked forward to flying. She was always in first class and enjoyed the pampering. However, as she headed to the airport, dread hung over her like a rain cloud. Amsterdam was the last place she wanted to be. She refused to acknowledge, even to herself, where her heart wanted her to be.

As the plane lifted off and the ground fell away, apprehension filled her. Something felt off, wrong, but she couldn't put her finger on it. The flight attendant served her an orange juice, and Jenn settled in for the long flight. She'd just pulled out the last report on the project when the plane nosedived, dumping her juice off the back of the seat tray and down her legs. The RETURN TO YOUR SEAT sign flashed on with a loud ding.

"This is your captain speaking. We've experienced a bird strike to one of our engines. Please remain in your seats. We will be landing shortly."

The plane's pitch deepened, and the plane shook. Oxygen masks dropped. Jenn reached for her mask and placed it over her nose, as did the people around her. She looked out her window to see the ground rising quickly.

"Brace! Brace! Brace!" came the shout over the plane's intercom.

Twenty-One

M arc looked into the mirror and straightened his lapel.

"Are you okay, son?" Lon asked.

Their gazes met in the mirror. "I want to apologize to you."

Lon frowned. "Apologize? You have nothing to apologize for, especially not today."

Marc turned around. "Yes, today. I forget sometimes that life is short, and holding on to juvenile and petty grudges does more to hurt me than the other person."

Lon frowned. "I'm not sure I'm following you."

"I'm talking about calling you Lon after calling you Dad for sixteen years. That was petty and mean of me."

Lon's face was sober. "Son, it never mattered what you called me. I knew what you were doing. Your mother and I discussed it. We decided what you called me was only an issue if I let it be. I didn't. Just because you were fathered by Cora's first husband didn't make me feel any less for you. I love you as much as I love Dax and Sami. You weren't going to drive a wedge between us with something as flimsy as what you called me."

"You have been a wonderful father to me, Lon. When Cora wasn't around for whatever reason, you were there. You were always there for me. And today…"

"I'm here for you today."

"You're my rock, Dad…Is it okay if I call you that? I feel like I need my dad today."

Lon's eyes teared, and he put his arms around Marc for a hard hug. "Oh, I'm sorry. Did I hurt you?"

Marc shook his head. "No. Those wounds have healed."

"Cora told me that, but I wasn't sure if you were telling the truth."

"Well, the right shoulder's still a little stiff, but my hair's grown back, and my side has healed, so I'm good."

"You know I'll probably cry today, right?"

Marc nodded. "Yeah, I might too, but I need to be strong for Chloe."

"Your daughter is made of you and Jenn. She carries both of your strengths inside her. She'll be fine."

There was a quiet tap on the door.

"Dad?"

His daughter's voice filtered through.

"Come in, Chloe."

"It's almost time," she said as she walked in. "I wanted to see if you were ready."

She looked so grown up, he thought. She and Annabelle had gotten to be as tight as sisters.

"You look beautiful," he said.

She wore a long, dark blue dress. Her makeup, which she'd begun to wear regularly thanks to Annabell's tutelage, was flawless. Her red hair was set in waves and curls.

"Thanks. Annabelle did my makeup. My hand was shaking too hard to hold the eyeliner."

"Well, she did a fabulous job."

"Hey, G'Pa." She'd decided to call his dad G'Pa and not Lon.

When Marc had asked him about the name, he'd said that he didn't mind what she called him. It was only a name. The actual name was irrelevant as long as they were closed and talked often. He thought about that now and realized Lon was right. While Marc loved being called Dad by Chloe, he would have accepted Marc too, as long as she called and they talked. His stepdad was a smart man. How had it taken Marc so many years to appreciate his wisdom?

"Have you seen Dax and Cori? Are they here yet?" Lon asked.

"They're here. Cori is showing."

Cori and Dax had finally told everyone that they were expecting a baby. "Squirt" was due in mid-March, and Marc was looking forward to meeting his niece or nephew. They hadn't told anyone the sex of the baby yet.

"She probably is," Marc said, agreeing with Chloe's assessment of Cori's protruding belly. Cori was a petite woman, and this baby was taking up a lot of room inside her.

Another knock interrupted their conversation. The door cracked open again, and Dax put his head in.

"It's time."

Chloe took his hand. "You've got this."

He squeezed her fingers. "You too, baby girl, you too."

Chloe hurried from the room to get ready for the ceremony.

"I never thought I'd see this day...again," Lon said.

Marc grinned. "It was up in the air for a while, but..." He blew out a long breath. "I'm ready. Past ready. Let's go."

Marc and Lon followed Dax from the back of the ballroom at the Whispering Springs Country Club to the front. The rows of chairs were overflowing with friends and family. He was touched so many Whispering Springs citizens had made time this close to Christmas to come out and support him and Jenn.

His mom sat in the second row, a handkerchief in her hand as she dabbed at tears. Across the aisle sat Jenn's mom, also clutching a handkerchief for tears. Both women wore bright smiles on their carefully made-up faces. Now he understood why Chloe had insisted on introducing her grandmothers to waterproof lotion to wear under their makeup.

Jenn's dad occupied the second row next to his wife, while Marc's dad stood beside him upfront.

The rear door opened, and Chloe walked in. She carried a nosegay of orange and white roses. She'd insisted on those colors since she'd be attending the University of Texas. With her dark blue dress as the background, the rose color combination worked.

She stopped by Marc to kiss his cheek before walking to the other side of the ballroom.

The doors had closed after Chloe's entrance. The music stopped momentarily. Instead of Mendelssohn's "Wedding March" accompanying Jenn's walk down the aisle, she'd chosen the instrumental version of Dolly Parton's "I Will Always Love You."

As the first notes played, the doors opened again, and Jenn stepped in. She hadn't wanted her dad to walk her down the aisle. She'd talked about having Chloe do it, but in the end, she'd decided she wanted to walk to Marc all on her own. She'd told him this was the last thing she was doing by herself before becoming his wife again. She didn't need anyone's help going to him.

Her dress was different than the first time they'd married. That dress had been long and white—a classic formal wedding gown. Today's dress was different. She'd told him it was champagne-colored, but he hadn't understood until he saw it.

The dress hit below her knees. The top of the dress had a couple of pleats that crisscrossed side to side. The top cut in at her waist and then flared out again. There were some pleats in the skirt. She carried a single rose that matched the color of her dress. She'd left her hair long, and it hung in waves down her back.

She'd never looked more beautiful. Never.

Love for this woman swamped him. For the rest of their lives, he promised he would tell her every day how much he loved her and how glad he was that her plane hadn't crashed but had only landed hard. It was the ill-fated plane trip that had convinced her that life was too short waiting for something awful to happen.

He smiled as she stepped up beside him.

"You are stunning," he whispered. Of course, with the audio system that'd been set up at the front, his voice carried through the room.

She smiled. "You're not bad yourself."

They joined hands and turned toward Dax, otherwise known as Dr. Finally, or as he'd explained it, It's-Finally-Time-You-Two-Got-Married-Again.

In six months, he'd gone from finding out he was a father to marrying the woman he'd always loved. The mayor and city council had refused to let him resign as sheriff, so his job continued, but the cattle rustling was over. All the stolen cattle had been located at Judge Yeats's ranch. The judge had tried to claim that he'd known nothing about the scheme, and that he'd bought those cows, but that bull story hadn't held up long. One thing about hiring unscrupulous accomplices...no scruples meant they had no problems turning on each other.

Jenn had left Stroker against their wishes. They'd promised her the moon to stay, but she'd said that being in the operating room with Marc had reminded her of why she'd gone into Orthopedic surgery in the first place. The OR was her home, and she'd ready to go back after she and Marc finished the house renovations and moved there. Drs. Caroline and Lydia Montgomery were begging her to joint their practice. She promised them an answer as soon as she and Marc returned from their honeymoon in the Maldives.

As Dax pronounced them husband and wife, Marc looked at her with a smile, his heart so full of love he could barely breathe.

"I'll love you forever," he said and kissed her.

Who would have guessed that a bombshell thrown on his birthday by an angry teenager could explode his life into perfection? Today, his life started anew with a daughter he adored and the only wife he ever wanted. Bring on more bombshells if they were always this good.

A Note From Cynthia

Thank you for reading Texas Bombshell.

If I haven't told you, I appreciate my readers. Without you, I wouldn't be here.

Readers are always asking: What can I do to help you? My answer is always the same: PLEASE give me an honest review. Every review helps.

Are you curious about the other couples in the story? They each have their own book! Check out all the books in the Whispering Springs, Texas Series.

Check out the Also By for a list of all Cynthia's Books.

THANK YOU again for all your support.

Cynthia

About the Author

New York Times and USA Today Bestselling author Cynthia D'Alba started writing on a challenge from her husband in 2006 and discovered having imaginary sex with lots of hunky men was fun. She was born and raised in a small Arkansas town. After being gone for a number of years, she's thrilled to be making her home back in Arkansas living in a vine-covered cottage on the banks of an eight-thousand acre lake. When she's not reading or writing or plotting, she's doorman for her border collie, cook, housekeeper and chief bottle washer for her husband and slave to a noisy, messy parrot. She loves to chat online with friends and fans.

You can find her most days at one of the following online homes:

Website: cynthiadalba.com
Facebook:Facebook/cynthiadalba
Twitter:@cynthiadalba
Newsletter:NewsletterSign-Up

Or drop her a line at cynthiadalba@gmail.com

Or send snail mail to: Cynthia D'Alba PO Box 2116 Hot Springs, AR 71914

Other Books by Cynthia D'Alba

WHISPERING SPRINGS, TEXAS
Texas Two Step – The Prequel
Texas Two Step
Texas Tango
Texas Fandango
Texas Twist
Texas Hustle
Texas Bossa Nova
Texas Lullaby
Saddles and Soot
Texas Daze
A Texan's Touch
Texas Bombshell
Whispering Springs, Texas Volume One
Whispering Springs, Texas Volume Two
Whispering Springs, Texas Volume Three

DIAMOND LAKES, TEXAS
A Cowboy's Seduction
Hot SEAL, Cold Beer
Cadillac Cowboy
Texas Justice
Something's Burning

DALLAS DEBUTANTES

McCool Family Trilogy/Grizzly Bitterroot Ranch Crossover
Hot SEAL, Black Coffee
Christmas in His Arms

Snowy Montana Nights
Hot SEAL, Sweet and Spicy
Six Days and One Knight

Carmichael Family Triplets Trilogy (coming soon)
Hot Assets
Hot Ex
Hot Briefs

SEALs in Paradise
Hot SEAL, Alaskan Nights
Hot SEAL, Confirmed Bachelor
Hot SEAL, Secret Service
Hot SEAL, Labor Day
Hot SEAL, Girl Crush

Mason Security
Her Bodyguard
His Bodyguard
Mason Security Duet

Other Books
Backstage Pass

Texas Two Steps

WHISPERING SPRINGS, TEXAS BOOK 1 ©2012
CYNTHIA D'ALBA

Secrets are little time-bombs just waiting to explode.

After six years and too much self-recrimination, rancher Mitch Landry admits he was wrong. He left Olivia Montgomery. Now he'll do whatever it take to convince Olivia to give him a second chance.

Olivia Montgomery survived the break-up with the love of her life. She's rebuilt her life around her business and the son she loves more than life itself. She's not proud of the mistakes she's made—particularly the secret she's kept—but when life serves up manure, you use it to mold yourself into something better.

At a hot, muggy Dallas wedding, they reconnect, and now she's left trying to protect the secret she's held on to for all these years.

Texas Tango

WHISPERING SPRINGS,TEXAS, BOOK 2 © 2013
CYNTHIA D'ALBA

Sex in a faux marriage can make things oh so real.

Dr. Caroline Graham is happy with her nomadic lifestyle fulfilling short-term medical contracts. No emotional commitments, no disappointments. She's always the one to walk away, never the one left behind. But now her grandmother is on her deathbed, more concerned about Caroline's lack of a husband than her own demise. What's the harm in a little white lie? If a wedding will give her grandmother peace, then a wedding she shall have.

Widower Travis Montgomery devotes his days to building the ranch he and his late wife planned before he lost her to breast cancer. The last piece of acreage he needs is controlled by a lady with a pesky need of her own. Do her a favor and he can have the land. She needs a quick, temporary, faux marriage in exchange for the acreage.

It's a total win-win situation until events begin to snowball and they find, instead of playacting, they've put their hearts at risk.

Texas Fandango

WHISPERING SPRINGS, TEXAS BOOK 3 © 2014
CYNTHIA D'ALBA

Two-weeks on the beach can deepened more than tans.

Attorney KC Montgomery has loved family friend Drake Gentry forever, but she never seemed to be on his radar. When Drake's girlfriend dumps him, leaving him with two all-expenses paid tickets to the Sand Castle Resort in the Caribbean, KC seizes the chance and makes him an offer impossible to refuse: two weeks of food, fun, sand, and sex with no strings attached.

University Professor Drake Gentry has noticed his best friend's cousin for years, but KC has always been hands-off, until today. Unable to resist, he agrees to her two-week, no-strings affair.

The vacation more than fulfills both their fantasies. The sun is hot but the sex hotter.

Texas Twist

WHISPERING SPRINGS, TEXAS BOOK 4 © 2014
CYNTHIA D'ALBA

Real bad boys can grow up to be real good men.

Paige Ryan lost everything important in her life. She moves to Whispering Springs, Texas to be near her step-brother. But just as her life is derailed again when the last man in the world she wants to see again moves into her house.

Cash Montgomery is on the cusp of having it all. When a bad bull ride leaves him injured and angry, his only comfort is found at the bottom of a bottle. His family drags him home to Whispering Springs, Texas. With nowhere to go, he moves temporarily into an old ranch house on his brother's property surprised the place is occupied.

The best idea is to move on but sometimes taking the first step out the door is the hardest one.

Loving a bull rider is dangerous, so is falling for him a second time is crazy?

Texas Bossa Nova

WHISPERING SPRINGS, TEXAS BOOK 5 ©2014
CYNTHIA D'ALBA

A heavy snowstorm can produce a lot of heat

Magda Hobbs loves being a ranch housekeeper. The job keeps her close to her recently discovered father, foreman at the same ranch. She is immune to all the cowboy charms, except for one certain cowboy, who is wreaking havoc on her libido.

Reno Montgomery is determined to make his fledging cattle ranch a success. Dates with Magda Hobbs rocks his world and then she disappears, leaving him confused and angry. He's shocked when he learns the new live-in housekeeper is Magda Hobbs.

When a freak snowstorm cuts off the outside world, the isolation rekindles their desire. But when the weather and the roads clear, Reno has to work hard and fast to keep the woman of his dreams from hitting the road right out of his life again.

Texas Hustle

WHISPERING SPRINGS, TEXAS BOOK 6 ©2015
CYNTHIA D'ALBA

Watch out for chigger bites, love bites and secrets that bite

Born into a wealthy, Southern family, Porchia Summers builds a good life in Texas until a bad news ex-boyfriend tracks her down. Desperate for time to figure out how to handle the trouble he brings, she looks to the one man who can get her out of town for a few days.

Darren Montgomery has had his eye on the town's sexy, sweet baker for a while but she's never returns his looks until now. He's flattered but suspicious about her quick change in attention.

Sometimes, camping isn't just camping. It's survival.

Texas Lullaby

WHISPERING SPRINGS, TEXAS BOOK 7 ©2016
CYNTHIA D'ALBA

***Sometimes what you think you
don't want is exactly what you
need.***

After a long four-year engagement, Lydia Henson makes her decision. Forced to choice between
having a family or marrying a man
who adamantly against fathering
children, she chooses the man. She can live without children. She can't live without the man she loves.

Jason Montgomery doesn't want a family, or at least
that's his story and he's sticking to it. The falsehood is less
emasculating than the truth.

On the eve of their wedding, Jason and Lydia's well-
planned life is thrown into chaos. Everything Jason has
sworn he doesn't want is within his grasp. But as he
reaches for the golden ring, life delivers another twist.

Saddles and Soot

WHISPERING SPRINGS, TEXAS BOOK 8 ©2015
CYNTHIA D'ALBA

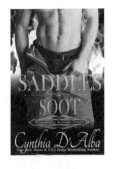

Veterinarian Georgina Greyson will only be in Whispering Springs for three months. She isn't looking for love or roots, but some fun with a hunky fireman could help pass the time.

Tanner Marshall loves being a volunteer fireman, maybe more than being a cowboy. At thirty-four, he's ready to put down some roots, including marriage, children and the white picket fence.

When Georgina accidentally sets her yard on fire during a burn ban, the volunteer fire department responds. Tanner hates carelessness with fire, but there's something about his latest firebug that he can't get out of his mind.

Can an uptight firefighter looking to settle down persuade a cute firebug to give up the road for a house and roots?

Texas Daze

WHISPERING SPRINGS, TEXAS BOOK 9 ©2017
CYNTHIA D'ALBA

A quick fling can sure heat up a cowgirl's life

When a devastating discovery ends Marti Jenkins' engagement, she decides to play the field for a while. A ranch accident lands her in the office of Whispering Springs' new orthopedic doctor, Dr. Eli Boone. And yeah, he's as hot as she's been told.

Dr. Eli Boone is temporarily covering his friend's practice and then it's back to New York City and the societal world he's lives. He's not looking for a wife, but he wouldn't say no to a quick tumble in the sheets with the right woman.

Due to ridiculous challenge, Eli has to learn to ride before he leaves town. He turns to the one person who can help him win the bet, Marti Jenkins.

As he learns to ride a horse, Marti does a little riding of her own...and she doesn't need a horse.

A Texan's Touch

WHISPERING SPRINGS, TX BOOK 10 (C) 2023
CYNTHIA D'ALBA

From NYT and USA Today best-selling author Cynthia D'Alba comes a steamy romance with a hot cowboy, a smart heroine and two meddling mothers who scheme the perfect meet cute.

Army Major Dax Cooper's life blew up with the IED that took his leg and most of his Delta Forces team. Medically retired, nightly dreams torture him, not only forcing him to relive the explosion time after time, but also the loss of the future he desired and is now denied. Unfocused and adrift, he follows his brother to Whispering Springs, Texas to lie low and think.

Psychologist Cora Belle Lambert understands what it's like to be an outsider. Sandwiched between two gorgeous and successful sisters, one a former Miss Texas and the other the current high school homecoming queen, and blessed with a stunningly beautiful mother, she considers herself to be the ugly duckling in her family. Determined to prove her worth, she takes on broken kids who need an avenging angel on their side. Kids. Never adults and definitely not an ex-military alpha male with sexy hard edges and mesmerizing azure-blue eyes.

Forced together on a mercy date set up by their mothers, each recognizes untapped promise in the other. Can these two broken people overcome the cruel hand of fate or will they allow their demons within to gleefully dance on their dreams?

17447355R00179